Under Blood Red Skies

By

Kevin R. Kotara

Daniel Gomez L.L.C

Under Blood Red Skies
by Kevin R. Kotara
Published by Daniel Gomez Enterprises LLC / September 2025
Contact Info: (210) 663-5954 / Email:
Info@DanielGomezGlobal.com
Copyright © 2025, Kotara.
All rights reserved.
ISBN: **979-8-9931375-1-3**

Under Blood Red Skies

& Other Old West Stories

Author Kevin R. Kotara

1

Under Blood Red Skies

Snow covered the ground. The morning sky was bright and sunny, but the air was heavy with a brisk chill. A frigid breeze whipped around the wood-clad building, piercing through Flanaghan's threadbare coat. Missing buttons from years of wear and tear, he gripped the two sides of his coat at his chest with his left hand and held it closed to protect himself from the exposure of the cruel northern wind. His right hand held his revolver with three bullets left in its chambers. The others had been fired a few moments before.

Flanaghan peered around the corner of the building. He was following a trail of blood in the snow. He looked down to see where it led. There was one more section to the back of the building, which ran perpendicular to the dirt street out front. It stuck out from the rear of the building about another thirty feet. The trail of blood continued around the building, right down of the middle of the nascent footprints. The footprints and blood droplets meandered from the corner where Flanaghan stood to the other back corner of the building. The gunshot victim had obviously stumbled all along the way and had been hurt enough that he could not keep his path straight.

Flanaghan continued cautiously along the bloody path. He gingerly nuzzled himself against the corner to avoid revealing himself to whoever was waiting on the other side. The whole scene was eerily quiet except for the bustling wind.

He had ridden into town at daybreak, after hearing that this man was back in the territory. The small town was located on a high point between two mountain ridges. A wide valley vista sat beyond the lonely town. Only about a dozen buildings lined the street. The buildings provided the bare necessities of commerce and services for surviving frontier life. Several houses dotted the landscape just beyond the reaches of the commercial buildings. There was nothing behind this particular building except a higher ridge of land dotted with a sizeable copse of trees.

Flanaghan looked up the ridge for a moment, and then he eased his face around the corner of the building. First, he looked forward to seeing if anyone was there. No one. He looked down; the blood trail continued along the back of the building. It looked as though the victim hugged the wall, using it to support himself as he walked. There were smears of blood along the wall. The blood droplets in the snow had grown more numerous per footstep. His target was bleeding out.

Flanaghan slowly edged himself slowly along the wall, listening for anything. Only the winter wind howled. He got to the next corner of the building and peered around it. He saw his victim on the ground, about thirty feet away. His head was up, and he was clutching his leg. The white snow was stained blood red all around him. His other hand was pressed against his abdomen. Flanaghan had thought at least two of his shots had hit their target. That was now confirmed. The dying man did not notice Flanaghan standing at the edge of the building; he was looking in the other direction. Flanaghan noticed the man's head seemed to be watching something beyond his line of sight. He thought he heard the crunch of snow coming from between this building and the next one, like someone was walking up to the dying man.

The gunshot victim put up one of his bloody hands, as if to show surrender or a last-ditch effort to shield himself from something or someone. Then a shadow extended from beyond the far corner of the building. Flanaghan could see a long shadowy line extend from the body of the shadow. A rifle muzzle. The wounded man said something, but the wind drowned out his words. Flanaghan could hear the wounded man whimpering and begging the shadow to put his gun down.

A blast penetrated the howling wind, almost causing the wind to be silent for a brief moment. The gunshot echoed off the ridge behind Flanaghan. The wounded man was definitely dead now. The rifle blast had taken off the back half of his skull. A scattered pattern of blood stained the pure white snow for about six to eight feet behind the man's head. Brutal. The man had clearly been about to bleed to death in a moment or two. The bullet could have been saved for another time.

Flanaghan kept watching. A figure appeared from around the corner – the gunman walking closer to his kill. He was tall and lean. He wore a black duster and black hat; a rifle cradled in one arm. As he approached, his shadow covered the dead man. He kicked the body with his boot, and it flopped on its back. Surely the gunman knew that he had delivered the death blow. There was no need for him to confirm the man was indeed dead. His brains were scattered all over the snow.

Flanaghan pressed himself against the back of the building, staying out of view. He didn't know what to do next. He cautiously glanced around the corner. The gunman was crouched over the dead body, rifling through the dead man's jacket and pockets. He must have noticed Flanaghan out of the corner of his eye because suddenly, he stood up swiftly and pivoted on his boots to get behind the other corner of the building. Flanaghan flinched backward.

The man in the duster called to him, "Who are you?"

Flanaghan didn't answer. The man peered around the corner and waited for Flanaghan to do something. Flanaghan braved a glance. When he had just had his head slightly around the edge of the building, the man fired at him. But Flanaghan had noticed the raised rifle. He recoiled behind the safety of the building just in time to not be shot. The bullet glanced off the very edge of the wooden stud corner. Splinters flew.

Damn good shot, thought Flanaghan.

The bullet continued toward the ridge behind the building, and the echo bounced back, again overpowering the sound of the wind and announcing its presence, which was the more lethal at this moment.

The man in the duster asked again, more forcefully this time, "Who are you?"

Flanaghan was still silent.

No friend was ever silent to that question, only foes. The man in the duster fired another shot at the building – about a foot to the right of where his first shot went – but it didn't find Flanaghan's flesh. Flanaghan had crouched down. The second shot pierced both corner walls but went over his head. He was shaking in fear, but he did not want to reveal that he was still alive. He remained silent, hoping it would buy him some time to think of something.

8

"I'm coming to get you, you bastard." The man in the duster reloaded his Winchester, stood up, and walked toward Flanaghan. Flanaghan could hear the man's footsteps crunching on the snow.

"All right, stop." Flanaghan finally answered. "My name is Flanaghan."

The man in the duster stopped for a moment. He retreated slightly, probably expecting a gun to appear around the side of the corner. "What do you want?"

Flanaghan answered, "You're full of questions, aren't you?"

The other man had made it back behind his corner, safe for the moment. The wind persisted.

Flanaghan broke the silence, "You know who I am, who are you?"

"The man who is collecting the bounty on this dead man." There was a hint of sarcasm in the man's voice.

Flanaghan glanced around the corner. He saw that the man had retreated to his corner. "There's a bounty on him?"

"Yeah. You didn't know?"

"No."

"Who put the other two bullets in him?"

"I did," Flanaghan said.

"Why did you shoot him?"

"He killed my wife and my son!" There was silence from the other side. "I didn't know there was a bounty on him."

"He's killed a lot of people," the man said.

"I'll ask again, who are you? A lawman?"

"No."

"I don't have any beef with you. And I don't have a bounty on me. Are you going to shoot me? Can I come out safely?"

"That depends."

"On what?" Flanaghan asked.

"Are you going to shoot me?"

"Why would I shoot you?"

"Now that you know there's a bounty on this dead man, you can collect it if you shoot me."

"How much is it?"

"Two thousand dollars."

Flanaghan hesitated for a moment. He was not sure he could even count that high, but he knew it was a lot of money. "Why don't we split it?"

"Now, why would I split it with you?"

"Seeing as it is, I got the man halfway to hell before you came along. All you did was get him there about a minute or two faster."

"I don't split any bounty," the man said.

Flanaghan grimaced. He knew that he was going to have to fight his way out of this situation. He thought for a moment and quickly glanced back around the corner. The bounty hunter was still behind his corner of the building.

The gunman toyed with Flanaghan with his next statement. "Seeing as you got the revenge you were seeking and didn't know he had a bounty on his head, I think you can just mosey along and I'll forget I ever ran into you."

Flanaghan knew that the man in the duster wasn't going to let him safely walk away from the potential two thousand dollars, and he remained silent.

"I'll give you a minute to run the other way," the man said.

No answer.

The gunman emerged slightly from around the corner, rifle raised, poised to fire.

Flanaghan peered around the corner.

A shot rang out and echoed off the ridge. More splinters flew from the building. Flanaghan heard footsteps in the snow. He knew that the gunman was advancing toward him. He gripped his revolver, clutching it in terror. "That wasn't a minute!"

"It'll take me another half minute to get to you. Why haven't you started running yet?"

Flanaghan stood up. He knew this was it. Kill or be killed. He cocked the hammer of his pistol, whirled around the corner of the building, and fired.

The shot was errant.

The gunman fired his rifle at Flanaghan, a mere twenty feet away.

The shot hit its mark. Flanaghan's body reeled from the gunshot. He took the last couple of steps of his life backward, blood spewing out of his chest. The gunman fired his second shot before Flanaghan's body hit the ground. Another shot to the chest.

Flanaghan's body went limp as it plopped on the frozen ground. Blood was all over the snow. The gunman relaxed, put his rifle down, and stared down at the fresh corpse.

From the ridge, behind one of the trees, a shot rang out.

A bullet hit the man in the duster in the head. He fell straight down, dead. Another pool of blood began staining the snow.

Five minutes ago, there was nothing but pure white snow behind the building, and now the snow was soiled with red pools of blood from three fresh dead bodies.

A man emerged from behind a tree and looked around. He scanned the back of the other buildings. The town was still quiet. The residents were probably cowering in fear in their homes, waiting for the gunfire to stop.

He walked up to the dead man in the duster and kicked him over to look at his face. Half of it was missing and a bloody mess.

"I don't split any bounties, either."

2

The mystery man from the trees picked up the dead man with the bounty on his head, carried the body to his horse, and draped the corpse over his horse's rump. With a rope, he tied off to the back end of the saddle, securing it from falling off. He left the other two bodies. The whole thing looked like just another gunfight. There was not really anyone around to count bodies or record the events. He saw the whole thing from his secure location and decided to let everyone settle their differences, and he would clean up if he had to.

There were two other dead bodies farther down the street. He wasn't sure what happened there or who they were, but it wasn't his problem. He looked at their faces. They were not anyone of interest. At least, not monetarily. There was another dead body farther down the street. He knew who he was, but it did not matter anymore. "Good riddance," he murmured. His words lost in the wind, he rode on out of town.

He was lucky the face of his dead bounty was not too damaged from the rifle shot from the man with the duster. The bullet had gone through his eye socket. His face was still recognizable. A face worth two thousand dollars – dead or alive.

He headed towards the valley. He heard there was a US Marshal's office in the next town, down along the river.

The bounty hunter arrived in the town along the river mid-afternoon. He rode down the street that entered town and passed several buildings. He pulled his horse up to a hotel, got off, and tied his horse to the railing. There were two doors on the front of the building. He went in through the one on the left.

It was the saloon to the hotel. A couple of cowboys were playing poker at a table on the left.

A bartender was behind the bar on the right side of the room. "Howdy, sir."

"Howdy."

"How can I help you?"

"Is this your hotel?"

"Yes, sir."

"Is there a room available tonight?"

"Yes, sir."

"How much?"

"Three dollars per night."

"Expensive."

"We have indoor toilets in some rooms. Installed them last year. Best hotel in town."

The stranger shook his head. "OK. I'll take it. It's kind of quiet in here for a saloon."

"It's early yet. Things will pick up after sundown. Can I get you a drink or something to eat?"

"What do you have for food?"

"Some meat and potatoes. My wife has a stew – or we can cook a steak for you. We have a restaurant next door, but the kitchen is right here behind this door." He pointed to a door just off the to the side of the bar. "I can have them make you a plate and you can eat here, or in the dining room next door, whichever you prefer."

"I'll eat here. I could use some warm stew on a day like this. How much for a plate?"

"Fifty cents, sir."

"Fire it up."

"Yes, sir."

The bartender went back through the door, and the man could hear him talking to the cook. Some pots and pans starting clanking around. The man turned around to look at the poker game. He scanned the faces of the cowboys and didn't recognize any of them. He turned back around.

The bartender came back through the door. "Anything to drink?"

"Just a whiskey."

The bartender poured the man a swig of whiskey.

The man downed it in one gulp.

The saloon was warm and toasty. A Franklin stove in the corner next to the kitchen door was doing its job on this frigid day. There was a large fireplace on the other side of the saloon. It needed another log or two on it as the embers were dying, but it was still putting out heat. The poker-playing cowboys were sitting at the table closest to it, for obvious reasons.

The man figured the bartender probably started the fire first thing that morning. He pointed at the empty glass and motioned for another swig.

The bartender obliged and poured another shot.

"There's a marshal's office here, ain't there?"

"Oh, uh, look out the window there. You see that other street, two buildings down, that tees off this one? Take that street down to the next corner and turn right. The marshal's office sits on the ground floor on the second building to the right. He's across the street from the bank."

"Thanks."

"You need the local sheriff, by any chance? He's just down the street from here."

"No. Federal marshal. I've got a bounty to collect."

"Oh…" The bartender knew better than to ask too many questions of strangers, but he was curious where his bounty was located at the moment. "Is that your horse right there outside the door? With the man's body on it?"

The stranger looked up from his glass, figuring the answer was obvious and answered itself. and replied, "Yes."

"Dead?"

"Yes. Deader than dead."

"I wouldn't leave him out there too long by himself, if you know what I mean. Around here, even dead men have been known to get up and walk off." He chuckled at his own wit.

"Thanks for the warning. I'm just going to eat and then head over to the marshal's office."

"OK. Let me see where your food is, sir." He turned around and went to the kitchen.

The stranger could hear the bartender asking, "Where's the man's food?"

A minute later, the bartender emerged with a plate of stew and potatoes.

"Thank you." The stranger started eating, famished from a long day chasing down men now dead. "Why do you have a separate dining room next door?"

"Some townsfolk don't like 'entering a saloon' to eat. Churchgoing people. You know."

"Are there a lot of them here? Churchgoing people?"

"Enough of them, yes, sir. Enough to keep the town in check. The saloons are really just here for the cowboys and the miners that come down from the hills once a week. The locals stay out of the saloons for the most part. I decided to keep the dining area separate. You got to know your clientele."

"That's for sure." The stranger kept eating.

"My wife and daughter run the kitchen. You like your food, sir?"

"Yes, very good." He took another few bites. "You said there's mining operations nearby?"

"Yes, up in the mountains. There's a private rail line that the mine owns that runs along the river. The main railway is about fifteen miles upriver. If you go out down this street you eventually get to the end of town and you'll see it run up the side of the mountain over there. There's a wagon trail that follows it up there, too. If you stay on it, you'll get to the mine. It's about five or six miles up."

"Oh, I don't need a job – least of all at some mine. I was just curious. If you have a mining operation close by, that means you probably have a good mercantile in town."

"Oh yes, sir. Turn up at this street that I told you about, like you're going to the marshal's, but take a left at the corner instead of a right. It's down at the next corner. Can't miss it."

The stranger finished up his plate of food. "Good food. How about a livery stable?"

"Grossbar's down the street from the marshal. In fact, it's where the marshal and the sheriff keep their horses. He's about a buck or two more expensive than the one over here behind me, but there's always someone on guard over there since the lawmen keep their horses there. Jonesy, behind me, is cheaper."

"Thanks. I'll be back in a little while. Going to drop off my bounty before it walks away." The stranger smiled.

The bartender laughed. "Let me get you your room key." He reached under the bar and pulled out a wooden box, unlocked it with a key he had in his apron, and took out a key. "Room 6. Up the stairs there and to your right."

"Thanks." The stranger paid for his plate, his whiskey, and for the first night at the room and walked outside.

The wind had calmed down from earlier, and the afternoon was more pleasant than the lethal morning had been. There was still snow all over the ground and on the rooftops of the bustling town, but the sun was dipping low now. Long shadows were creeping across the street. There was but a sliver of sunlight still shining on the wooden plank sidewalks before the vertical rise of the western walls of the buildings.

The stranger mounted his horse and rode the short distance around the block to the marshal's office. He walked in the door and saw the marshal and two deputies sitting at their desks, boots propped up. The stranger had interrupted a conversation.

All three faces turned to the door, as it creaked open and a rush of the outside winter cold invaded the toasty confines of the office. A wood-burning stove was strategically positioned in the middle of the large room and was working to full capacity. The three men inside did not look like they were expecting any more business to happen on this waning winter day.

The deputy closest to the door said, "G'afternoon, may we help you?"

"I have a bounty to collect." He unraveled a wanted poster from his coat pocket and laid it down on the desk.

"You have him?"

"Yes."

"Dead or alive?"

"Dead."

"Where?"

"Outside. On my horse."

"Well, let's go get him."

The three lawmen grabbed their coats, and all four men walked outside.

The marshal grabbed the dead man by the hair and lifted his face up. The dead man's hair was matted and stiff from his own coagulated blood. He studied the picture on the wanted poster and looked back at the dead man's face. "Yep. That's him." He dropped the dead man's head, and it flopped back down. "Where'd you nab him?"

"Up a ways. Just outside a little town up the valley. Sour Creek? Is that it?"

"Sour Springs. Yeah. We heard there was a gunfight up there in the street. The sheriff and his men went up there to check it out. I don't know if they've returned yet."

One of the deputies asked, "Were you part of the gunfight?"

He shook his head, "Nope." And he was telling the truth. "Heard the fracas, though."

"How'd you know he was there?"

"I'd been tracking him and following him for some time. Always a step behind. I guess he got caught up in that gunfight. He was fleeing the scene, and I got him." That part wasn't true.

"He's got multiple gunshots in him."

"Yep."

"Not all your bullets?"

"Nope."

"Well then, it doesn't matter. Here he is. You've stopped a cold, hard killer. Boys, let's get the body inside."

The marshal and the stranger went back inside, and the deputies hoisted the body down from the stranger's horse and carried it inside. They had a holding area in the back of the building for corpses until the funeral home could take them. They carried the body through the office to the back. The body was stiffening up; it had been in the frigid mountain air all day plus rigor was setting in. Both deputies were needed to manhandle the corpse.

"How did you know about him? Where did you run across him first – or where did you start tracking him from?"

"Guy named Flanaghan told me all about him. Shot his wife and kid."

"Yep. This is a two-grand bounty. I have about a thousand here in the safe, but the bank across the street keeps the rest of the money to pay out these. However, I think McCarthy already locked up the bank for the day." He went up to the window and peered out. "Yeah, the shutters are closed. I'll have to pay the rest of it to you tomorrow. Are you sticking around town until the morning?"

"Yeah. I got a room around the corner."

"Carpenter's Inn?"

"I didn't catch his name. Has a restaurant separate from the saloon; wife and daughter are the cooks."

"Yeah, that's Ennis Carpenter. Good. It's going to be another cold night tonight. I imagine you slept on the ground last night."

"Yeah. Past several nights. Up in the foothills. Damn cold for sure."

"I tell you. Tracking a guy down like this and getting him, that's something. Not too many are either foolish enough or skilled enough to do something like that. He came up from Texas by the last report I saw. We weren't expecting him all the way up here. Mind if I ask your name?"

The stranger took another piece of paper out his coat pocket, unfolded it, and handed it to the marshal. "Here. In case you thought I was foolish enough. Some credentials."

The marshal took the paper from the stranger, which was on US Marshal letterhead, and began to read. He glanced up at the stranger's face once or twice while reading it with a look of amazement.

The deputies reentered the room.

"Carson, Stephens, take a look at this."

Carson reached the desk first.

To any sheriff, marshal, deputy, or lawman of any jurisdiction within these United States or any territories thereof:

This paper is notification that the gentleman that possesses it, Kyle M. Foster, is a friend of law enforcement far and wide. Mr. Foster is the man responsible for bringing to justice the outlaws Kenneth Garson, Sherman Rogers, and Gerald Stock of the infamous Garson-Pecos Gang that rampaged through western Texas. Mr. Foster singlehandedly cornered them in El Paso and brought them to justice. Weeks beforehand, he had also killed and brought in Zechariah "The Pariah" Jepson and Alfonso "El Toro" Munoz, a.k.a. "The Bull" Munoz.

Please do all you can to accommodate this man if he asks. He is a friend of the law in this lawless world.

Signed,

Marshal Jefferson "Lefty" Gorman.

El Paso Division, US Marshal's Office

"Whoa. You were the one that brought in the Garson Gang?"

The other deputy added, "And Pariah Jepson? Damn!"

"You're legendary in our circles."

Foster just nodded his head in acknowledgment of the praise.

"Mr. Foster," the marshal said, "Let me thank you for all you've done out there." He stuck his hand out for a handshake.

Foster obliged.

"You've undoubtedly made a small fortune in bounties bringing all those men to justice. I remember the reward amounts of a couple of those guys. I'm not sure why you are still chasing down men like this guy."

"Just still am. Sometimes I just run across trouble."

"Look, let me pay for your lodging over at the inn. I hope that doesn't insult you."

"Not at all."

"If you don't mind, and I don't know your business in town, if there is more business, but if you don't mind, I'd like to pay for your lodging for at least a week. I could use a brave man whose a crack shot in town for a while." The marshal looked down at the paper and back up at Foster. "I know old Lefty Gorman well; we were deputies together down in San Antonio back during the war. Worked under him in El Paso before I came up here. He's an old trusted friend."

Foster winced a bit. He wasn't sure how long he was going to stick around, but he didn't plan on being around for too long. He never stuck around anywhere for too long. "Expecting some trouble coming to town?"

The marshal sighed. Obviously this man saw right through the request. "Well… maybe."

Deputy Stevens piped up, "We got word just this morning that a gang out of Kansas is in the territory. Might be coming this way. We don't know for sure."

"Kansas?"

"Lance Pickford. Heard of him?"

"Yeah. Ran across him once."

"Yeah. I guess you made it out alright."

"I'm here and in one piece."

"So you are."

"It was a poker game in Dodge. Got a bit heated. I folded, wasn't in the hand anymore, but guns on the table were drawn. After some tension Pickford shot the guy across the table. Him and his goons bailed. Took all the money from the table. No one protested. Our lives were worth more."

"Well, he's still a cold-blooded bastard, and he's on the loose and in the area."

"I'll think about it. Let me get back to the hotel. I'll come back in the morning for the rest of my reward and give you an answer. Speaking of reward…"

"Oh yeah, let me get that for you." The marshal unlocked his safe and handed Foster a fistful of bills. "Count it… make sure what I'm giving you. Should be about a grand."

Foster turned to the desk and counted out the money:

"$1,120."

"Oh, there's more there than I thought. OK. I'll get you the rest when you come back in the morning."

The men shook hands and Foster left.

He rode down to the livery behind the inn and stabled his horse. He walked back to the inn. The evening was growing colder, the wind starting to pick back up. Carpenter was serving drinks behind the bar. The saloon was starting to fill up for the evening. Several poker games were in process. Foster looked around the room and approached Carpenter.

"Yes, sir. How can I help?"

"You, you have… Are there any women around? Y'know? A woman to help a man after a long ride?"

"Um. Yes. Not here. Well, not in the hotel. Uh, head around the corner, like you're going to the livery. Did you stable your horse over here or over at Grossbar's?"

"Back here."

"OK, just head back that way and stay on the path. There's only one house past Jonesy's stable, about a quarter mile down the road. You can see it when you pass the barn. Two-story house. White fence around it."

"Thanks."

Carpenter leaned in closer to Foster and motioned to him with his finger.

Foster leaned towards the saloon owner.

Carpenter looked behind him quickly and half-whispered, "Tell Gertie that Jimmy sent you. She'll hook you up with the best girl at half price."

"Thanks. Gertie is the madam?"

"Yep."

"I thought I heard from the marshal your first name was Ennis?"

"It is. Middle name is James. Only Gertie and a few others even know that name. And I'd like to keep it that way."

"Gotcha."

Foster walked up to his room, unloaded some of his paraphernalia, and hid his money. He washed up and headed back out the door and down the snowy path past the stables. The mountains in the distance were silhouetted against a thin ribbon of red, the last of the sun's rays for the day. The sky above his head was a dark indigo and clear. A few dozen stars started to shimmer. A chill was in the air. The wind was cold.

3

Foster was standing outside the marshal's office early. He was watching the early-morning hustle and bustle of the town as it woke up and started to move about. His night had been satisfying. He spent some time at the whorehouse down the way and then returned to the inn. Tempted by other vices in the saloon, he had two drinks at the bar, but he just observed the poker players from a distance, not joining in. He turned in early and had his best night of sleep in weeks.

Morning came, and he had a hearty breakfast in the diner. Instead of saddling his horse, he just walked over to the marshal's office and waited for the lawmen to start their day. He was surprised they weren't early risers. He saw the sheriff office was already open as he walked down the street. He guessed that's the difference between the locals and the federals.

The morning sun was bright. Some thin, wispy clouds were high in the sky, but much of the sky was a vibrant blue. The sun accentuated the white, snow-covered town, brightening the landscape more than it really was. At least the wind was no longer blowing. The morning was just crisp and bright. The snow in the streets was crunched into a dirty mush from horses hooves and wagon wheels, but the snow in other areas, along the margins of the sidewalks and streets was still a virgin white.

The marshal and Deputy Carson showed up at nine o'clock sharp, both riding in side by side. There was a clock tower on the bank building across the street.

"At least you got here before the bank opened." Deputy Carson laughed at the whimsical comment. Everyone entered the office.

"We'll head over as soon as McCarthy opens the bank."

"Sleep good last night?"

"Yes. Yes. Beats sleeping under the stars on cold nights."

"Carpenter has a good place. Nice beds."

"There's Edward. He's opening the bank."

"One question, Marshal."

"Yes."

"You mentioned you needed someone to stick around who was a good shot. How did you know I was a good shot?"

"I just assumed. It looks like the kill shot on Pearson went straight through his eye. That's a pretty good shot. Or lucky."

"Oh yes."

"Let's head across the street."

They walked out toward the bank. As they crossed the street, the marshal asked Foster, "Given any more thought to sticking around for a week or so?"

"I have given it a thought or two."

"Well?"

"I'm still considering it. I'll be here at least one more night."

"I visited Ennis Carpenter. I went ahead and paid forward your room until Sunday night."

"Yes, I know. I went to him this morning to reserve tonight. He told me."

They reached the door of the bank, and the marshal paid up the balance owed to Foster.

"Let me know what you decide. I haven't heard anything more on the Pickford gang, but if you need to hang your hat in town for the rest of the week, we welcome you. I never know what other trouble comes along. You just never know. Every day can be an adventure."

"I'll let you know. Thanks."

They went their separate ways. The marshal crossed the street back to his office, and Foster went down the street to the mercantile. He needed some provisions and more ammunition.

Foster got his horse out of the livery and meandered around the growing town. After exploring the half dozen streets, still half-covered with snow, he rode down to the docks on the banks of the river. The docks were constructed of fresh wood and pilings. Much of the town was of recent construction. The mining outfit was recent, but fueling the town's rapid growth.

He looked off in the distance across the river, up the other side of the valley. The foothills of the other mountain ridge had fresh-cut tree stumps, and the landscape across the mountain side was a patchwork of old growth, medium growth, new growth, and saw-cut stumps. A warehouse along the riverbank on the other side filled with lumber planks, ready for use or shipment down the river. He could hear the harsh sounds of a sawmill echoing across the river, probably in the building just behind the warehouse. There was another roofline, taller, visible behind the open warehouse. It looked like the lumber operation had been around for some time. It was probably the prime mover of the town. It probably predated the town itself. He'd have to ask Carpenter. He seemed to know everything.

Between the lumber, cattle ranching, and the mine, there was a lot going on here.

He kept riding along the river. There were two places to cross the river, both providing manned rafts for a nickel to get across, each way. The river was deep enough that you couldn't cross on horse. The banks were steep, too. The underwater terrain was probably steep and possibly had loose rocks. Treacherous to attempt.

He rode on farther, about another mile or two, and he could hear rapids. The river took a sharp bend toward the right behind a forested area. He rode into the trees, still following the water. The river widened out and become much shallower for about a quarter mile. He was right about the river bottom, which was made of very loose river rock. The water was only about as deep as the belly of a horse is high. It would be difficult for the horse to cross, but it could be done—if you had to.

The water was crystal clear, fresh, and frigid. His eyesight tried to follow it upriver to see where it came from. He could see it for several miles across the wide valley and up into the foothills. The river disappeared at a higher elevation beyond a ridge, obscured with pine. He was curious where the headwaters were. It probably meandered across and through the mountain slopes for quite a ways.

It seemed wide enough in the valley to have been a longer river that collected snow melt for quite some distance away. He doubted the headwaters were just in these mountains. There must have been higher mountains beyond what he could see.

Much of the landscape in that direction appeared untouched. The only visible evidence of humans was that one long, sweeping hillside about a mile or two on the other side of the river, where the trees were being cut for lumber.

There were some wagon wheel indentions across the ground leading up to the shallow area. He could see a continuation of the wagon wheel tracks on the other side. Someone saved a nickel and crossed here. There must be something on the other side, farther down, that was worth getting to. He kept to his side of the river and explored more.

The river bent back toward his left and the elevation decreased sharply in a few places. The path he was on became less of path and more of just a level, rocky area on the side of a mountain. His horse, while astute to this kind of terrain, had to step gingerly as he traversed the rocks. He found himself on a ridge overlooking the river. The ground leveled off, but the river continued beneath him. He looked back. The mountain ridge on the western edge of town, beyond the whorehouse, was still visible over the tops of the pine trees he had just wandered through. He looked to the north and saw the full extent of the forest providing the lumber operation its raw material. It stretched for miles along the mountain ridge.

The river kept flowing beneath him as far as he could see. The landscape over his other shoulder spread out into a flattened plain area a mile or so beyond his precipice. There were some fences stretching at right angles to each other in the distance. It looked like there might be some farming going on out there in the springtime, and cattle dotted the plain. There was some bison in the distance.

He took in the vista in for several minutes, basking in the beauty of the scene.

He turned his horse around and looked to the south, which was mostly up a ridge. Somewhere up that ridge was the mining operation. He surveyed the hillside and looked down the incline. He could see a creek at one point peek out of the hillside, rushing downhill. He couldn't see where it ended; farther down, it disappeared into more trees. Undoubtedly, it found its way to the river in the distance. He couldn't advance any farther, other than back the way he came, and he rode back to town.

4

Foster arrived back in town and ate some lunch at the dining room of the hotel. He figured he should poke around and try to find out what the local sheriff's investigation of the gunfight revealed. He wanted to make sure no one had any contrary theories to what he told the marshal. If he had to, he could get out of town quickly.

He was not sure why he was even staying in town any longer. He had his money. *Curiosity, mostly*, he thought. *There might be an opportunity or two for some more financial gain. Also, just to get a lay of the land.* He might return one day. It seemed to him a lot of the commerce of this territory flowed through here. Whatever information he can get and store in his brain might prove useful one day. Also, the man in the black duster he shot at Sour Springs was someone he knew. He wanted to know what business he had up here. He might as well poke around for a few days.

And he wanted to spend at least one more night in a hotel before heading back to the wilderness and sleeping under the stars in the winter night air.

The dining room was busy with patrons, but it was not completely full. He had eaten more in the last two days than he had all the week leading up to the capture of his bounty in Sour Springs.

Carpenter came into the room from the kitchen. He saw his newest favorite customer sitting alone at a corner table. "Howdy, stranger."

"Hello Ennis."

"How are you today?"

Foster chewed his bites of food and swallowed before answering, "Fine. Rode down to the river earlier. Busy town, it is."

"Yes."

Foster pointed at the other chair at the table with his fork. "Sit down."

"Oh no. Thanks. We're awfully busy right now."

"Sit, for just a minute. I have a question for you."

Carpenter was a bit taken aback at the command, and Foster sensed it, but he wiped his hands on his apron and took the seat. "OK."

Foster took another bite of food, chewed it, and swallowed. "What do you know about the gunfight up at the Sour Creek town?"

"Springs. Sour Springs."

"Yes, that's it."

"I haven't heard much. The sheriff was talking to the mayor in the saloon last night. Not much they could figure out. Probably some rival gangs got into it in the street. The townsfolk scattered or hid. No one seemed to have any information when the sheriff interviewed all he could. That little place up there seems to invite that activity, why, I don't really know. It seems like there is a gunfight up there once a month. This town is too big to get away with much, plus with both a sheriff and a federal marshal, it keeps us a bit less desirable for ne'er-do-wells to attempt anything.

"That's not to say it hasn't happened, or won't happen again, but I reckon it depends on what an outlaw is after. If they want to hit a big bank, this is the place, but the marshal is across the street. If you're just after some petty theft, or seeking revenge, or stealing horses, Sour Springs is prime for it. There's no law presence there."

"I gathered that. The sheriff is down here."

"Yes, sir. Correct. Usually about once a day, one of the deputies rides up there just to check on things. I think Carson was going up there the other day, but hadn't left yet. It all happened early in the morning from what I heard. A guy named Blanton, he runs the store up there, rode down here and told the sheriff. They all rode back up together."

Foster kept eating his meal.

"I heard you got your man from up there. Your bounty."

Foster gulped. He didn't make eye contact with Carpenter. "Yeah."

"Forgive me for asking, sir, but were you a part of all that?"

"Not really. No." He looked up from his plate, and his gaze pierced Carpenter.

Slightly questioning the man's response, Carpenter sat frozen in his chair. He stared back at Foster, surveying his face and watching for a nonverbal sign that suggested otherwise. Carpenter sensed tension between the two for the first time since they had met. He fidgeted with his apron, worried he may have just angered his current best patron. Ennis Carpenter was never in the business of making customers angry, especially ones that had not shot up the saloon or a hotel hallway, and ones that paid up front without him begging.

Foster swallowed the last of his food, set down his fork, and pushed the plate an inch or two away from him. He leaned back in his chair and crossed his legs. He took a sip of water and looked Carpenter in the eyes.

Carpenter started tapping his right leg while still fiddling with his apron.

"I was following the guy. For… a while. A week or longer. Well, more than that, nine or ten days. I was camped out just above him for the night, waiting for him to move on. He must have gotten up early and roamed into that town. He had been traveling alone. I never suspected he knew I was following him the whole time. He didn't seem to be wary or cautious at all. However, he did seem to be purposeful in his travel. I don't know what he was doing or where he was going. I was just following him. I didn't want to take him too quick. I didn't want to take him too far away from a town without a sheriff because I didn't want to have to carry a dead body around for too long.

"I'm not familiar with this territory up here. So, I wasn't sure where I was, but I knew the moment would present itself at some point. I just needed to stay close behind him. Honestly, I wanted him alive, too. I'd rather he come to justice, but that wasn't in the cards.

"I got up, looked down at his camp, and he was gone. I saw that little town down the way and figured he was down there. There was a bunch of gunfire I could hear before I got into town, and I just hunkered down, out of view, and waited to see what was going on. I figured he was the cause of it. When it was all settled down, he just happened to come up on me suddenly. He startled me, I had my rifle in my hand, and I fired. Took him down. He had a pistol in his hand. I only realized afterward he had been shot a couple of times already."

"How did you know to come down here?"

"I didn't. But I had seen the tracks the day before and the river. I figured there was some town down along the river here somewhere. I was not sure if whatever was going on in that little town was still going on. I didn't need to walk into someone else's gunfight. I had him. Dead. And I got out of there. As I got closer, I realized there was a bigger town down here. Call me lucky."

Carpenter looked around the dining room to see if any of his customers needed anything and then looked back at Foster. "Well. You might want to tell the sheriff. He's mighty perplexed about the whole incident. No one that was shot and killed was from Sour Springs. They were all strangers. Except for one, Flanaghan, he was from there. The rest were outsiders. They must have all rode in that morning."

"The marshal knows my story. I'm sure they've compared notes by now."

"Probably. You need anything else, sir? More water? Whiskey?"

"No, I am fine. Thank you. What do I owe you?"

"Nothing. The marshal is paying your bill as long as you're in town."

Foster smiled. He put a quarter on the table as he stood up. "There's a tip."

"Thank you sir." Carpenter stood up and grabbed the quarter, put it in his pocket, and grabbed the man's dishes and cutlery. "If'n you need anything, I mean anything, you just let me know, mister."

Foster walked up to his room.

Carpenter cleaned the table and wondered how much of what he told him was true. The last man standing in any gunfight is the one who records the history of it. He knew the folks up there. They usually stop watching when a fight breaks out. They never wanted any trouble. They always turned around and hid until the shooting is done. He didn't blame them either.

Foster cleaned up in his room and then walked down the street towards the sheriff's office. He looked around at some of the businesses. He was being nosy, but he wanted to see if there was a casual way to catch the sheriff's eye. They must have known about him by now, but he was curious about what they knew. Carpenter was the headwaters of town gossip, but he could not have known everything—even if what he knew was accurate. He knew Carpenter would repeat what he told him to the sheriff, or to the mayor, or to the marshal, or Gertie, or whomever, which is why Foster told him his false version of what happened. He also knew that Carpenter wouldn't remember all the details exactly and would get some of them wrong. Everyone does. That's how gossip works. The key thing of the story was he was outside the town when he shot Pearson. That was the same part of the story the marshal knew too.

If they compared stories, and he figured they would at some point, they'll arrive at the same point. It was all a lie, but it was unprovable. That's all he needed... for now.

5

He looked at the store directly across the street from the sheriff's office. He turned around and looked towards the sheriff's office for a moment. The sheriff's office had big windows on the front. It was their way of keeping their eye on the street. Several lawmen were milling about inside the office, clearly seen through the windows. He then turned back around.

Townsfolk kept passing him on the street, going about their business. The sun was at its apex for the day, and it felt warm on his skin, despite the ever-present seasonal chill. It was warmer than the day before, and some of the snow started to melt. The street was a slushy mess of half-melted snow and dirt. He looked around, tried to look as much like a stranger as possible standing in the middle of the street for a minute or two, and then entered the business. Hopefully, the sheriff or one of the deputies noticed him.

The proprietor greeted him as he walked in.

Foster returned the greeting with a nod. It was a hardware store. He looked around, and before the man could say anything else, Foster walked toward the back of the store. His boots clunked along the wooden floor and made a hollow thump with each step as the floor was raised up on wooden girders to keep the floor up off the ground. The space in between the ground and floor acted like the cavity of a drum, amplifying each step. There were several other patrons inside. When a group of three or more moved at the same time, it sounded like an orchestra of drums.

Foster heard the door squeak open and turned slightly around to see one of the local lawmen walking in. Good. They had taken his bait. The building was full of noises: the creaky door hinge, the clump-clack of boots percussing the resonant floorboards, and the jingle of the deputy's spurs as he moved with a purpose towards Foster. He stared straight ahead at some bins with nails in them, but he knew the deputy was headed straight for him. Footsteps came up behind him on the wooden floor. He could feel the deputy behind him. He glanced over his left shoulder subtly, and the two made eye contact.

"Yes, sir. Can I help you?" Foster turned completely around.

The deputy looked him square in the eyes for a moment but didn't answer.

"Deputy?"

He finally answered, "Are you Kyle Foster?"

"Yes, sir."

"Mind if I ask you some questions?"

"Not at all."

The deputy looked around the store. "Care to come across the street?"

"Am I in trouble for something?"

"No. Just have a few questions."

"Can you ask them here?"

The deputy looked around the store. The proprietor was now looking in their direction.

"I suppose."

"OK."

"Were you up at Sour Springs two days ago?"

"Sort of. Close by."

"You brought in that Pearson fellow to the marshal, right? Collected a bounty for him?"

"Yes."

"I heard you had been following him for some time."

"Yes." He swallowed; his throat was getting dry. He wondered what version of the story the deputy knew, but he kept his cool.

"How did you know he had a bounty on him?"

"Ran across a guy who told me. The Pearson fellow had shot his wife and kid. I inquired. Heard he had shot several people."

"And where did you acquire this information?"

He swallowed again and rubbed the back of his neck, "Um. Not sure anymore. Really."

The deputy stared him down.

Foster was silent. He heard the door squeak a couple of more times.

The old man who owned the place emerged from the counter and locked the front door. As innocent of a sound as it is possible for a door latch to slide into its groove, it seemed like an explosion to Foster's ears when the old man engaged it. He didn't want to be suspicious and look around the store, but he figured out that all the other patrons had bought their goods and left. It was just the three of them in the store. The hardware store, with all its creaks and thumps was now a chessboard; Foster was a chess king standing alone, facing another king and queen chess piece. There was no way out, except perhaps that it was a fair bet a backdoor existed.

The deputy spoke, "Chester Flanaghan?"

"Uh. What?"

"Chester? Chester Flanaghan? Was that man who told you Pearson killed had his wife and son?"

"I don't rightly know what his first name is, sir."

"Sir, I'm going to ask you one more time… where did you meet up with Chester Flanaghan?"

Foster stood there silent. He was desperately trying to avoid checkmate. He did not find any options that he could weigh. He looked toward the front door.

The old man was staring and watching the whole thing from the end of the aisle.

Foster looked beyond him, out the windows, at the sheriff's office. He could see another lawman standing in the sheriff's office window, watching from across the street. The deputy's backup. Foster wasn't sure if it was the sheriff himself or another deputy.

Too far away to tell, but it didn't matter. He knew things were about to go down—fast and dirty.

Foster made eye contact with the deputy, "Why does it matter to you?" Keeping his eyes pinned on the deputy, Foster discreetly eased his hand to his revolver. He could see the lawman's eyes narrow, and the veins in the man's temple started to beat rapidly.

"It just does." The deputy already had his hand near his holster.

"Look, I brought a man to justice. What else matters?"

"The truth."

Foster stood there silent.

"Chester Flanaghan is from here. He worked at the sawmill. Billy Pearson had been in Sour Springs for a couple of days. He used to work up at the mine. He went on a killing spree, killed Flanaghan's family for no reason that anyone can figure. And then he killed some people in a bar that night. That was about a year ago, maybe longer." He turned to look at the old man for confirmation.

The old man nodded in agreement.

"Pearson fled to Kansas, allegedly, but I guess he came back. Someone noticed him and came down here to tell Chester. Chester told his brother and went up there that morning to kill him, and ran across some other bad guys. You suspiciously look like you might have been one of them.

Foster looked over at the old man and back at the deputy. The deputy moved his hand to the grip of his pistol, still holstered. Foster moved his hand away from his gun, purposefully enough so the deputy would see. "I want this man as my witness." He pointed at the proprietor. "Are you an honest man, sir?"

The old man swallowed at first, nodded, then found the courage to finally speak, "Yes... Yes, sir."

"He's a pillar of our community if that's what you're asking."

"Fair enough."

"But, whatever you are going to say, you can do it across the street."

"No. I'd rather he hear it. All you can come over here and listen, but I'd rather do it here... with a witness."

"You don't trust us?"

"You trust me?"

"No, but I'm the man with badge."

"That doesn't always mean much from what I've seen over all my years."

"Go ahead and tell us what you want to say. You can trust Collins here. He's more honest than a preacher."

"I didn't know Flanaghan. There is a dead guy up there... or was. You probably collected him behind a building on the east edge of town, dead with the Flanaghan guy, wearing a black duster coat and a black hat. He was the guy I was following."

"Yep. We didn't know who he was."

"Well, I do."

"Who is he?"

"Doesn't matter to you."

"It does. He was killed in our jurisdiction."

"He deserved it. Ruthless man."

"I don't know that, sir. Vigilante justice might prevail elsewhere, but in these parts we don't embrace it. Killing is killing."

"Fair enough. He's part of the Pickford gang y'all been hearing about."

"Go on."

"There's a long story and a short story."

"I got time. Tell the long version."

There was a knock at the door. Everyone turned to see who it was. It was the deputy that had been watching from across the street. The old man let him in.

"Everything all right in here?"

"This man was about to tell his version of the story, Mac. Why don't you join in on the entertainment?"

Foster rolled his eyes. This guy wasn't going to believe him—no matter what he said. "As I said, the man in the black duster is part of the Pickford gang. I know him. There's no bounty out for him alone, or anything. The bounty is on Lance Pickford himself."

"Go on."

"I was actually following him. I'm not sure what was going on in the street. Filson, that's his name, went into town alone, and I can only assume he killed those other guys. I honestly don't know who they are. I stayed out of sight to see what was going to happen. I only wanted something from him. I wanted him dead, but if someone else was going to do my dirty work for me, that's fine. I wouldn't complain.

"There was an exchange between this Flanaghan guy and Filson. Filson was the one that killed the Pearson fella, and then the two of them were in a standoff behind the building. Filson told Flanaghan there was a bounty on Pearson. Flanaghan told him he don't know that. Filson asked him why he shot him then. Flanaghan said out of revenge and said he had killed his wife and kid, son, whatever. Flanaghan was the one that put a bullet or two in Pearson, but he was crawling, stumbling away, and Filson came up from around the other corner. Filson put the bullet in his eye.

"I probably could have gotten involved and it's possible I could have saved Flanaghan's life, but this was between them. I didn't know the man, and, quite frankly, I didn't care. I wasn't sure if he had a fighting chance or not, but if this Flanaghan fella took out Filson, then my dirty work was done. I had just found out at that point that Flanaghan was only in it for revenge. Perhaps him and I could have split the bounty on that Pearson guy. Anyway, Filson advanced on Flanaghan's position. He strategically was in a good place behind the building. I let it play out. Flanaghan turned abruptly and faced off with Filson, and Filson blasted him. It was a risky and boneheaded move on Flanaghan's part to face him straight up at point blank range and it was his last move.

"I should have known Filson was the better gunfighter, because he's one of the best in the land, but I didn't react because I knew one of them was going to be out of the picture in a matter of seconds. I didn't want to reveal my presence to them and have to deal with both of them."

"I understand that. Go on."

"The Flanaghan fella was dead and Filson didn't know I was there. I put a bullet in his head. Revenge was mine. So, there, I'm admitting to you that I killed the man—a man you know nothing about—but his death was justified. That should go for something. I need to return something to someone to prove this Filson fella is dead. That was what I come for, and that is why I killed him."

"And, what is that?"

"A silver crucifix."

"Let me see it."

"I don't have it on me; I hid it away for safe keeping."

"What's the story with the cross?"

"It's stamped on the back 'For Mabel'."

"Who's Mabel?"

"The daughter of Pappy Carmichael."

"Who's Pappy Carmichael?"

"The man currently holding Lance Pickford hostage."

6

"What? Where?" Both deputies suddenly perked up interest.

"Kansas."

"Tell us more."

"Mr. Collins, you still following all this?"

Old man Collins nodded.

"Mabel was Pappy Carmichael's daughter." Foster swallowed and his face showed a slight flinch of emotion as he glanced down at the floor for a moment and then back at the deputy. "And I was engaged to her. I was off in the war when all this happened. I was in Vicksburg under General Grant's command. I didn't know until I returned home about a year later."

"That was a long time ago. You've been chasing him ever since?"

"No. Pappy didn't know exactly who the guy was at the time. They were just a young outlaw gang that ran up on the house. Pappy never forgot the man's face and ran across him in Dodge City years later. Pappy found out who he was and we've been after them ever since."

"They killed his daughter?"

"Filson raped her first. Right in front of Pappy. The other two gangsters held him at gunpoint while he did it. A neighbor of his, not knowing what was going on, came riding up to the house. It startled the gangsters, and they went up to the window to look out. Pappy reached for a gun. Shot one of them. Wounded him. Filson fired back, missed Pappy, but then shot Mabel, point-blank, and killed her. He pulled his pants up, and Pappy fired again, missed Filson, and the whole gang ran out the door, firing at the neighbor, who was still on horseback. They shot him, didn't kill him, but knocked him off his horse. The horse was spooked and ran off. Pappy chased them, but they got on their horses quickly and got out of there. Pappy hit one them in the shoulder while they were riding off. He doesn't remember if the first one he shot was who he hit again—or the other one—but they got away."

"And this crucifix?"

"A silver crucifix Mabel's grandfather gave her for her sixteenth birthday. She wore it on a necklace. Filson ripped it off her neck."

"And he had it on him?"

"Yep. Pappy wants it back. It's proof Filson was dead."

"Can you take us to this Pappy Carmichael to corroborate the story?"

"Sure. It's a long ride."

"I'm going to talk to the sheriff about this. He's out of town until at least tomorrow. He's serving a warrant down in Shannon Creek. We might need to post a bail for insurance you won't flee."

"I can do that."

"We need to talk to the marshal… not sure if you rightfully can accept that bounty money now."

"Why not?"

"You admitted you didn't kill him."

"Right. But I brought his body in."

"Yes, but, you didn't kill him…"

"Dead or alive! It doesn't matter how he died. His dead body was brought in… by me!"

"Not my decision to make. Just mine to report. The marshal needs to decide."

The other deputy added, "You better come with us now."

Foster looked at the old man, "You got all that, right?"

"Yes."

"I want your file to note the witness."

"It will. C'mon. Let's take him over to the marshal."

7

The marshal looked at Foster, "How can I prove this Pappy fellow has Pickford? How can I prove your story isn't a load of bull?"

"I guess you can't unless we ride off to Kansas."

"I thought you were from Texas?"

"I am... now. After I got home from the war and found out Mabel was dead, I moved around and settled in Texas. Found work. Wrote to Pappy for Christmas every year. He discovered who the guy was and wrote me back one year to tell me, and asked me to help find him. I owed that old man at least that."

"Found work? Bounty hunting, I guess?"

"Whatever pays."

"And how did you get this Pickford guy? I mean how is this old man holding a ruthless outlaw hostage?"

"I brought along some men to help. We ambushed them and captured Pickford. Filson got away. I think one other guy got away too, but Filson was the one I wanted. My guys stayed to guard Pickford, and I followed Filson. It's easier to follow someone when you're just one person. A crowd attracts attention. All I wanted was to return that crucifix to Pappy. Closure for his daughter's murder."

"Why didn't you tell me this when I told you we had word that Pickford was riding into the territory?"

"I don't know. I didn't want the word to get out. Filson was heading this way for a reason. I'm not sure why. I think he was after Pearson… maybe. When he got away from us, he came this way. I had to find out what he was doing out here. Even though I killed him, I wasn't sure who he was here to see or do. If I had said something, word might have gotten out to the wrong people, and then next thing I know, I'm dead. I had to protect my back. I don't think anyone out here knows me or my face—or that I was even after Pickford in the first place—but I couldn't be too careful and say anything to you.

"I know how things are in small towns when people start talking about the 'stranger' that just came to town. Not that I'm blaming you for gossip or anything, but I figured word would've gotten around. That old Carpenter guy has told me more about this town in two meals I've eaten in his presence than I can even remember. It was apparent to me that the sheriff and him talk about the goings-on in this town. I gathered you and the sheriff talk for professional reasons. I had to keep quiet. In the meantime, I had to lie low and see what was going on around here. I'm sorry I lied to you Marshal, but it was just to cover my own ass."

The marshal grimaced and sighed. "Boys, Mr. Foster here is relegated to his room and the hotel dining room—but *not* the saloon. I want one of you to post a watch on him the entire time. He is not to step outside. You guys figure out the schedule and rotate. Ask the sheriff for help from his deputies if you have to. Mr. Foster, this will be temporary until I figure out what to do about this matter. Boys, escort Mr. Foster to his room. Good day, sir."

The deputies obliged their boss's command.

Foster went grudgingly, but quietly.

The marshal sat down at his desk and pondered the situation further.

The deputies walked Foster down the sidewalk and over to the hotel. The sky was now overcast, and it looked like a threat of snow. The mountains in the distance were shrouded in thick clouds, all that could be seen was the base of them. A northern wind had begun to blow, and the air was brisk and chilly. Long shadows spread across the street. Foster was quiet the whole way.

When they got to the hotel, Carpenter was cleaning up a table of glasses in the saloon. A group of cowboys had just finished a poker game.

Carson addressed him, "Mr. Carpenter, Foster here has been sequestered to his room for the interim. He is allowed to eat in your dining room, but not be here in the saloon. One of us will be posted outside his room in the hallway. Could you kindly provide us with a chair? We will accompany him when he needs to eat. I just want to inform of you what we're doing."

"Yes, sir. I'll get a chair up there for you. Is he under arrest?" Carpenter made eye contact with a smirking Foster, bemused by his situation.

"Not exactly. Maybe. I don't know what category we are classifying it as. Marshal's orders, that's all." He looked back at

Foster, "I'm not sure what the Marshal thinks he's doing. If it was up to me, he would be locked up in our jail cell until we figured this story out."

"I'll get you that chair shortly."

"Thank you."

The three men walked up the stairs to Foster's room. As Foster unlocked his room, Stephens said, "We'll need your gun too."

"What? And leave me defenseless in this outlaw country?"

"We are armed and will be beside you should anything happen."

"What if you get shot? Then what?"

"Sir, your gun."

Foster gingerly produced his revolver from its holster and handed it to them.

"And I understand you have a rifle also."

Foster entered the room. "It's in here." So as not to start any violent flare-up, he simply pointed to the corner of the room and allowed them to pick it up. "It's over there in the corner."

Carson grabbed it.

"And the silver cross."

Foster sighed. He reached under the bed, and pulled out a saddle bag.

Carson and Stephens both drew their guns. "Easy now."

Foster paused and put up one of his hands up. "I got it. Not going to do anything stupid." He reached in, rifled around a bit, and produced an ornate silver crucifix with a large turquoise gemstone in the middle, a few smaller ones around it, and with an engraving on the back: "For Mabel".

Carson, with his revolver still pointed at Foster, reached over and grabbed it. He rolled it over between his fingers a couple of times. It was just as he had described it. Carson pocketed it.

"Careful with that. It's the only thing in this evil world that means anything to me. And it belongs to a broken-hearted father in Kansas. It must be returned."

"Don't worry."

Stephens added, "I'll be right outside. Just open the door when you are ready to go to dinner."

The two men exited his hotel room with Foster's guns—the ones they knew about.

Foster put his bag back under the bed. *Sloppy law enforcement. A quick search of that bag would have produced another pistol. They'll learn... the hard way.*

Foster plopped down on his bed and stared out the window. It certainly looked like it was going to snow.

He had a knife he always had tucked away discreetly in his right boot. That would also prove useful when the time came. He contemplated what to do next. He figured he would make a play on one of them at some point, but he would give it some time. Make sure they have earned his trust that he is complying with their demands. Hit them when their guard was down. He also knew he shouldn't wait too long. Time was not on his side. Probably late tonight after the fervor of the saloon died down. He could hear all the activity through the walls. His room was directly above the bar.

He could probably just stab whichever one is on watch in the middle of the night and make a break for it. He liked the sharp blade of a knife. Quiet killer. Doesn't raise any attention. The ultimate weapon, but you have to get close to the guy. Eventually the saloon would be closed for the night. Everyone should be asleep late night or early in the morning. Even that creepy Carpenter had to go to sleep at some point.

He could get his horse out the stable and ride out of there.

He still had all the cash money. The marshal hadn't taken that away from him—yet. More sloppy law enforcement. At least if the deputies had confiscated the money, he would have no reason to make a break for it. No matter the situation, no one would just escape and leave two grand behind. If they had taken and held that money, it would make it less enticing to leave town. Money is its own prison and greed holds the key to the lock. They were probably too trustworthy to think he would try to escape. How naïve of them. Night would fall in a few hours, and the darkness of night is always the perfect cover.

And he did not need the crucifix back. He won that in some poker game several years ago. It was worth something for its value in silver—but not the sentimental value of the story he told. He wasn't sure why he had held onto it all these years. Maybe he considered it some talisman that kept him living up to this point. He didn't know. He just hung onto it. The cross meant nothing to him.

No. It was all a lie. There was no Pappy Carmichael. There was no Mabel that he knew—nor was ever engaged to. Pickford was not being held by anybody in Kansas, but he *was* being held. Loosely. In a hotel room. In this hotel room.

He was Lance Pickford.

8

The marshal was still thinking about this Foster guy. The credentials from Lefty Gorman. The first story Foster told. The second story Foster told. Which was true? Was either true? Hard to tell. Carson walked back into the office.

"He's secure. Stephens is on watch. We got his pistol, rifle, and this…" He reached in his pocket and pitched it irreverently onto the marshal's desk. The silver crucifix adorned with turquoise gemstones clattered and clinked and came to rest two inches from the marshal's hand.

The marshal picked it up and turned it over a few times in his hands, admiring the silversmith artistry of it. "Beautiful workmanship." He paused and gazed at the engraving on the back. He set it back down on the desk and turned to Carson. "What do you think about this guy? His story? His stories? What's your opinion?"

Carson took off his overcoat, set Foster's rifle in the corner of the room right behind his desk, and sat down. "Not sure. Hard to know what to believe. The cross is there. That's about it. But he may have had that for some time. Made up a story on the fly... maybe? He knew if we had to ask, he had this trinket and he could produce it, hopefully adding some credence to his story. I don't know. Maybe he was the rapist of a girl named Mabel? Maybe he got it in a poker game? Maybe his story about Pappy is true? Who knows? How do we plan to prove his story correct without riding out to Kansas?"

"That's a tough one."

"What do *you* think?"

"Not sure. I can't arrest him for nothing. What we're doing with him in the hotel room is borderline breaking protocol. I acted a bit out of emotion, but I knew I had to figure out a way to keep him under our control. I should have had the sheriff do it. Let him worry about the legal regulations. He's out of town?"

"Until tomorrow—or maybe back late tonight. Went down to Shannon Creek."

"Doesn't matter. I don't think this Foster guy is going to do anything."

"What if he had balked at your request to hold him in the hotel room?"

"I'd have played my hand and said, 'Well, you can spend the night in the jail cell.' He would have agreed to his hotel room. When presented with two choices, a man will always take the lesser of two evils."

"True."

"Well, I guess a gunfight and possible death would have been the third choice, but he was woefully outnumbered and on our turf. He's not stupid, that's for sure. He's one smart dude. I have to take him at his word. The letter from Lefty is enough to offer him some trust. We show him trust, and he may trust us. Besides, if this cross has that much meaning to him, he won't leave town without it."

Carson thought for a moment and said, "Are we not holding him under suspicion? Isn't he a suspect?"

"A suspect for what?"

Carson had a confused look on his face, but answered, "Um... well... he did admit to killing that one guy up at Sour Springs."

The marshal had his head hung low pondering the entire situation and the facts, or lies, that were in front of him. "Yeah, but that dude, for all we know, probably deserved it. It might have been outlaw killing outlaw, but if it meant he erased one more piece of human debris from the face of the earth, that's a favor we didn't ask for. I have to go with the fact he helped out with some bounties down in Texas. I have to respect that, and I have to respect Lefty's opinion of him. I need to allow some room for that. I'm not worried about that killing up at Sour Springs. That's a local thing. The sheriff has all the information we got from him. If the sheriff wants to hold Foster for that, he's got a jail cell over there—and he knows where to find him."

"I'm getting the impression the sheriff doesn't want to deal with this guy at all. He heard the story from his deputies and then takes off to go serve a warrant? One of his guys could've done that."

"I get that impression also. Sheriff Donnelly is a helluva shot. Brave man in the line of fire. Courageous. Honest. Loyal to the law. A man you want on your side in a gunfight. All of that. But when it comes to investigations and mirky details and such, he freezes on his decision-making. And he doesn't like the paperwork. I can't blame him. I don't like all the paperwork either. I'd rather justice be administered by the bullet. Quick. Swift. Decisive. If I'm wrong, I'm wrong. Let God figure it out in the end. This world is too evil for any sane man to tolerate anyway. Besides, by not throwing him in our cell gives him a little bit of a trust factor in us. It's just one night I'm asking him not be in the saloon. He will appreciate it." He picked up the crucifix from his desk top and put it in his pocket for safekeeping. He needed to take a stroll to the outhouse. "I'll be right back." As he passed by Carson's desk, he stop momentarily and added, "By the way, next time you recover a religious symbol, I don't care what your beliefs are, don't call it a 'trinket' and don't toss it on my desk like it's some common coin. Some of us still believe in being respectful."

Carson scowled at the criticism as the marshal walked away.

The marshal was heading down the hallway and sarcastically shouted back towards him, "And don't give me that look."

Carson sighed and shook his head. *God? Doing this job and seeing what I see, how can you actually expect me to believe in God?* He shook his head again and added this thought to his internal conversation. *How does the marshal believe in God after doing this job every day for all these years?* He propped his feet up on his desk and leaned back. His felt his lack of faith was justified almost every day he woke up. He couldn't see it any other way.

The door of the guarded hotel room opened.

Stephens was in the chair and looked back at him.

"You want to go to dinner?" asked the voice of the sequestered man.

"I could use a bite."

"We'll put it on the marshal's tab."

The two went downstairs to the dining room. Carpenter was in his usual spot behind the bar. As they passed through the forbidden zone of the saloon, they each nodded at him. They walked out the salon door, stepped on the sidewalk for about ten steps, walked into the dining room door, and sat down.

A light snow was falling.

Carpenter, feeling a need to cater to the men himself and volunteer himself in the name of civic duty, passed through the kitchen to the other side and trotted up to their table to take their orders. "Did you know you can come down the staircase at the end of the hall and it leads right down to here?" He turned over his left shoulder and pointed at a door in the corner of the room. "You don't have to go through the saloon and out one door and back in the next one—unless you want to."

"Thanks for letting us know. Say, just out of curiosity, when do you close the restaurant?"

Stephens glanced at Foster, "You plan on eating again later?"

"Just curious."

"About eight or nine. I keep the kitchen open for the guys in the saloon."

"And when do you open for breakfast?"

"Whenever we get up. I'm usually up by daybreak and in the kitchen for any early-risers."

"Thanks."

They ordered their food.

The marshal came back from the outhouse. "It's damn cold out there."

Carson acknowledged, "I see it's snowing." He shuffled some papers on his desk, stuffed two sheets of papers in an envelope, and closed it.

In the middle pf the room, the marshal staring out the window at the street. It looked to Carson like he was deep in thought. "Look, sir. I'm sorry about the cross thing. It's just that, well, I guess I don't have much faith in this world anymore. This job is just, well, you know, more than any of us can take most days. It's hard facing the evil we face sometimes."

The marshal shook his head slightly as if Carson disrupted his train of thought. "Carson, you think I have any faith left in this world? No. I do not. That is why I have faith in what comes after this world. I have to hold on to that faith. I have faith in justice and in prudent law and in my men to do the right thing at the right time when the time comes. I have to have faith in a judge's decision to rule justly. And I have faith in my wife. That's about it. If I had any faith in the rest of this world, in any man out there, especially after what I have witnessed doing this job year after year, I'd be lying to myself. But, if I don't have any faith in a God that put us here to do what is right—to steer men of a community and lead a community into a life bound by law instead of lawlessness—then what good is that?"

"I don't know, sir."

"There has to be more than just this. That's what I believe. If I have to hold on to the notion that if this is all there is, then why even have laws in the first place? How many men have escaped our grasp? Dozens. They are out there somewhere, doing dastardly things to others. They are not bound by anything other than their own evil thoughts. They live day-to-day with no care for others because they don't think there's any consequence to their actions unless they are caught by lawmen like us. Those are dangerous men in this world. I cannot live that way. That's why I keep doing this damn job. I have to make this world a safer place for those law-abiding people that do care. The ones that just want to be left alone and live their lives quietly. When evil comes to town, it's our job to take care of it. If this is all there is, then why even bother? We should be as lawless as the outlaw and pillage and plunder."

"I understand, sir. It's just hard to see the goodness of world most days."

"I know. Just do me this favor. I know Gretchen is a rock for your family, and I know she makes sure your two little boys go to church every Sunday and say their prayers at night. Just, don't ever lead them astray from that ideal. You can be the curmudgeon all you want and a doubter all you want. You've seen true evil in this world. I have also. We have to live with it. We will continue to live with it, but don't spoil it for the innocent minds that are your children. Let them figure it out as they grow older.

"If they see the same evil when they grow older as we do, and they make an adult decision to question God or reject him, so be it. At least they've done it for reasons they've seen. Like you, I gather. Don't corrupt their young minds at an early age though. If they get a good perspective on life as children, hopefully they'll carry that as long as possible into their adult life. You've said that's how you grew up, and I think that's why you do this job and do it well. I don't think you've lost faith in God; I think you've lost faith in men."

"I will, sir. I get what you are saying. Gretchen will always raise those boys right. She'll do a better job than I will ever do."

"I don't mean to preach, but it might help a little if you go with your family every once in a while and sit in the church pew with them. Show your boys what a man is all about—whether you are going through the motions for their benefit or you are actually moved by the experience. Pastor Mark might teach you a thing or two. It helps me get through the week until the next Sunday. Trust me."

"I'll take that advice, sir."

"Now. I had an idea before we started this conversation. I always do my best thinking in the outhouse. I need to go down to the telegraph office. I'll be back." He walked down the street and asked the telegraph office send a message to the El Paso US Marshal's Office:

Marshal Lefty Gorman.

Could you provide a description of Kyle Foster? The man you said who killed the Garson gang. He is up here. I have doubts about his story.

Frank Fuller

It was late in the evening, and he was not expecting a response until the next day. "Thanks, Morgan. Let me know as soon as there is a response." He paid the fee.

"Will do, sir. I'll let you know right away when I get it, sir."

"I'll be at the office for about another hour or so. Then I'm headed home."

"G'evening, sir."

"Good evening, Morgan."

The marshal returned to the office. "I wish I would have thought of that earlier."

Carson looked up at him, "What's that?"

"I sent Lefty a telegram asking him to provide a description of Foster."

"Oh. Good idea."

"Yep. I thought so. Just wish I had thought of it earlier."

"Probably won't hear back until tomorrow."

"Probably not."

"I'm going to relieve Stephens about midnight. So, I'm going to head home and get some sleep for a couple of hours. Gretchen will wake me up."

"You do that."

Carson gathered his things and headed out the door. Marshal Fuller sat down and decided to finish some paperwork to fill his time.

Foster and Stephens finished their meal and sat and talked a little. Stephens did most of the talking. Foster asked him a few questions about his life and such. He wanted to seem friendly to his captor—and he did not want to talk very much in case he said something to counter whatever they knew about him already. Or thought they knew about him.

The marshal finished what he was doing and decided to head out. He was going to stop by the hotel first and make sure everything was going well.

He saw Stephens and Foster through the window of the restaurant as he walked down the sidewalk. A heavy snow was now falling. "I guess I didn't expect to find you two in here, but it is warmer here than anywhere else."

"Marshal."

"Marshal, have a seat."

"That's alright. I'm sure Julia has food on my table back home. I'm heading out. I sent a telegraph to Lefty in El Paso." He looked at the man he thought was Foster, "I'm not saying I don't trust you; I'm just verifying something. I wouldn't be a good lawman if I didn't."

Foster stared back at him stoned-faced. The poker game for his identity had begun—and he was going to bluff his way all the way to the end.

"We'll load up with provisions and leave for Kansas in the morning. Stephens, Carson will relieve you at midnight. Gentlemen, have a good evening."

They all doffed their hats at one another, and the marshal left.

"Shall we retire to upstairs? It's been a long day."

"You're the boss."

They walked back up the stairs that Carpenter told them about so they did not have to go out outside and then back through the saloon. As they went down the hallway, the clatter of the nightly activities of the saloon drifted upstairs.

Foster opened his door, and Stephens returned his watch to the chair outside. Foster smiled and closed the door. "*Fate*," he said under his breath. He formulated his plan on the way up the stairs. He was going to wait for Carson and Stephens to switch places in the middle of the night and make his escape. Stephens would live to see tomorrow, but Carson would not make it to morning. Even if the saloon patrons were still rollicking after midnight, he could make his flight down this newly discovered staircase.

The plan was coming together.

9

He started packing up things. He gathered all his paraphernalia together and put everything in his saddlebag. He slid it under his bed as before just in case there was a "bed check" by the deputies. He had stashed his money under and behind the few pieces of furniture in the room. He retrieved it all, discreetly packed most of it in the bag, and strategically stashed the rest on his person. A long time ago, he had learned to stitch a few hidden pockets on the insides of a few articles of clothing that were difficult to detect.

It was a nice hotel room this far out in the frontier. Wallpaper. Comfortable mattress. Curtains. A porcelain wash basin and pitcher. Frilly doilies on the furniture. Good, solid, hardwood pieces, probably crafted locally. It looked like pine. He noticed a furniture maker on one of the back streets. An ornate kerosene lamp. All the accoutrements had a woman's touch to it. He still had not met Carpenter's wife, but had seen her through the kitchen door a few times.

He felt as though he had been in this town for an eternity. It really had only been two full days. He was not going to be around much longer. He had everything in place. He kind of would have liked his rifle back, but he knew he couldn't retrieve it from the marshal's office. He'd have to acquire a new one. Stephens had a rifle on him and a revolver. He hoped Carson had the same. After he killed Carson, he take whatever firearms he had.

He was ready. He just had to wait.

The voices, raucous piano playing, and merriment could be heard from downstairs. There was a light thumping in the room. It was not too loud to keep someone awake or to possibly wake up someone who had fallen asleep, but it was noticeable enough if you were still awake. The occasional loud laughter and singing from the drunkards downstairs would crescendo to a point of breaking someone's concentration if they were reading a book. Drunk people always laugh and talk and carry on louder than anyone sober.

Foster/Pickford propped himself up on the bed against the wall and kept his mind busy dealing himself solitaire with a well-worn deck of playing cards on the quilt. He had kicked his boots off. He figured if Stephens and Carson did a bed check when the shift changed, it would only look right if his boots were off; otherwise, it would give the impression he was going somewhere.

The merriment downstairs continued. At times, there was a crescendo; at others, it died down to almost nothing. The waves drifted in and out.

He heard footsteps in the hallway and two men talking. It was the deputies. He quickly gathered up the cards and tossed them in the nightstand. He grabbed a book he had and put his head down as if he dozed off reading. His door was locked, but he was sure Carpenter had given the deputies a pass key.

There was a light knock on the door. He remained motionless for a moment to see if they would enter. He knew they could see the lamplight through the crack under the door. There was a second knock. The doorknob was jiggled. He didn't hear a key. *Huh, amateurs, these guys.*

He stood up. He needed to see what was going on to make sure he knew he could execute his plan. A hard knock came on the door. He opened it.

Both deputies were standing there.

"Sorry… I must have dozed off." His hair was ruffled.

They both peered into the room, saw him in his socks. The kerosene lamp was lit, and the book was still in Foster's hand with his fingers holding it partially open somewhere in the middle.

"I was reading."

They walked in and brushed him off to the side.

"Problem?"

"No. Just checking. You cleaned up in here."

"Passing the time."

"All right. Stephens here is relieved of duty for the night. I'm on watch now. Mind if I use that fancy toilet in there?"

"Go ahead."

The Carpenter Hotel was one of the only places in town that had an indoor toilet—a recent invention, but still rare on the

American frontier. Stephens stood guard one last time while Carson relieved himself.

He washed up in the basin. "You're almost out of water in the pitcher. Stephens, why don't you get some more from Carpenter before you leave for the rest of the night?"

Stephens grabbed the pitcher and went downstairs.

"Leave the door unlocked. I'm on guard; there's no need to lock it."

"Whatever you want." He yawned. "I guess it's going to be a long night for you."

Carson looked at him side-eyed. "I got a few hours of sleep at home. I'll be all right."

Pickford sat back down on his bed. "Right. I'm going to turn in for the night." He reached for the kerosene lamp. "Oh, right, I guess we have to wait for Deputy Stephens."

Carson didn't say anything. He continued to look around the room, looking for anything suspicious.

Stephens returned with a full pitcher of water. "All right guys. That's it. I will see you tomorrow."

"Thanks Stephens."

"Can I extinguish the lamp now?"

"Yes."

He reached over and turned the pilot knob closed. The wick burned out slowly, and then it was dark in the room. He pulled the quilt over him and put his head down on the pillow.

Carson watched him for a moment and then closed the door.

After a few minutes, Pickford quietly pulled the quilt back and sat up. He didn't want to fall asleep and miss his window of opportunity. He reached for his boots quietly and gently slid them on his feet. He pulled the knife out and laid it on the bed to his side. The room was almost pitch-dark. A kerosene lantern outside his window illuminated Carpenter's marquee. It was reflecting light off the falling snow back into his room. His stared straight ahead, looking out the window in silence. His face was clothed in the blue of the light coming in from the outside. It was the face of a killer. All could be hear was the continuing sounds of amusement from downstairs as they faintly drifting upstairs.

He waited in silence and darkness.

10

He estimated he'd been sitting there for about an hour. The sounds from the saloon were dying off. His greatest concern was Carpenter. The nosy hotel owner was the one wildcard in his whole plan. As luck would have it for him, he actually heard his voice in the hallway. It was muffled through the hotel wall, but since the mirth form the saloon had died away for the evening, he could hear what they were saying.

"Hello, Deputy. Is all well?"

"Just fine." The deputy's voice sounded as if he was startled by Carpenter's presence.

"You need some coffee to stay awake? You look a bit sleepy."

Pickford heard Carson shift in his chair. He was probably dozing and slouched in it. His response sounded groggy.

"Thanks. No, I'm fine. Not my first time. I'm all right."

"Good. Things have shut down in the saloon. My son is cleaning up the tables, a couple of drunkards are sleeping on the floor. Normal. They'll be fine. The saloon door is unlocked in case they wake up; they can let themselves out. Everyone else has gone home. I'm turning in for the night."

"Good. We'll see you in the morning."

Carpenter has a son? He never mentioned that before. Carson sounded about as annoyed by Carpenter's nosiness as Pickford always felt. This one time, though, it served Pickford right. Now he knew Carpenter was not going to be around. He was not concerned with his son. Probably just going to wash the glasses and mugs and go to bed. Pickford would use the dining room stairs anyway to steer clear of the saloon.

Pickford crept as silently as possible toward the door as the conversation was going on. His knife was in hand. He heard Carpenter's footsteps head down the hall and eventually faded away. He crept back. He put a chair halfway between the door and the bed, and he sat down in it. It kept him fully alert if he sat straight up. He glanced out the window again. The snow had stopped.

He waited some more time, what he thought was probably about half an hour. It had to be about two o'clock in the morning, which was probably the best time to attack and escape. Pickford had not heard any more noises coming from anywhere within the hotel. Just the wind outside.

He slowly stood up and gracefully walked towards the door with his knife in hand. He took a deep breath. He had no backup plan if Carson was still awake when he opened the door. He softly grasped the doorknob and delicately turned it open. He eased the door open enough for him to look out into the hallway.

74

The deputies had made another amateur move by positioning themselves on the side of the door with the hinges. That way, all he had to do was just barely open the door and peak out to see them. Had they chosen to sit on the other side, the door would have to be almost fully opened in order to look at them. Bad idea on their part.

He managed to crack the door open without any sound. A sliver of light from the hallway poked through the minute opening. It was just enough for him to notice that Carson's head was drooped down. He was sleeping. He could hear him half breathing and half snoring. He continued to ease the door open. No squeak or noise. He re-gripped his knife, solidly held in his hand, took another deep breath, and pounced!

With two graceful steps and a minimal amount of sound, Pickford plunged the knife deep into Carson's stomach, beneath his sternum.

Carson's eyes opened wide, and he belched a painful groan.

Pickford quickly ran the knife across his abdomen, up toward his rib cage, and around the side to his back. Carson's body went limp. Pickford quickly grabbed his body, brought it inside his room, and laid him down on the floor next to the toilet. Carson was struggling for breath. Pickford grabbed the knife from Carson's abdomen, and struck Carson in the neck, and sliced. His blood spewed out and ran all over the floor.

Pickford grabbed his knife and wiped off the blood with a towel. He went outside and looked at the floor. No obvious signs of blood. The hallway was carpeted a dark red with a repeating pattern in it. It hid the first few drops of blood very well that fell before he got Carson's body inside the room. They were not obvious to any casual observer that might happen to walk down the hall in the middle of the night. All they would notice, if they had noticed anything earlier, was that a deputy was not sitting in the hallway.

He grabbed the chair and quietly closed the door to his room to avoid disturbing anyone sleeping down the hall. He glanced back at Carson. *Definitely dead.* He looked at his boots, and there was no blood on them. He didn't want to track anything while going outside. In the morning, everyone was going to know who killed him, but he didn't want someone to find out too soon. He needed all the time he could get to get away from this town.

He grabbed Carson's rifle and pistol, and he put Carson's pistol in his empty holster. He grabbed his saddlebag, cradled the rifle under his arm, quietly exited the room, and locked the door. He crept down the side stairs he had found out about earlier that evening and snuck out through the dining room. No one was around. Once he was outside, he threw the hotel key in a snowbank. He made his way around the corner of the hotel and to the livery stable.

Pickford secured the saddlebag to his horse, put the rifle in a sheath attached the saddle, and mounted him. Man and horse quietly walked out the stable and made their way out of town toward the south, the way he came in from Sour Springs a few days earlier. He knew the northern path presented some issues with the river. He got out of town a ways and spurred his steed to bring him to a trot in the darkness.

The skies had cleared. The wind was blowing fiercely from the north, and a waning moon was providing enough moonlight for him to see the path before him. The fresh snow-covered ground seemed to glow in the scant moonlight. It was enough for his horse to feel comfortable enough to keep a solid pace for the rest of the night. He had to get as far away from here as he could.

11

The first thing Carpenter did after he woke up and washed up was walk down the hallway towards the ad hoc jail cell that was room 6. He assumed Deputy Carson would want some coffee. As soon as he turned the corner and saw no deputy and no chair, his heart began to beat rapidly. He rushed down the hallway toward the door. He tried the knob. Locked. He banged on the door. No answer from inside. He rushed downstairs to the saloon.

The sun had not risen above the mountain range yet, but faint light of dawn was illuminating the frozen ground and the buildings in town. The dawn skies were reddish closest to the mountainous horizon and the snowy predawn ground had a slightly bluish hue to it.

Carpenter rushed to behind the bar and fiddled with the lock on his lockbox with his key. He grabbed a key to room 6 from the box, grabbed his Colt .45 from the hidden cubby on the underside of the bar, and rushed back upstairs. With his adrenaline coursing through him, he fumbled all along the way, stumbling twice as he rushed back up the stairs. With his hand shaking in fear, he had trouble getting the key into the lock.

When he finally unlocked the door, he rushed inside and looked around. He noticed the borrowed chair from the saloon, out of place in the room, next to the room chair and then glanced to his left and saw Carson's boots sticking out of the doorway to the toilet. He took two cautious steps toward him, and in the faint light of morning, saw the pools of blood. Carpenter gasped, pushed the door all the way open, and saw the horrific crime scene.

He turned around, grabbed the kerosene lamp, lit it, took it into the little room, and surveyed the scene. His adrenaline was still coursing through him, and his heart pumping. He had to get with the marshal, but it was still too early for him to be in town.

He set the lamp down, blew it out, and rushed back down the hall to wake up his son.

"Son? Son!"

"Yeah, what is it?"

"Get dressed and ride out to the marshal's house. Foster killed the deputy, and Foster is gone."

"What?"

"Just go get the marshal—and the sheriff!"

Carpenter went into his room. His wife was just getting ready to head down to the kitchen for breakfast. "Dear. Please don't go into room 6. Don't send Catherine in there either. Just stay out of it."

"Why?"

"There's a dead deputy in there. Blood everywhere. I sent Charlie to go get the marshal."

She gasped.

He kissed her on the forehead and left the room. He thought maybe one the deputies from either law enforcement branch might be in early. He walked out into the cold street with only his apron over his clothes. His son, having gotten the horse from the stable and saddled quickly, rode past his father as he stumbled through the snow to the marshal's office.

Carpenter glanced back to the sheriff's office. It looked dark. No lamps were on. He turned the street corner and headed down to the marshal. No one was there either. The air was blustery cold. The freshly fallen snow from the overnight snow shower glowed with an eerie bluish hue in the nascent sunlight. There were a few meandering footsteps in the snow-covered street of some of the late-night drunkards. He was tracking his own fresh footsteps in the snow. He cinched up his exposed neckline on his shirt to the bottom of his chin with his left hand. He should have put his overcoat on before he went outside. He rushed down to the sheriff's office just to confirm. No. He was right. No one was in yet. He rushed back to the hotel.

As he opened the door of the saloon, Morgan from the telegraph office was yelling at him and rushing toward him from down the street.

The two men got out of the cold and walked inside.

Morgan asked, "Have you seen the marshal this morning?"

"No. I was just looking for him. Why?"

"I got a cable from El Paso. Frank sent them a message yesterday at the end of the day asking about that Foster character."

"Yeah?"

"This just came back. We need to get to him."

79

Carpenter looked at the message, and his mouth fell wide-open. He was silent for a minute. "Um… uh… I just sent my son to go get him. I found Deputy Carson dead in the room. Foster is gone."

Morgan took a step backward in disbelief.

Both men stood in silence.

Carpenter's wife came downstairs.

"G'morning ma'am," Morgan tipped his hat towards Mrs. Carpenter.

"Morning Morgan." She nodded at him and turned to her husband, "Is it all right if I fire up the kitchen?"

"Yeah, yeah. Sure. Of course. Let's not make it look like anything is wrong here. Once the sheriff or the marshal gets here, they'll take care of everything. Until then, it's business as usual. Serve any customers—but don't let on to anything."

She hurried into the kitchen and started the daily chores.

"My son won't be long. It's about a five-minute ride out to the marshal's place. They'll be here soon enough."

"I'll stick around. It's my duty to deliver this to him. If you think he's coming already, I'll just wait."

"All right." Carpenter, frazzled by the early morning chain of events, turned around to the fireplace in the saloon and started up a fire. Morgan assisted and handed him some fresh logs. Acting busy and unsure of what to do next, he also went over to the woodburning stove next to the bar and started a fire there. The saloon started to warm up slowly.

Pickford rode all night. He bypassed Sour Springs while it was still dark and rode up the ridge. There were no trees up there, and the ground was relatively flat. He kept riding, guided by moonlight on the snow, until the red glow of dawn provided more light to see. Dawn was peeking up over the mountain peaks. He stopped his horse for a moment, dismounted, and let him forage through the snow and find some grass or other nourishment. He paid for hay at the stable and knew his horse had received some good meals while he was there.

Pickford looked back down the valley which he had been riding up all night. He could not see Sour Springs anymore. He was fairly far out of range of everyone that was going to be coming after him—if they even knew what direction to go in. He probably left horse tracks in the snow. Since it had stopped snowing before he left, they'd probably assume whatever tracks they could find would be his. Who else would have left town in the middle of a frigid night?

He walked around, stretched his legs, and then got back up in the saddle. He glanced backward one last time. Old Carpenter had probably noticed a hallway free of a deputy and had probably entered his room by now. He probably went to the marshal or sheriff, and they were about to figure out he was long gone and would ride out after him. He was about four hours or more ahead of them, but he needed to keep going. This seemed to always be his life. Always on the run.

He spurred his horse lightly and he galloped off toward the red sky coming up over the range. Now that there was more illumination for both him and his horse to see, his horse would trust him when he commanded him to gallop. He took off across the snowy high plain, covering more ground faster than in the shear darkness.

12

Charlie Carpenter and Marshal Fuller came galloping up to the front of the hotel.

The marshal tossed his reins at the Carpenter boy and stormed inside. "Carpenter! What happened?"

Morgan was standing there and impishly handed the marshal the telegraph.

"I thought you were to summon me as soon as this came in?"

"It had just come in, sir. I was coming down the street when I saw Ennis. He said his boy had just left and gone to get you."

The marshal unfolded the message.

To Marshal Fuller

No need to have to describe Foster to you. Kyle Foster, who killed the Garson gang, died last year. He was shot and killed by some outlaw. I went to his funeral. Who you have there is an imposter!

Signed,

Lefty Gorman

Marshal Fuller folded the message and put it in his pocket. "Thanks, Morgan." He looked at Carpenter and took a deep breath. "Take me to the room." They started towards the stairs.

"Wait." The marshal turned around. "Charlie, can you ride out to the sheriff's place and see if he made it back in town? Tell him what happened. Then ride out and get Deputy Stephens, you know where his place is, right?"

"Yes, sir." Charlie nodded and rushed out the door.

Fuller and Carpenter ascended the stairs.

The marshal eased open the door to room 6. He was a professional, but this was also his deputy—and a friend. It was difficult to face this crime scene. He walked over to his body, and a sense of strong emotion came over him at the sight of the blood and his guts spilled out through wide gash in his abdomen. It was like the floor of a slaughterhouse. Since the day was beginning, more sunlight was illuminating the bathroom than when Carpenter had initially entered the room.

Carpenter gave the marshal some space. For once, decent decorum took the place of his usual nosiness. He stepped out of the room and pulled the door slightly shut, leaving just a small gap. He could hear the marshal weeping. He didn't blame him. He was still trying to process the whole scene himself. It felt to Carpenter that Marshal Fuller was in there for an hour, but it was only a few moments.

Fuller came out of the room, visibly shaken by the gory death that had befallen his deputy. "You got someone that can clean that up? I mean, you probably don't want your wife or daughter to see that—or would you want me and Stephens to do it?"

"No sir, I couldn't ask you to do that. Too personal for you. My son and I will clean it up."

"Thank you. I'll wait for the sheriff to get here, and then we'll get Carson's body out here."

They went back downstairs.

"I know it's early, but do you mind if I get a drink?"

"Not at all, sir." Carpenter pulled a bottle from the back of the bar. "It's been awhile, but you still drink whiskey?"

"Yes. Just a swig. Not too much."

Carpenter handed him the shot glass.

"Thanks." Fuller took the shot in one motion and put down the glass. "Now I have to figure out where this damn fellow went." He sighed deeply. "Damn. If I had only sent Lefty a telegraph earlier. I don't know what took me so long to think about it."

"Don't blame yourself, Frank. This man was going to do whatever it took to save his own skin. You probably weren't going to see it coming."

"Thanks Ennis." He looked back down at his empty glass. "Let me have one more, but just one more."

Carpenter obliged the request and put the bottle back in its place after he poured the shot.

Fuller drummed his fingers on the bar for a minute or two, deep in thought, and then he grabbed the shot. "He took off with all the bounty money, too. I was going to get that from him first thing this morning. Damn." He took the shot. "Where'd he stable his horse? Out back here?"

"Yeah, I think so."

"I should've locked the son of a bitch up! This is all my fault. Damn. I didn't think this through. I was just trying to… well, I don't know what I was thinking. I really fouled this up."

Jonesy was in the stable and had already noticed one of his patrons had grabbed his horse and ridden off in the middle of the night. "G'morning Frank! Come to your senses yet about stabling your horses here instead of at Grossbar's?"

"Funny. I'm assuming that Foster fellow grabbed his horse and skedaddled out of here in the middle of the night."

"Appears that way. Left a twenty in the stable. That's one heck of a tip."

"No way of knowing which way he might have gone?"

"Snow is still fresh out there, I'm sure there's some tracks you can follow out of town."

"Right. I was thinking the same."

"What's he wanted for?"

"Lots of things I don't even think I know about, I'm sure, but I do know about one thing: Deputy Carson's death last night."

Fuller did not even wait for a response from Jonesy. He just turned around and walked out the stable. He was still shaking from the crime scene. He'd seen a lot of dead bodies in his day. He was responsible for many of those deaths. He had sent probably two dozen or more outlaws to their grave, but he had not ever seen that kind of carnage, least of all that much carnage of one of his own.

The marshal was blaming himself for the entire course of events. He should have locked the stranger up. This guy had obviously killed Kyle Foster and found that letter on his body. There's no telling how times he may have used it to get away with or out of something. He did not see this coming. Not even remotely. Maybe he was getting too old for this job. He was no longer thinking crisply and fully. He had grown too trustworthy in his later years. His keen sense of suspicion had waned, and that failure to recognize certain things or to act more decisively had cost the life of one of his deputies. Tragic.

Fuller shook the thoughts away from his brain and re-focused himself. He then noticed some hoofprints leading down the street in the snow out towards the south and east. He followed them for about fifty yards and saw they went up over the rise and disappeared at the horizon.

The sun has just peeked above the ridgeline. Orange and yellow skies were turning bright morning blue. He heard some horses galloping and turned around and saw the sheriff and one of the sheriff deputies dismounting in front of the hotel. Fuller started walking back. By the time he walked back to the hotel, Charlie and Stephens were also riding up.

"Deputy, I'll advise you not to go see it—unless you feel compelled—but I'm warning you. Remember, it could have just as easily been you."

They all walked inside. The sheriff turned to Fuller, "Marshal. I've heard. So sorry. What can we do to help?"

"Well, we have a murder in the hotel. This is your jurisdiction, so do what you have to on your end. Let me know when you're done and I'll get with his wife. I guess we'll have to bury him in the next day or two."

"Show me where he is."

"Ennis will show you. I've seen all I care to."

The sheriff and his deputy followed Carpenter toward the stairs. Stephens started to walk with them. Fuller grabbed his arm and stopped him, "I'm warning you. It's gruesome. You don't have to see it."

"It's… It's all right. I can handle it."

Fuller let go of his arm and Stephens followed the group upstairs.

"Fellas!" Fuller shouted up at the group when they got to the top of the staircase.

They all stopped in unison.

"Might want to make it quick. I have an idea what direction he went. He's several hours ahead of us. We should get going if we want to catch him."

The sheriff nodded, and the group continued toward the room.

"Oh! Jesus, that's horrible." The sheriff came out of the room.

Stephens stepped to his side and tried walking in. The sheriff stopped him, "Son. I don't think you need to see that."

"Yes, I do."

Stephens walked in. Almost instantly he stumbled back away from Carson's body. He found the wash basin and vomited in it. He cried out in emotional pain.

The sheriff shook his head in utter disbelief at the violence of the scene—and of someone he knew personally.

Stephens grabbed the pitcher of water, the very pitcher he had filled seven hours earlier, and poured some water on his hands over the basin. He wet his face, wiped it, and glanced at the mirror.

"It's all right, son." The sheriff put his hand on his back. "Why don't you head back downstairs. We'll take it from here."

Stephens wet his hands once more and rubbed the water on his face. He shook his head and descended the stairs. His face was as white as the snow outside.

Fuller looked at him as he approached. "I told you not to look."

"Yes, sir. You did." Stephens kept walking past him.

"Stephens."

He stopped and turned around to face the marshal.

"Are you going to be all right?"

"Yes, sir."

"Good. Head to the office. Put out some signs around town in the usual places that we need some volunteers for a posse. Roust up the usual boys that help us out. Tell them we leave in one hour. I think he went east. There's a set of fresh hoofprints leading from the stables out of town that way. Has to be him."

"Yes, sir."

"Stephens. We're going to get this son of a bitch. I promise you."

"I'll also check the other streets to see if there are any other fresh hoofprints leaving in a different direction." Stephens walked out the door to get to work.

Charlie Carpenter came into the saloon from the kitchen.

"Son, come here for a second. I appreciate all the help this morning."

Charlie dried his hands on his apron. He had already donned his normal work garb and was working. "No problem, sir. Happy to help. I'm sorry to hear about Deputy Carson."

"Thanks, son." He paused. "Listen. Tell your father and the sheriff when they come back down that I sent Stephens to round up a posse. We're leaving in an hour. I'll be back by then. I need to ride out and talk to Gretchen Carson."

13

About two dozen men on horses had gathered in the street between the bank and the marshal's office. The sheriff, all three of his deputies, and Stephens were there too. Many of the same faces answered the call when the time arose, but this was the first one in quite some time for the burgeoning town. The snowy streets had started to fill up with daily activity, and news of the events of the night were spreading across town.

The marshal came back from his visit with the grieving Carson widow. He rode up through the middle of the pack of horses and well-armed men. He stopped to address the volunteers.

Stephens came up beside him, "No other fresh tracks leading out of town that I could see, sir."

The marshal nodded.

"Men. Thanks for volunteering. One of my deputies, Phillip Carson, was murdered last night in the Carpenter Hotel while watching a captive. A man who had claimed to be Kyle Foster, a well-known bounty hunter from Texas, gutted Carson with a knife from his stomach to his spine. Simultaneously to me finding out about my deputy's murder, I got a telegraph from my peer in El Paso that the real Kyle Foster was shot and killed a year ago. This man is an imposter. He also was involved to some degree, though not entirely known how, with the shootout at Sour Springs a few days ago. He did admit to killing one man up there. You may have seen this man around town in the last day or two or in Carpenter's saloon.

"He wears a brown cowboy hat and a long gray overcoat. He rides a pinto horse. He is armed with at least the firearms he lifted off Deputy Carson. He has probably been in a fast gallop out of town since sometime after midnight. I saw some horse tracks fresh in the snow leading east from the Jonesy stable. I suspect they're his tracks. I think we can follow him.

"If anyone else has a better idea, I'm open to it. If some of you want to split off in different directions, that might help. But I think east is the direction. I'm going to head that way. I'd like Sheriff Donnelly to follow alongside me and our deputies to flank the group in case he spots us and a firefight starts. It is obvious he is a cold-blooded killer. Sheriff, you have anything to add?"

"No marshal, I think you covered it."

"All right then. Shall we, gentlemen? Let's go. I think we need to ride our horses out hard to try and gain some ground on him. We also need to follow the tracks. I hope we don't lose the them. Let's ride!"

Marshal Fuller saw Gretchen Carson's father in the bunch. He rode up to him. "Sir, I appreciate you volunteering, but you don't have to do this. We'll get him."

"That's all right, marshal. I have to do this."

"I understand."

The marshal turned to one of the sheriff deputies, "Did y'all get Carson's body to the funeral home?"

"Yes, sir. I saw Collins ride up a minute or two before you got back. I asked him to help Gretchen with the funeral arrangements."

"Thank you for that. We'll probably be out riding for a few days."

He readdressed the group of volunteers, "Let's go!"

The marshal took the lead of the group and galloped out of town with everyone following. He pointed out the tracks in the snow to the sheriff as they rode out past the end of town. The sheriff nodded to him in agreement.

The group rode for the rest of the morning, still seeing the tracks fresh in the snow. The path was clear for some time. A few of the volunteers split into two smaller groups and decided to ride about a quarter mile or so on either side of the main group, just to cover more ground. One deputy joined each group. As they rode across the high, snowy plain, all three groups could see each other in the distance.

Most of these men had been accustomed to doing this. They all brought their own provisions, jerky, and canteens of water. No one stopped to eat or anything for a few hours; everyone just kept riding.

The tracks were starting to disappear in places as the sun started to warm the snow. The direction of Pickford was fairly straight. When they lost the tracks for a bit, they simply continued in a straight path and picked up the trail where they become visible again.

He had ridden in a straight line as long as he could to get as far away as he could quickly. They kept up a furious pace in pursuit. Sometime midafternoon, they lost the trail. The marshal put up his hand for everyone to halt.

The bevy of horses slowed down and came to a stop. The flanking groups kept going until someone noticed the main group had halted. They headed in to rejoin the main group.

"What do you think sheriff?"

"Not sure. I thought there was a set of tracks back about a mile that headed toward that ridge over there… not sure. We could send a couple of guys out that way to see if they can pick up a trail."

"Do it."

The sheriff turned around, whistled at his deputies, and told them to take a few men with them to check it out. If it looked promising, they were to send the fastest horse back to them to turn around and follow them.

"I'm not sure if we're accurately following any lead at this point. At some point, he had to have veered off in one direction or another." The marshal led his horse around the group a ways to look at where they came from. He looked at the path they had trodden through the snow. The path of twenty horses through the snow was much more obvious than the path of one. It was as straight as an arrow. "Seems highly unlikely he rode this straight for this long." He looked ahead and said, "Isn't there a creek or a river up here about a mile or so?"

"I think so. Up towards over there… before those hills up yonder." The sheriff pointed to where he meant.

"Let's ride up to it and rest the horses and let them get a drink. It'll allow them to check out the trail you think is back there. They'll find us. We're not too far out of sight."

They rode toward the creek and rested their horses.

Sheriff Donnelly approached Marshal Fuller. The two had not had much time to talk to each other that morning, and the sheriff was curious about a few details. They talked a for few moments, and Donnelly eventually asked the question, "Why did you put him in his hotel room? Why didn't you lock him up for the night?"

Fuller sighed deeply. "I believed his story."

"What story was that?"

Fuller told him the Pappy Carmichael story and the story of his daughter Mabel, and then he produced the silver cross from his pocket. "He gave us this. Matched his story. Between that and the letter from Lefty, I had no choice to believe him."

Donnelly grabbed the cross from Fuller and turned it over in his hands. "Oh my God."

"What?"

"I know who this belonged to." A tear ran down his cheek. An odd emotion from the sheriff.

"You do?"

"Yeah. Nothing to do with anyone from Kansas, I can assure you of that. Mind if I keep it? I know someone who will want it back."

"No, sir. Go ahead and keep it."

Sheriff Donnelly pocketed the silver cross. Another tear or two fell dripped off his cheek, and he grabbed his bandana and wiped his face.

Pickford had veered off the trail they thought they were following *way* before the trail Sheriff Donnelly thought he had seen. He was up in the foothills of the mountain range about three miles back. He had turned toward a bison herd that was grazing about a mile away. He knew the bison tracks in the snow would mask his pathway. If they were following his tracks in the snow, which he figured what had gotten them that far, the bison herd would mask his horse's hoof tracks.

Pickford ran through the loosely packed herd and found a secluded spot up in the foothills. He led his horse up over a ridge to keep him out of sight in case one of them had good eyes and saw a saddled horse up the hillside. He was easier to hide than his horse. He tied him up to a tree about fifty yards away, trekked back up the ridge and back down behind a rock outcropping next to some large trees, and watched to see how good these guys were.

He figured if they made it out that far, they would probably ride past him, and then he could head farther up into the mountains, perpendicular to where they were going. If somehow they determined where he was and started coming his way, he had plenty of time to get to his horse and get out of there. On the other side of the ridge, there were several paths he could go down to lose them, depending on where they might come from. He had already surveyed the lay of the land.

He saw the one group split off and head to the same ridge he was on, but they were about a mile away from him. He wasn't sure what tracks they were following. After he rode past the bison earlier that morning, they advanced themselves in that direction. In fact, he wasn't sure where they wandered off to. The bison were out of sight.

He continued to watch the splinter group riding toward the ridge. They stopped suddenly, and all their heads turned back and forth as they looked at the ground. Whatever they thought they were following, they had lost the trail. Probably they ran across the multitude of bison hoof tracks. Two of them rode a bit farther, possibly assuming a straight line again, and then they rode all the way up to the base of the foothills. They stopped for a bit and looked around.

One rider, it looked like one of the deputies, ran a few hundred yards up the hillside. Pickford lost him for a moment or two, but he reemerged in a clearing. He scanned the hills for a few minutes.

Pickford was well hidden behind an outcropping. His hat was off his head, and only his forehead to his eyes poked up over the rock he was hiding behind. Even the keenest of eyes couldn't detect his presence at that distance.

The rider turned around and rode back to the splinter group.

The splinter group had been watching the hills the whole time. When the rider rejoined the group, they all rode away toward where the main group was down by the creek.

The main group had ridden off and slowly disappeared as if going down a hill in the far distance, possibly two miles or more from where Pickford was. He was convinced they had lost his trail. It was time for him to make another move. He went back to his horse.

He gave his horse some water, climbed into the saddle, and rode up the mountain. He followed a path that went behind an area they could not see from way out where they were—if they were even looking back in that direction anymore. The path followed a crease in the mountainside that curved away from them. It was a very wooded mountainside at that point, but sometimes you can see a man on a horse moving up a mountain from a long distance off. He was still on the shady side of the mountain, but that was not going to last much longer. He was going to top over the next ridge before the afternoon sun was to hit that side of the mountain.

And he was right. He could not have timed it out any more perfectly. He crested the ridge just as the afternoon sun emblazoned the mountainside he had just traversed. He popped over the edge and saw another wide valley before him and a wooded ridge about two miles in the distance. Down and then back up. Perfect. Even if this posse took a sharp right turn at this very moment and came his way, they wouldn't catch up to where he was at the moment for another hour, possibly longer. He'd be over the following ridge by then. They would have no idea where he was. Too many options for someone to travel. There was a stream at the base of the valley he could refill his canteen and let his horse have some fresh snowmelt water. All was working out in his favor.

The splinter group joined back up with the rest of the group. The main group decided to keep going straight east in the general direction they had been going all day. They knew they had a few hours of daylight left. They would ride until dusk, camp out for the night, and ride for another day if they had to. If they didn't have any luck, they would turn around and head home. One of the sheriff deputies got two other volunteers to go with him back toward the mountains.

"I just think that if I were fleeing, going up into the mountains—knowing I can be hidden by the crevasses and trees—would be strategically beneficial to me. I think a few of us should go that way and see if we can find him."

"Go ahead. I encourage anyone that has an idea to express it. He's several hours ahead of us and could have gone anywhere at this point. There's enough of us here that we can split up into several groups and cover more ground."

Another small group decided to go all the way down to the river valley. There were some farm houses and barns down that way, which would be tempting for someone fleeing the law to use as a hiding place. The guy was a killer, too, and anyone living down there might be in danger of his ruthlessness should he cause some trouble.

Pickford got fresh water for him and his horse and crested two more ridges before nightfall. He found a great spot to rest for the night in a tight clump of trees hidden in a little alcove not visible from any vantage point more than twenty yards away. They would have to be the luckiest posse in the world to stumble across him right there. He knew he had to be over five—if not closer to ten—miles away from them. He padded down for the night. He had not slept since the night before last. He was anticipating a good night of sleep in the impending frosty night. Facing the opening of the alcove, he had all the guns loaded and at his side. His horse bedded down ten feet from him. The frigid cold set in for the long night, but he was bundled up tight. The horse was covered in a blanket. Clear skies. At least no more snowfall.

The volunteer group rode another day to the east. Nothing. They were just going by luck at this point. By the third morning, most of the men wanted to get back to their wives and families. They had had enough of this. It was fruitless. The marshal didn't blame them, but he was going to press on.

After the fourth day, he decided the sheriff and all the deputies needed to head back. They had left their town unprotected, and he hope nothing had happened in their absence. That Pickford gang was allegedly still out there. The small group that had headed down into the river valley spent a day and a night there, and then they turned around. At this point, if he was still progressing eastward or downriver, he was probably out of the territory or in someone else's jurisdiction. What usually happens at this point, since it's an outlaw that is being chased, if the outlaw gets out of the area, he'll get somewhere else and cause more trouble and find himself in someone else's jail or dead. The odds are against him at this point—and against them for finding him. They were riding blind at this point. They headed back to the high plain and eventually saw the main group in the distance, heading back to town themselves. They all headed back with the remainder of the volunteers in tow.

The marshal wanted to press on alone, but Sheriff Donnelly insisted on travelling with him. Fuller convinced Donnelly to head back to town with the group. "I can handle it. Besides, you might want to get that cross to whomever it belongs to."
"You're right, Frank. Be careful."

He knew what direction he was going—and what was ahead. He told Stephens he'd send a telegraph when he got to the next town. He would stay there one night and wait for a response from him just to see if all was alright in town. Depending on that response, he would either keep riding and chasing this phantom outlaw or return home empty-handed.

The group that went up into the mountains went a foolhardy way that slowed them down. Rocky terrain, needing to make some tricky switchbacks and such to move forward, was treacherous in a few places and it was difficult to make good time. They got to the valley below, alongside the water, and pitched camp for the night.

Pickford had a great night sleeping. He walked up to a higher vantage point and scanned the valley. He saw no evidence of other humans. He saddled up his pinto and kept heading south. He didn't stop until he got to the next town.

Unbeknownst to him or to the splinter posse, only a large mountain ridge separated them all. But for the posse to go up and over that ridge and get to the valley Pickford was in would take almost another day's travel to catch up to where he was at that moment. It was several miles distance, but they would have to travel down one side and up another—across some treacherous terrain.

Pickford was halfway up his ridge on the other side and just needed to find his way up and over and then down the other side. After about an hour scaling up his mountain, he found a gap that led to the other side.

High peaks were on all sides of him, covered in snow. He came out of the shadows of the peaks, and sunlight warmed his face for the first time that morning. The sky was bright. He stopped at one point to look back and see if he saw anyone traversing the valley below. He had perhaps the best vantage point of any time since he had gone into the mountains. He spent several moments looking up one side and down the next, carefully, just to make sure. He knew how long it took him to get there; anyone blindly following would take longer.

Pickford saw no one. He looked ahead, went over the ridge through the gap, and found himself on the southern edge of the mountain range. The vista opened up before him as he crested over the top. Below him, lied a vast lower plain engulfed in morning sun. He felt like he could maybe see the Mississippi if he squinted hard enough. Well, that was not possible—but maybe the Platte, or the Missouri.

He surveyed the plain below and then looked down the mountainside he needed to move down to get there. Way off in the distance, he could see some towns. He picked a spot on the horizon and set toward it as a visual guide as he traveled down the mountainside.

The splinter group travelled for another half day and did not even make it up and over into the valley where Pickford spent the night before, so they decided to turn around and go home. They rested their horses, gave them water, ate some food, and refreshed their canteens with pure mountain stream water. They went back up the mountain spent the night on the top ridge. They then endured the longest day of their lives riding all the way back to town.

14

Pickford came into the next town quietly. It was bigger than Sour Springs, but not by much. He went to a hotel, ate a meal, and got a room for the night. He stabled his horse. They both slept with a roof over their heads and ate a nourishing meal.

After a good night of sleeping indoors, he ate some breakfast, collected his horse, and rode back out of town. He had no desire to stop for long. However far he was from Marshal Fuller, it was still too close for comfort. He rode south, and Fuller was travelling east; there was no way for them to cross paths again.

Marshal Fuller arrived in Simmonstown, near the edge of the territory. There was not much to this town. It was on the rail line to Denver and served as a stop for the locomotive to get reloaded with water and such. It was also a stop on the Oregon trail. A localized cholera outbreak had occurred a few years earlier and wiped out a sizeable percentage of the town. The town had not grown after that. Many buildings remained vacant. Fuller rode up to the sheriff's office. No one was there.

He rode through the town and stopped at a restaurant. Three patrons were inside. He went in and ordered his first hot meal in days.

"Y'know where the sheriff might be?"

"Naw. Hadn't seen him all day. He usually eats lunch here, but I didn't see him today. Probably out somewhere taking care of something."

"Probably. Thanks. You know where I could send a telegraph?"

"Uh, rail station. I think that's it."

"Seen any strangers in town in the past day or two or so?"

"Naw. Don't think so. You're the first new person I've seen in weeks. You got a badge on. Marshal?"

Fuller nodded. "You have a hotel in town?"

"Up the street. Edge of town."

"Thanks." He finished his meal and paid up and headed to the rail station.

Simmons was a railroad magnate who owned much of the ranchland around this town and orchestrated to have a railway stop there so he could bring in supplies for the ranch. The town grew up around the rail stop. Nothing else was a commodity in the area except ranching. He sold his portion of the rail to a larger railroad entity for a fortune. Fuller knew the whole story. He probably ridden across half of the Simmons ranch that morning to get to town.

He went to the rail station and looked for the telegraph operator. No one was inside the station. He walked out the back door.

An elderly gentleman was scattering chicken feed on the ground. About a dozen chickens were following him around. He saw Fuller and waved. "I'll be there in a moment!"

Fuller waves back, walked back inside, and waited.

The old man came inside a few minutes later. "Yes, sir. How may I help you?"

"By any chance, have you seen the sheriff today?"

"I can't say I have. Any trouble about?"

"Just need to talk to him. Area Marshal." He pointed at his badge.

"Oh yes, sir."

"Just an outlaw on the run, and I need to talk to the sheriff."

"I haven't seen him today. You been by his office?"

"First place I went when I rode into town."

"Ah, yes, I suppose you would. Did you check the diner, he usually eats lunch there."

"That's what the waiter told me."

"Ah. I don't know then. Your guess is as good as mine."

"Fair enough."

"If I see him, can I tell him you are looking for him?"

"Yes. I'll spend the night at the hotel and head out in the morning. I'll drop by his office before I leave. Seen any strangers come around? Not off the train. Rode up on a horse. Maybe came to send a telegraph or something."

"No sir. Not even from the train. No one has gotten off that train here in weeks."

"I understand. Thank you, sir."

"Not a problem. Any time."

"Oh, I almost forgot… I need to send a telegraph."

The marshal rode back into town and checked the sheriff's office again. There was still no one around. He went back to the hotel and got himself a drink in the saloon. When he walked in about half the poker players inside left abruptly, seeing the badge or just recognizing his face. It was the most movement of humans the marshal had seen since he got in town. He did not care who may have been there; he was on a mission to find one man at the moment.

The bartender looked at his new customer, "You really know how to clear out a room."

"Sorry… I didn't mean to. It's the badge… and some of them may recognize me. Can I get a whiskey?"

"Yes, sir."

"Have you seen the sheriff?"

"Not today."

"Seen any strangers in town? The past day or two?"

"Not any other than the regular strangers. No." The bartender put the whiskey in front of the marshal.

"Thanks." He downed the glass in one gulp. "How about another?"

The bartender poured another.

The marshal checked the sheriff's office one more time before the sun went down, and then he went to the restaurant for dinner. He went back to the hotel, had two more drinks, and went up to his room for the night. Exhausted, he fell asleep almost immediately.

An hour later he had a knock on his door. "Marshal? It's the sheriff!"

Fuller got out of bed and opened the door. "Sheriff. Good to see you."

"You were looking for me?"

"Yes, sir. Come on in."

"What's going on?"

"Any suspicious strangers in town in the last day or two? Bushy mustache outlaw in a brown hat and gray coat... rides a pinto horse."

"Can't say I've seen a fella by that description. Can't say I've seen anyone unusual other than the normal suspects."

"I'm putting out a three-thousand-dollar bounty on him."

"Wow. What did he do?"

"Murdered one of my deputies. Gutted him with a knife from his stomach to his backbone. Then he fled. He apparently was in a gunfight a few days beforehand in Sour Springs."

"Sorry to hear that marshal. Sour Springs? That's hell and gone from here—two- or three-days ride. It's horrible to lose one of your deputies. I lost two last year myself."

"Sorry to hear that."

"Thanks. This whole damn world is going to hell."

"Mind if I ask what happened?"

"Some said it was the Pickford gang that came riding into town. Wiped out my boys and several other men."

"Heard about that. They're supposed to be back in the territory."

"I'll be on the lookout."

"Thanks. Cable me any time you may need some help."

"Will do. Thanks."

"We're a three or four days' ride out. But, you're in my jurisdiction."

"Thanks, marshal." He reached out and shook his hand.

"I'm heading out in the morning. If you need anything before I leave, I'll probably eat some breakfast at the diner and then I'm going to ride back. I won't be anywhere but here or the diner. I'll check with the telegraph operator at the rail station before I leave. I need to get some sleep. I've been out on the prairie for several nights."

"I understand. Have a good night, marshal."

"Good night, sheriff."

Fuller did not have any telegraph messages in the morning. He ate breakfast and rode out of town.

The ride back was long, and he was exasperated by the loneliness and of being alone with his thoughts. He had his faithful horse, but he had lots of time to think. He kept turning the outlaw's story over and over in his mind. *How much may have been true—and how much may have been concocted to fill in the blanks or to throw them off the trail. Was there anything about that story that was true at all?* He was fixated on the name Mabel. Now that he had some time to think about it, it sounded a bit familiar.

He wished he had thought more about the situation at the beginning. He should not have given the stranger the benefit of the doubt, and should have locked him up in the jail cell instead of leaving him in his hotel room. That was foolish, and it proved fatal. He knew he would never forgive himself for that. *Maybe it's time to retire and ride off into the sunset as it were. Maybe I'm too old for this line of work. A man doesn't always know when to quit until it's too late sometimes. Maybe it was too late now?* He kept thinking about his short-term future and long-term future. There were a lot of things to sort out, but he needed to get back to town first.

Two days later, the marshal made it back to. He rode hard back across the prairie and spent only one night on the ground. Nothing had changed. The guys had not stumbled across the outlaw on their way back. He was disappointed. He wanted more than anything to get him. Justice was the primary driver—as it was every day of his life—but revenge for his deputy's life was the secondary driver. He really wanted to get that guy. What was worse was that he did not even know who the guy was.

Pickford was long gone from the territory. He rode south with the eastern edge of the Rockies to his right almost the entire way. He remained incognito the whole way. With all his illegal activities in Kansas over the years, he knew he needed to get through Colorado as quickly as possible. Some of that outlaw activity bled over into Colorado. He only stopped in Denver to get provisions and rest under a roof for one night. He kept to himself and out of the saloons. He kept riding south.

He knew the New Mexico territory well, but thankfully, for his sake, the New Mexico authorities did not know him. He had come this way a few times, and the blood of at least five men fell on the dirt and sands of New Mexico at the end of his gun.

South of Denver, he knew a cut back to the southwest through a pass in the mountains to get himself into the valley that would lead to Santa Fe. The Sangre de Cristo Mountains to the east and the Rockies to the west, all the rivers ran east until you found the one that ran south: the Rio Grande. He got to the banks of the big river and kept riding south.

When he arrived in Santa Fe, he rested another night in a hotel and ate two good meals: a dinner and a breakfast the following morning. He loaded up with provisions again and went to a telegraph office on his way out of town. He sent a telegraph to a bartender in Ft. Worth to tell the bartender to contact his second-in-command and where to meet up with him. His gang needed to rendezvous with him at a specific hotel in San Antonio. They had another score to settle.

Pickford also sent a second telegraph from Santa Fe. This one went to Marshal Fuller.

Marshal Fuller

Lance Pickford was the man who killed Deputy Carson.

I was under your nose the whole time. Come and get me if you can find me.

L. Pickford.

There was a gun pointed at the telegrapher because surely, he could turn him in after he sent the telegraph. Pickford put a bullet in his forehead right after it was sent. He left the dead man in a pool of blood on the floor of the telegraph office and rode out of town as quickly as possible. Heading east from Santa Fe, all Pickford had to do was to keep going in the direction of the morning sun and keep the afternoon sun at his back, and he would be in Texas before too long.

He reached the flat wasteland that is the Llano Estacado. Flat, desolate, and with few landmarks, a rider had to keep his perspective heading across the monotonous landscape. The weather was more hospitable as he came down to the vast plain shared by the New Mexico Territory and Texas, but the water sources were more scarce. He had bought two extra canteens in Santa Fe and filled them up with mountain stream water for the last time before he dropped down in elevation, heading east.

It had been about a year since he had been in Texas. His last time there was when he murdered the Kyle Foster guy he had assumed his alias from. Foster and his crew ran down Pickford's gang, and a gunfight ensued. Pickford and Foster were the last two men standing, and Pickford won the gunfight. Among the many items he lifted off Foster's body was the US Marshal letter that Lefty Gorman had written. Pickford knew it would come handy, and it did—several times. Obviously, his luck using it had finally ran out.

He assembled a second crew of outlaws, and some had done many jobs with him in the past. They were a backup bunch, but since his primary group were all killed in the skirmish with Foster, these guys became his main group. They had gone into Indian territory before Pickford sent them back to Texas. Before he had gone to follow Filson by himself, he told them to check in with the bartender and wait for a telegram from him before they went on to the next job.

It took Pickford a few days to cross the West Texas plains and then drop down into the hill country above San Antonio. He rode along some of the railroads to help him navigate the terrain. All the railroads ran to San Antonio.

When he arrived at the hotel in the center of town, his gang had already been there for two days, waiting for their leader.

The skies were turning violent in San Antonio. Thunderheads tinged with pink, orange, and red were off to the west as a cold wind from the north was blowing in. It was as if Pickford had brought the norther with him, but for the first time in months, an extreme weather event Pickford was in the middle of would not bring snowfall. No, this was South Texas, and it was getting late in the season. The torrential downpour of rain would last until morning.

Pickford and his gang sat on the porch of the hotel as the rain fell, smoking cigars and drinking whiskey. Lightning flashed and lit up the streets, and thunder disturbed the rhythm of the rain. At times, the rain roared as it fell from turbulent skies. It crashed on the roof of the porch, but despite the cacophony of the storm, the group still managed to carry on a conversation.

"Filson's dead."

"D'you get him?"

"Yep. Bullet in the head."

"Just like Jackson would have wanted."

"Yep."

"We took care of Charles up in the Indian Territory—just after you left to go chase Filson down."

"Good."

"What are we going to do down here?"

"One last job, guys. Bankston is down here. He's the last one. When we take care of him, we're done with everyone."

"How do you know he's here?"

"I ran across Sumter in a poker game up in Kansas. He told me Bankston hooked up with a local girl down here, married her, and bought a parcel of land outside town—with my money, no doubt."

"Sumter? Johnny Boy Sumter!?"

"Yep."

"I didn't know he was still around."

"Apparently he had been hiding himself up north for a few years. He wasn't all too thrilled to see me, but he was a wealth of information to me about several things, like Filson. You know how he gets when he's drinking? He told me everything. Lost a bundle to me on that table."

"How much did you get from him?"

"Eight hundred dollars. Everything he had. He had just collected a bounty up in Idaho and was coming back to Kansas to settle in. Foolish man. His last hand, he thought he had me on a straight—and I had a full house. He bet like three hundred dollars on that hand alone. Threw down two hundred as a final bet. He thought he could scare me out of the hand. I called him. I knew I had him."

"He was always more bold at betting than his hands were strong."

"Y'all remember that one game... where were we, up in Denver? He threw some silver cross on the table. You were in that game, weren't you, boss?"

"I remember."

"Got it from some gal he killed or something like that. He had some story behind it. Who won that hand?"

"I did."

"What did you ever do with the cross? Sell it for cash? It was silver, wasn't it?"

"No. I kept it… for a while. I don't have it anymore. Got me out of a jam. Saved my life."

"I think it was a whore he said he got it from. Some story he told. Who knows? Probably stole it off some old lady, knowing him."

"Yeah. He always had some tall tale."

"So, what happened to him after the poker game?"

"He tagged along with me for the next couple of days. He was broke, and I gave him a false sense of security that I needed an extra hand to collect a bounty. I told him I'd split the money with him."

"And then what?"

"I shot him along the way. He was holding me down—but not before I got the information on Bankston that he was now living down here."

"You know where?"

"Not exactly." He puffed the last of his cigar and extinguished it. "But I know where his brother works. We'll visit him in the morning. We will get the information from him—if it's the last thing he ever says."

Morgan delivered the telegraph; Marshal Fuller was devastated. He knew he had really fouled up the whole thing. He put the telegraph in his desk drawer. He'd tell Stephens when the time was right. Fuller went to tell Donnelly the news.

"I guess I might need some help from your guys for a while until I can get a new deputy."

"We're here to help in any way we can, Frank."

"Thanks Tom. Any of your boys want to become a US Marshal?"

"I'll ask… but I doubt it."

Fuller asked the sheriff about the cross.

"I hadn't said anything yet. I suppose I should. I've been working up the courage, know what I mean?"

Fuller knew what he meant. He said goodnight and left the sheriff alone in his office.

Donnelly reached in his pocket and grabbed the crucifix. He rolled it around in his hands several times. A tear ran down his cheek. He opened his desk drawer and pulled out his flask. He put his right hand on the cap, but he stopped himself before he opened it. He set it back inside the drawer and closed it. He looked at the cross one last time, stuck it back in his pocket, grabbed his coat, and walked out of the office. He had built up all the courage he needed, finally, and he did not need any liquid courage this time. He was stone-cold sober.

It was late in the evening, and some high clouds were dotting the sky over the mountains. The sun was setting, and the mountains were silhouetted against a red backdrop. It would be pitch-black soon.

The wind was brisk, but not as cold as the past several days were.

Donnelly walked down the street with his hands in his pockets. People passed him as he walked by and said hello. He stopped in front of Carpenter's Hotel and peered through the saloon's windows. The place was already busy. After a moment of reflection, he turned and continued down the wooden sidewalk. He turned right after the Carpenter Hotel and walked down the path that led to the Jonesy stable. However, he didn't stop there. He kept down the path.

He walked up to the two-story house with the white picket fence and pushed open the wooden gate. It had been a while since he had been there. He went up to the front door and knocked. A well-weathered, but still beautiful woman opened the door. She had on a low-cut blouse and her shoulders were draped with a stole.

"Tom?"

"Gertrude."

"What… what brings you here?" She studied his face. "Did one of my girls do something? What's wrong?"

He shook his head and removed his hat from his head. "May I come inside?"

She looked past him and glanced around the area beyond her yard that surrounded the house. "You sure you want to be seen entering here?"

"It's fine. It's business. Let me come in."

She stepped to the side, and he walked inside.

"Have a seat, Tom, please."

Thomas Donnelly sat down on the red velvet sofa. He felt uncomfortable despite being very familiar with the room.

"What's wrong Tom? Oh, I heard about Deputy Carson. I'm so sorry. He was such a nice fellow. I know he was in the marshal's office and not yours, but I'm sure you two knew each other well."

"We did. Thanks, Gertrude."

"What's wrong? You know I can tell when there's something on your mind."

Donnelly reached inside his pocket and pulled out the crucifix. He cupped it in his hands for a moment and then held it up with one hand for her to see. He held still for a moment longer and placed it in her hand. "Do you recognize this?"

She started to tear up. "Oh, my dear Lord."

The sheriff remained motionless and silent as Gertrude wept for several minutes. He reached over and hugged her. They were once very accustomed to each's embrace, but it had been a long time since they had found each other like this.

"My Mabel." She kept crying and buried her head on Tom's shoulder.

They embraced for a good, long moment and she finally picked her head up from his shoulder. "How did you find this?"

"The Marshal came across it with someone he had in custody, but then he got away. He showed it to me when we were out on the prairie. It had been such a long time since I had last seen it, but I knew it was hers as soon I saw it."

"It is. Who's the bastard that you got this from?"

"The same bastard who gutted Deputy Carson: Lance Pickford."

"The man y'all tried to chase down?"

"Yes."

They continued to embrace, and she kept her weeping face on his shoulder.

He stroked her long hair and held her tight, comforting her shaking body, which was quivering with grief. "I'll get him, Gertrude. I promise. I'll get him. I'll send him straight to hell for you."

The End

2

Hell's Half Acre

Lance Pickford peaked around a majestic oak tree. They were outnumbered six to four. Josiah Cole, his oldest compadre, was to his right, crouched behind a fallen hackberry. Jimmy Edwards was behind another oak, to Pickford's left. Greedy Mendez was to the left of Jimmy, hiding behind a grove of prickly pear cactus. Pickford was not sure who these guys were that were across the quaint meadow from them, but he figured they were trying to collect a bounty on him. Lance Pickford had bounties on him from Texas to at least the Dakota Territory. Cole told him he saw a wanted poster of him once in Winnipeg. Pickford did not know exactly where that was, but he knew it was even farther north.

"Who are you?" he yelled out across the meadow.

There was no immediate answer. The only sound was the rustling of the wildflowers and weeds, dancing in the early summer breeze, and the gentle applause of leaves.

He asked again, "Hey, who are you? If you are gonna kill me, I would at least like to know who my killer is."

Silence.

One of the horses whinnied softly, tied up to an oak about forty yards away. Pickford could hear a couple of rifle hammers cock—his opponents were that close. Pickford's gang was already cocked and loaded—and ready to shoot. This group across the way had chased Pickford's gang as they rode out of town after Pickford robbed the bank. That was when the chase ensued. They had already been on Pickford's trail for almost a week. Pickford gained some ground on them by riding all night, but they came into town in the morning to rob the bank, and these bounty hunters caught up to them as they were making their escape. The chase ended in this meadow, and now they were at a standoff.

Another horse grunted. It was a meaningless grunt, but seemed to break the ominous silence that hung over the peaceful meadow.

"Foster."

"What? Who?"

"Foster. Kyle Foster."

"Do I know you? I don't recognize your name."

"You will soon enough."

"What do you want with me?"

"Collecting a bounty."

"And you know who I am?"

"Yes. We've been following you since Fort Concho."

Pickford was an ardent poker player, and decided to call this bounty hunter's bluff, if there was one. "And who do you think I am?"

"Lance Pickford."

"And you think you know this how?"

"Someone at the poker game in that saloon outside the fort identified you. Remember the full house you dropped down on the old man's flush? You won about $150 on that deal?"

"I never forget a hand... Yes."

"You got up and left rather quickly after that. I asked who you were. I watched you play a good game of poker."

"I cleaned up all the money on that table—there was no more to win. I figured I'd get gone while the getting was good."

"Fair enough. I checked the next morning and found you had a bounty on your head. You've done some bad shit."

"And yet, here you are—most people run the other way when they find out who I am. You must have a death-wish."

"No. I have some of the best shots in Texas sitting here next to me—and we split the bounties evenly in my group—unlike what I've heard about you." Foster laughed at the end of his sentence.

A couple of Pickford's guys looked over at him. Pickford grimaced slightly. "My guys are rewarded nicely, thank you."

"That's not what I've heard." He let that statement hang in the air above the meadow so it would sink in with Pickford's gang, trying to play a little verbal poker with Pickford. "But, that's not my problem. Here—very shortly—you will all be dead, and all that money, whoever has it, will be ours. It won't matter a hill of beans. You ready?"

"Always… Come and get me."

There was another moment of silence—the calm before the storm. Pickford looked across the meadow and could see Foster motioning instructions to his men—strategically positioned behind certain tree trunks—on the other side of the meadow. He could tell their attention was momentarily distracted. Pickford lowered his rifle and sighted up Foster's tree trunk. He waited a few moments to see if Foster might foolishly let his guard down, or if a critical part of his body emerged from behind the security of the tree. No body part did. He decided to fire a warning shot anyway and try to rattle Foster's cage a bit.

Pickford fired. Foster froze at the shot. He was not scared and not even impressed. He thought Pickford was some two-bit fool for shaking his proverbial tailfeathers in Foster's direction.

Foster waited for what Pickford was going to do next.

"You coming out? You coming to get me?" Pickford yelled at Foster.

"Come my way."

Pickford laughed loudly, "Not a chance. You want your bounty, come and get it."

Foster's pistol barrel emerged from out from behind the tree, but was not aimed across the meadow, he was motioning to one of his guys to take another position. Pickford watched what was happening. He fired at the guy that was repositioning himself. The shot missed. Cole fired at the guy too. That shot was also errant.

Another of Foster's guys fired at Cole. Cole stood up, exposing himself, and unloaded his gun in the direction of the guy that just fired. Foster did quick math, realized Cole was out of ammo in his chambers. He glanced quickly from behind the tree, fired at Cole, striking his arm. Cole fell, bleeding, and writhing in pain. He dropped his pistol, which fell on the other side of the tree trunk. In order for Cole to reach it, he would have to expose himself.

"You alright, Josey?" Pickford asked.

He grunted, grimaced, and replied, "I'm hit."

Mendez stood up, fired two quick shots at Foster, but only hit the tree. Foster moved to the other side of the trunk, and returned the favor, hitting Mendez twice in the left arm.

"Greedy?"

No answer. "Greedy? You hit?"

He answered softly in agony, "Yeah."

Greedy Mendez ripped away his shirt sleeve, and looked down at his wounds. They were deep, and bleeding profusely. He reached around his triceps and felt an exit wound; also bleeding uncontrollably. One bullet may have remained in his arm. Even if some triage could be administered by his cohorts, Mendez feared there was a good chance he could lose his arm. He began to feel an intense pain come over him. He looked down again at his perforated arm, covered in blood. Reflecting on the wound for a short moment, distressed with the onset of intense agony, his mind went to a dark place. The pain was clouding his sensibilities—coupled with the fact they were outnumbered—he made the rash decision in what he perceived to be his final minute on the planet; to go out with a blaze of glory. He had always hated his life of crime, but thought he was lucky to have lived this long considering his life choices.

Blood was gushing from his arm, and after years of seeing others in the past bleed to death right before him, he knew his time was short. He picked up his gun with his good hand, put it in his bad hand to hold it, reloaded the two empty chambers, stood up for the last time, and ran towards Foster's group; his pistol blazing. His bullets found nothing but tree bark and dirt on the hill behind them— and hit no one. After his last shot was fired, one of Foster's men popped up from behind his spot, and fired one precise shot at Mendez's head. He was dead before he hit the ground.

Pickford was now outnumbered three to six.

"You had enough Pickford? Ready to surrender?"

Pickford looked over at Cole. He was still gripping his wound, trying to stop the bleeding. His gun was still unretrievable. It was really two and a half to six.

"Come get me! You're going to have to earn that bounty— if you think you can."

There was silence on Foster's side. There were some exposed arms, gun barrels were seen moving, pointing out strategic maneuvers. Jimmy took a shot at one of them, but missed. Pickford looked over at Jimmy after the errant shot. He motioned silently for him to go around to the left and see if he could get a shot off. Jimmy was reluctant, but assessed the situation. There was some underbrush off to his side that he could use as cover. He nodded back at Pickford that it was doable and began to move stealthily in that direction.

Pickford needed to help Josiah get his pistol back. Cole still had a rifle at his side. Pickford jumped quickly across from the safety of his tree to over behind the fallen tree trunk that Cole was behind. "Jimmy is going to distract them on that side. When he fires, I might be able to retrieve your revolver. How's your wound?"

"Still bleeding... Bad."

Pickford checked it out. It did not look good. "Here, take this pistol... I have two. When you hear Jimmy fire and cover me. I'll reach over and grab your gun."

Some silent moments passed. Pickford could not see Jimmy. He kept looking over to see if he could spot Jimmy's position. He was beginning to worry.

"Pickford? You there?"

He did not answer Foster.

"Hey, the bounty is dead or alive. I'd hate to kill you if I don't have to. Spare the lives of your gang and yourself... give yourselves up!"

"And spend the rest of my life in prison? Not on your life! I'd rather die."

"So be it... It all pays the same to me."

Now Pickford could see Jimmy for a brief moment. He was inching closer to Foster's gang as planned. Pickford looked around to assess the Foster group. He was not exactly sure where all six of them were, he knew six of them cornered them here, but two were hidden very well. He kept scanning the area across from them trying to find the missing men. He still could not see two—he had the positions of only four.

Jimmy accidently cracked a twig under his boot. It seemed like the loudest sound ever. His position was given away. Three of Foster's men reacted by standing up, and fired in the direction of the twig crack. Jimmy fired, hit the two men closest to him, and ducked back down. Instead of reaching over to retrieve Cole's pistol, Pickford raised up, and fired across the meadow hitting the now-exposed third man. Foster fired at Pickford, but missed him. Foster fired again, but Pickford ducked too quickly.

If the shots fired at Foster's gang were fatal, it was now three versus three.

Foster reeled around his tree trunk to look for Jimmy. Jimmy had hidden himself well. Foster was aware of the situation now. He looked at his three shot men to make sure there were any signs of life—there were none. Foster knew these outlaws were crack shots and he had underestimated them.

"Alright Foster! Now what? Do *you* want to give up?"

There was no answer.

"Still want that bounty?" Pickford's voice had a taunting demeanor to it.

Foster remained quiet. He knew one of Pickford's men was wounded and unarmed. Foster still had the advantage.

"I can feel the money in my hands, Pickford."

"Delusions of grandeur, Foster!"

"Prove me wrong! The sooner we get this over, the sooner I'm a rich man. A richer man!"

Overconfidence may have gotten the better of Kyle Foster in that moment: a mortal man's biggest weakness can be his own arrogance. Lance Pickford seemed to always bring out the worst in people, or their underlying weaknesses. He picked at the right scab each and every time. Foster raised up and took three quick pot shots at Pickford and Cole.

None of the shots hit human flesh. He dropped back down, and refilled the three empty chambers of his Smith & Wesson Model 3.

Pickford yelled across the way, "C'mon Foster! Come and get us!"

Foster was silent. He looked left and right at his two men left alive. They had moved closer to Foster from their hidden positions while Foster shot the three shots. Pickford saw the men move from their hidden positions—that was a mistake—now Pickford knew exactly where they all were. He glanced over toward Jimmy's position. He could not see him, but he trusted Jimmy was creeping up on them. Pickford was poised to make a move as soon as Jimmy opened fired or made a move.

Foster was still quiet and had not answered Pickford. Perhaps he was now scared. He was no longer outnumbered, but now evenly matched. Maybe that was weakness enough? Pickford had to guess that Foster had never been in this position before. He was ready to pounce as soon as the opportunity presented itself. Pickford knew it was either them or his guys—the losers of this gunfight were not getting out of this alive. This was either his last day on earth or they would live yet another day.

Pickford did not care. He had more than his fair share of menacing exploits controlled by avidity and lust: money, theft, rape, poker games, killing men—innocent or guilty—he did not care. Each day was a new adventure and the more dangerous, the better. Pickford did not believe in God. He thought this was it to life—death was the end and there was nothing more. He lived for the thrills, regardless of the outcome. If this was his last day alive, he would not care. He would die in the glory of a gunfight in a wildflower meadow on a sunny Texas day. He could not have scripted a better place to die. The one thing Pickford never relished in his entire evil life was to die in jail. He would die with his boots on.

If his fate was marked by a bullet in Foster's gun, and Foster ended up with all the money that was in Pickford's pocket, plus the bounty, what did Pickford care? He would be dead. The money in his pocket was ill-gotten anyway. It was all dirty money. Dirty money that just kept going around the world, from one person to the next. Pickford did not care. He breathed in the fresh spring air around him—this might be it. This might be the last breaths he ever takes. Would he even know? If his life were snuffed out by this Foster—and he died instantly—would he even know?

Would he even be aware of his life fading out to death? There was no way to know. There is no way to ever know until it happens. No one who has crossed that threshold can tell the living what death is like. Is there even a threshold? He did not believe there was an afterlife. Would it all just go dark? Why would it be all dark? Would it all be bright? How would he know?

A bullet whizzed above his head. It briefly interrupted his philosophical concentration.

He breathed deeply once more. He could smell the sweet scent of every wildflower bloom in the meadow. He was not one who generally appreciated the beautiful things in nature. Pickford thought nature was his foe. Humans, in his mind, were at the mercy of the weather and changing seasons. New leaves on trees, gentle spring breezes, the bouquet of seasonal flowers were never something he stopped to appreciate. Somehow, after all these evil years of life, and the threat of his own impending doom by the men across this picture-perfect field, his senses were fully attentive to the marvels of nature. His recognition of the beauty around him accentuated the danger nearby. Maybe this was it?

If this was his last hour on earth, he was going to be reminded of the beauty of this world and cursed to think about all the ugliness and evil he exacted on this world of beauty. Why would God, or the universe, or whatever supernatural power that might exist, be playing with his senses in this way? He turned and looked

Cole in the eyes. He had a look of drunkenness. Cole was not drunk; his life was just fading. He was still bleeding profusely and his whole body broke out in a sweat. Pickford realized it was time— time to face whatever lied on the other side of the threshold of death.

At that moment Jimmy stood up and let out a battle cry that pierced the air. Pickford was shaken from his musings, looked up, and saw Jimmy running full speed across the way toward Foster's men. His pistols were blazing and bullets were flying. Jimmy was on this side of the threshold at that moment, but his journey was about to take a different direction. He hit Foster's third guy in the head. Pickford saw the blood squirt in the air. The man dropped straight down. He hit Foster's second guy in the shoulder. As that man was recoiling in the pain of being shot, he fired back at Jimmy. Foster was also fired. One of those two shots hit Jimmy in the chest. He dropped in his tracks with a thud. Jimmy crossed that threshold of death—unable to let Pickford know what was on the other side— like every dead man before him.

Pickford stood up and advanced on Foster, his pistol blazing. Cole raised up halfway to cover his boss as he advanced on the enemy. Foster fired at Pickford. Somehow, his usually accurate shooting made no contact. Pickford fired toward Foster. Shots went back and forth across the way and no one was sure where the bullets were landing. Cole, his mind shaking off the fright of death, shakily stood up, mustering the last of the energy he had left in his debilitated body, put the stock of his barrel against his shoulder, and squeezed the trigger. His fired shot went astray. Suddenly Josiah Cole reeled backwards and blood spurted out of his chest. A bullet from across the way found its target and sent Josiah through that threshold also. Foster's injured compatriot stood up one last time, blood streaming down the side of his body. Pickford put a bullet in his head.

Pickford and Foster were the only ones left.

Foster was distracted when his last man fell and went through that doorway to death—a doorway that was busy this afternoon on a previously serene meadow—a meadow that probably never knew this volume of death before or perhaps any ever.

Pickford rushed across the field of wildflowers, skimming the blooms and weeds with his denim, strategically firing his pistol at Foster several times. His quick aim looked successful, as Foster flinched at the gunfire. Foster came back to reality just in time to duck back behind the security of his tree. He fumbled slightly with his firearm, but regained his grip, and fired a quick shot. It was off target, but enough to force Pickford to take cover. He had successfully run across the field and took shelter behind a thick oak trunk to Foster's right. It was where one of Foster's men was hiding previously. Ten feet separated the last two men left alive.

They were each sheltered behind two majestic oaks that had stood side-by-side peacefully on this calm meadow for a hundred years or more—two trees that never thought one would harbor the life of a sadistic killer and the other protecting the life of the bounty hunter trying to snuff evil out of a cruel world. The oaks just stared at each other not knowing the evil of the humanity that was playing out all around them. The two men were quiet for several minutes.

Pickford was not sure why Foster had been so quiet. Maybe a bullet hit Foster and Pickford did not know it. "Foster? You there?"

No answer. Pickford glanced back towards Josiah Cole. Cole was dead. He could also see Jimmy's body from where he was. Dead. Confirmed. He could see two of Foster's men from where he was. Dead, also. It was just him and Foster. Maybe?

"Foster?"

He finally answered, "Yeah?"

"Now what?"

"What do you mean?"

"What are you going to do now?"

"Still plan on killing you Pickford."

"Okay. Here I am. Come get me."

Again, silence.

Pickford glanced quickly around either side of the elegant oak to just check what Foster was doing. He could not see any activity on Foster's part. He wondered if he was shot and defeated. "Foster?"

No response.

Pickford double-checked his revolver. He reached in his belt and replenished the empty chambers. He checked, double-checked, triple-checked. He adjusted his belt nervously. His adrenaline was coursing through him. He wiggled his toes in his boots, making sure everything on his person was positioned properly and still functioning. He knew he needed to make a move and the last thing he needed was for something on his person to hamper him.

"Foster?"

No response.

"Foster... either you or me is about to die! There is no question about it. It's either you or me. I don't care. You probably have more to live for than I do. You have a wife? Children?"

No answer.

"Foster?"

Was Foster that coy? He took another deep breath. His third deep breath. Maybe this one will be his last deep breath of the sweet prairie air. He cocked the hammer on his revolver. He closed his eyes briefly and then let the rage take over—the rage that he allowed to envelope his senses—the rage he allowed to guide him through the world. It was a rage from deep within—an evil incarnate that took over his actions. He knew it was subconscious when he killed. He knew it was not right—he did have a sense of morality—he just did not think it mattered. He never answered to that small voice whispered gently inside his head—he only listened to the loud voice that screamed between his ears.

So many deaths. So much bloodshed. His soul, if it even existed, could not be saved. What did he care? He had been living a self-composed hell much of his life. There were days and nights he enjoyed the few luxuries that the hostile wilderness of the American West offered. He did not live the special life the railroad magnates and ranch owners lived, but he had a few nights that rivaled their lifestyles. He mostly languished on the open prairies, chasing after other deadbeats for money and robbing small-town banks. It was a better life than the mundane squalor his father and mother lived.

This was adventurous. It was sinful, but it was an adventure. Women, money, robbing, killing, drinking—doing what he wanted and dodging death all along the way—it all led up to this moment. All those raucous nights and all the empty feelings the next morning. It exacerbated the empty feelings he felt most days. He thought for a second, maybe there was more to a meaningful life. Maybe if he had pursued an honest life instead of an outlaw life, he would not be here on this beautiful, sun-kissed meadow, with eight dead bodies lying about, awaiting a ninth. Maybe this meadow was a message from God? Maybe this was what he had missed out on?

Maybe this was what he had misunderstood in catechism classes when he was a kid? Maybe this was what the nuns meant? He shook those thoughts off. He could not understand why was having these thoughts at this moment. It did not matter anymore—

his path brought him here to this moment—kill or be killed—he had one life between him and his impending death. It was either Foster or him that would continue to live a few short moments from now—but not both—he took another deep breath.

Pickford quickly reeled around the massive tree trunk and advanced on his foe's position—revolver steady at hand—poised for action like a hundred times before, and came face to face with Foster.

Pickford froze.

Foster was still breathing, but barely. He had lost his grip on his gun and it was laying on the ground mere inches from his outstretched and trembling hand. Foster had merely the energy to move his eyes upward to look at Pickford. An unassigned bullet in all the gunfire found Foster's chest. His shirt was soaked in blood. His heart was probably hit. Pickford was not about to investigate or do a thorough search. He only saw Kyle Foster struggling to grasp any last few breaths he could.

Foster was drawing in the same fresh breaths of prairie air that Pickford thought were his last. Instead, they were to be Foster's last. Death's door was opening for Foster. Pickford watched the eyes of a dead man watching that door open for him. With his gun still pointed at Foster's face, Pickford paused, as if having a philosophical dilemma as to what to do. His evil instinct took over. He had no use for a bounty hunter to remain living, even if that bounty hunter was unable to reach his own firearm, and defend himself. Foster was grasping to inhale his final breaths.

Cold and with no remorse, Pickford fired. The bullet went right through Foster's skull like it was nothing. Foster's body slumped over and his blood oozed out of the wound. Another soul crossed that threshold. Pickford was still processing whether there was anything worthy on the other side of that doorway. Still, he quickly dismissed the notion of any further philosophical musings—now was not the time. He looked around—nine dead bodies.

Pickford scavenged each dead body—seventy-nine dollars total.

What was of more interest was a curious letter tucked away in Kyle Foster's overcoat—a letter from a US Marshal in El Paso.

Lance Pickford read the letter two or three times.

He recognized it might be more valuable than money. It identified Foster as a friend of any law enforcement, deputy, or official out on the open range of the western territories, and that he was to be trusted.

This would change things for him. It also meant a name change. Lance Pickford was now Kyle Foster.

He needed to regroup. His men were all gone. He looked over at Josiah Cole's body. Pickford and Cole had been through hell together for over ten years. Jimmy had been with him for about five years. Mendez was one of the few men who had seen the end of Pickford's gun barrel and lived to tell about it. He ratted out his boss for his own life, and his quick thinking on that occasion saved his life. But today, his life was gone.

Pickford buried his men about a mile away on top of a hill. Three crosses marked the three graves. He left Foster and the other men to rot in the field. He unsaddled a couple of the horses and let them loose. He took the saddles, stacked them on top of a couple of the other horses, and lead them to the nearest town. Not to seem too suspicious, he sold four saddles and two horses for money. He left that town, regrouped with the other horses he had tied up to some trees outside town, and took them to the next town.

One or two at a time, he sold them until they were all gone. He had a few excuses if anyone questioned the riderless horses in his possession. "Friends of mine that died." "Fever." "Rattlesnake bite." "Want to give the money to his widow when I get back home." "Found them roaming the open prairie." Eventually all he had left from that deadly day were all the firearms and ammunition of nine dead men neatly tucked away in a bag on his horse, the money of the dead men, along with the money from selling the horses and saddles, and a valuable letter from a marshal in El Paso.

Pickford found his way back to Ft Worth. He visited The Trinity Bar, his usual hangout, and after two nights ran into Timothy Crawford. Tim was an old friend of Jimmy Edwards and helped Pickford's gang from time to time. He went where the money was best.

"Timmy?"

"Lance."

"How are you?"

"Good."

"What are you doing nowadays?"

"Same old… You know."

"I need a new right-hand man. I want you."

"Josey? What happened?"

"They got him. Death caught up to him. Jimmy, too."

Timmy was quiet for a minute. He took a swig and motioned to the bartender to pour two more shots. He turned and handed Pickford one. They clinked glasses together, "To Josiah and James."

Lance acknowledged, "To Josiah and James."

They gulped back their shots.

"Damn. Sorry to hear about them."

"Yeah. Had a shoutout with some bounty hunter. They were looking for me. Obviously, I made it out. We were outnumbered four to six."

"Lance, you old son of a bitch, you always make it out alive."

"Yep, killed all six of them. Bad about Josey and Jimmy, though. They put up a fight."

"You said four, who was the other?"

"Guy named Greedy Mendez. I picked him up a year ago in Santa Fe."

Tim motioned to the barkeeper for two more drinks. They arrived, and Tim said, "To Greedy. I didn't know him, but I would've wanted to fight alongside him."

"To Greedy." They clinked glasses again. "He was a good shot. Good guy, but reckless. Time just ran out on him too. Death caught up to him too quick."

"It catches up to all of us at some point or another, doesn't it?"

"Yes, it does."

They ordered another round of drinks.

"I need to rebuild my gang. You in?"

"Yes."

"You're my guy. I'm going to put my trust in you. I want you to assemble the team. We need about four or five. I figured you know the right guys in town, and that would be best. I've got some scores to settle."

"I'm your guy."

"Good. I was thinking Sam Taylor. And that Andy Newman, Norman, what's his name?"

"Newman. He's still around. He'd be interested. Sam and I just got back from the Indian Territory. He was asking about you not too long ago... He'd be in."

"Good. We need to get back up there. That'll be ya'll's first job up in Indian Country—settling some scores for Jackson—a promise is a promise. Let's get the team assembled and we'll ride. I need about four more probably."

"Whatever happened to Filson, or that guy Sumter?"

"Well, they moved on. Not dead, at least not that I know. Sumter is an idiot. Probably wouldn't surprise me if his own stupidity hasn't killed him by now."

"Terrible poker player."

"And he doesn't even know it."

The two laughed.

"And Filson?"

"I gotta find him... He double-crossed Jackson. Last I heard he was heading up north of Denver to find some new bounties placed up there. I might have to follow him. I hate going up into the snow country, but I think I have to."

"He was a shifty one. Hey, speaking of poker, there should be a game getting started here soon, you in?"

"Yeah, I got some money to burn."

"Good, Taylor might be here… we can all talk."

"Here comes another fella that might work for us, Henderson."

"He looks familiar. Does he know Jackson?"

"Yep. Worked for Jackson's brother for a while up in Missouri until he was killed. I'm sure he's looking for work. Ruthless bastard."

"Sounds good."

"We might be halfway to being ready before the end of the night."

"Looks like it. Let's deal some cards."

The End

3

The Evil That Men Do

He could hear the flies buzzing around the carcass long before he could see it. Thomas Donnelly walked across the pasture with his Colt .45 in hand, although he was certain he was not going to need it. The crime had long happened based on the stench that was now infiltrating his senses.

Two other deputies were trailing behind Deputy Donnelly. They were several years younger and fresh-faced. Donnelly had seen it all, or so he thought. He was looking down the hill and could see other dead carcasses in the distance. A pack of coyotes, grabbing a free meal, saw the trio walking their way, and scampered from the scene. The cloud of flies disturbed, they buzzed angrily, flew out of their rhythm, and attacked the encroaching lawmen. Their protest at the visitors went largely ignored. One deputy swatted casually at the mess of them buzzing about his head, but did not do much to scatter them. The flies persisted for a few moments and then went back to what they were doing before the deputies arrived.

Donnelly squatted next to the disemboweled bovine. He grabbed a stick off the ground and poked inside the abdomen. He was not sure what good he was doing; it was more out of curiosity. There was a bullet hole in the skull. Maggots had eaten most of the flesh from the face and were working their way through other parts of the body. Some buzzards flew overhead, and had, no doubt, feasted on the carrion also.

The other two deputies stood and watched, wondering what to make of the whole scene. They advanced to the next dead cow, and the next, and then the next, spending less time at each one, as it was not necessary to see every detail at each death—Donnelly got the point—there was a pattern. Outlaws had butchered nearly three dozen cattle in this pasture and cut each one of them open for reasons unknown.

They walked until they saw the last one, it was just like the first and all the others. The deputies heard two horses riding up and they turned around in unison so see the ranch owner and one of his ranch hands.

"Deputy Donnelly?"

"Yes sir, that's me."

The rancher dismounted and the two shook hands.

"I'm Jesse Albright."

"Pleasure to meet you, sir. Just not under these circumstances."

"Thank you, same here."

"These are all yours?"

"Yes, looks like it. See the *Rocking A* brand there? That's mine."

Donnelly grimaced and scanned the scene again, glancing up the hill, and then bringing his eye contact even with Albright. "Any idea who would do this? You have any enemies?"

"A few. But I can't even imagine how someone has this much hatred in them to do this to livestock."

"I can't either."

"I could understand if they stole them, or a few of them, or whatever—or killed a couple and took some of the meat with them—if they were outlaws riding through the area and hungry... taking some fresh meat. It's happened like that before. But this... this is just evil. I don't think there's any good meat cut out of any of them. They just did this... did this... for fun? I dunno? It's hard to fathom what possesses a man to do something like this for no good reason."

"Drunk, stupid, or insane. That's all I got."

The other two deputies stood in silence, not sure what else there really was to say. The ranch hand was roaming around investigating the carnage.

"I've been pretty drunk in my day. I can rightly say there ain't enough of the devil's water in the world to make me go around and cut up someone's cattle like this. But I ain't the smartest person in the world, neither."

"Insane then. I guess that's it."

"Or revenge." Albright let that terse statement hang in the putrid air for a moment. "Is the sheriff coming down?"

"He might. He was busy with something. He asked us to come up here."

"Cooper and I go way back. What did he say? Any ideas?"

"No. This is definitely stumping everyone. What are you going do with all them? Clean it up, or just leave them here to rot?"

"Not sure. One of my guys, Jorge, found them and told me. I waited for Smitty to get back to the ranch house and him and I rode up here late. It was getting dark, but light enough to see it all. I sent James into town this morning first thing to get you guys. I appreciate y'all coming out so quick. I haven't been back over here until just now. I don't rightly know what to do. I'm seeing all this in a different light now. Maybe we can pile them up and set a bonfire. It would take care of the smell. But, it's so far out here I don't think it's going to matter much. We could just leave them here as is—the wild animals will take care of them soon enough—some have been eaten up already. Those three back there and four or five up that hill—I imagine in a couple of days most of the meat will be gone— it'll save us the effort."

"Some coyotes were here when I walked on down. How many were slaughtered?"

He turned to his ranch hand, "Smitty? What did we count, 32? 34?"

"I think it was 32, but I saw three more up under the trees over there that I don't think we saw last night."

There was a pause in the conversation as everyone was still at a loss of words of the heinous act. Donnelly finally broke the silence, "Well, Mr. Albright, I'm not sure what else we can do. We'll look around a bit more if you don't mind and see if we see anything—maybe a dropped knife or something—although, I'm not sure how we can prove anything unless we see something unique."

"I appreciate that."

"You need Sheriff Cooper to come out?"

"Not necessarily. I'm sure you boys can investigate this. I'm probably going to just leave this be. My guys are too busy building a new barn and putting up some new pens. We really don't have time to be cleaning this up. It's so far out from the house that these rotting cows won't affect us in any way, other than that's about an eighth of my herd. That's a lot of money at market I lost here."

"I'll let Cooper know. He'll probably come by and pay you a visit."

"Thanks, Donnelly."

"Yes, sir."

The two men shook hands and Albright and Smitty rode off. They stopped about a hundred yards away and Smitty got off his horse to look at something. Donnelly saw him reach into the grass and pick up something silver. He rode back to the deputies, "Found this. It's a deputy badge."

Donnelly's eyes widened at the sight of it. He grabbed it from Smitty and rolled it around in his fingers to inspect it. Definitely looked like one of theirs. "We'll hang on to it. Thanks. We'll keep looking around and see what we find."

Smitty and Albright rode off.

The deputies walked the whole area and looked closely at each carcass for any clues but did not find anything else of interest. It was a grotesque scene. They counted the dead bovine just to get an official account for the report. Thirty-five cattle cut up, entrails all over the ground and a bullet between the eyes of each one. It was strange and a waste of livestock. They rode back into town.

Smitty approached his boss when they got back to the ranch house, "That deputy badge?"

"Yeah, I know."

"What do we do about it?"

"I'm still thinking. Part of me wants to sit and wait so as not to give away the fact we know who that belongs to, and part of me wants to ride on over there right now, and cut up every cow the sheriff's got. Let me keep thinking about it."

Smitty grabbed the reins of both horses and lead them back to the barn to unsaddle them. Jesse Albright went back to the house.

After Smitty was done with that chore, he stood outside the barn and gazed out into the distance across the prairie towards the scene of the crime. The Albright Ranch spanned several thousand acres, but the killing field was less than a mile in the distance, and he thought about the few dozen rounds of gunfire that was spent in killing the cattle. He wondered why they did not hear it. The hillside mesa off to the north and low foothills of the mountains off to the west of them should have echoed those gunshots back towards them.

Smitty doubted they were killed at night. It was two weeks until the next full moon, so the nights were pitch black. He figured they had to be killed during daylight. He was scanning his memory to try to remember the last day he saw some of those cows alive. It had been several days, but possibly less than a week.

And when did 35 or 36 head of cattle separate themselves from the rest of the herd? Most of the herd was over in the large prairie last Sunday. They were fixing a fence south of the horse barn all that day and he remembered looking out across the prairie and seeing the bulk of the herd out there grazing. He did not count them, but he figured almost all were there. If they drifted away from the main herd and that was the day they were killed, the ranch crew would have heard some of the gunshots.

Monday? Tuesday? One of those days the men went into town for provisions. The only one that stayed behind was Jorge and of course, the boss man. Jorge found them. Maybe Jorge heard the gunfire and that's what prompted him to head over there and discover the scene. Jorge never said that to anyone, at least to Smitty. Smitty went to ask.

He walked around the compound and did not see Jorge around. In fact, none of the other ranch hands were around. Smitty went into the house and approached Mr. Albright, "Where is everyone?"

"I guess making the rounds. I don't know. One or two guys went into town."

"Jorge?"

"Not sure." Jesse Albright was fiddling with his saddle bags on the table, taking inventory of his gear, and rearranging some the contents.

"Did Jorge ever say if he heard any gunshots? Why did Jorge head out to that field? I'm just curious. It would seem to me someone would have heard the gunfire."

Albright looked up from what he was doing, "He didn't say. I don't know if we'd have heard anything. It's quite a ways out there. You didn't hear anything, did you?"

"I'm thinking it happened the day we all went into town. I think only you and Jorge were here that day."

Albright never made eye contact with Smitty and kept fiddling with his saddle bags. "I never heard anything. Jorge didn't say he did. I think he was just riding. Maybe he noticed the herd was missing some cattle and went riding around to find them. I think that's how he found the dead cattle, now that I think about it."

Smitty remained silent and did not retort. He turned around and walked back outside.

The sun was dipping lower in the sky and the shadows were getting longer. He walked around for a few minutes to clear his mind, but the circumstances of the cattle slaughter weighed too heavily for him to shake it from his thoughts. He grabbed his tobacco pouch, hand-rolled a cigarette, and lit it. He sat off behind the bunkhouse and stared at the setting sun. He remembered what day it was—it had escaped for most of the day, as he was lost in his duties, and lost in the thoughts of the dead cattle—the guys all did go into town. They would be out all night. It was their day off—some might ride back to the ranch late tonight, others might find a woman in town and ride back in the morning. He was perplexed at the situation and had an idea of what to do in the morning.

He finished his tobacco and rolled a second one. The sun was below the horizon now. He ate some dinner, drank a few swigs of whiskey, and went to sleep.

He heard a few of the guys come in, staggering drunk, sometime late in the night. They made some noise, bumping around, but found their bunks eventually.

Smitty woke up early. Despite the disturbance of his drunk bunkmates coming home at whatever late hour it was, he slept well. The night was chilly, but comfortable. The morning was brisk with no breeze. Pink and orange clouds danced across the half-darkened morning sky. He made a small campfire outside the bunkhouse in the firepit and made a pot of coffee. He drank a cup and ate some jerky for a quick breakfast. The early sunlight that had penetrated the bunkhouse revealed that three ranch hands arrived at some point late in the night. Jorge and Wilson were still missing, their beds undisturbed. They must have found some women in town or passed out on a saloon floor—it was deathly quiet in the ranch compound— the only sound was the crackling fire.

Smitty walked to the horse barn, saddled up, and galloped off to the killing field. He'd be there in a few minutes, doubtful any of the drunken souls would be awake yet. The ground and rocks were still bathed in the blue glow of morning. The northern and western hillsides were still in the shadows. The morning was quiet but the wildlife were stirring. Several jackrabbits ran away from horse and rider as they approached. A small group of coyotes were trotting in the opposite direction as Smitty rushed through a horse-trodden path up one hillside and down the other. The sun advanced in the sky and the deep indigo of night had disappeared.

When he arrived at the edge of the death scene, a yellow band enveloped the crest of the ridge above him. The sky was cerulean blue and brightening up. The insignificant clouds were now white. Morning was fully engaged. Birds were singing and chirping, and the flies eagerly buzzed around the carcasses again.

Smitty tied his horse to a tree stump and walked off several yards away from his trusted steed. He walked down the hill to the approximate center of the death zone. He looked all around at the carnage again. He pulled his Colt .45 from his holster and fired three quick shots into the air. His horse reared up slightly, startled by the first one, and whinnied. He waited to hear the echo come back to him. He fired three more shots, at a slower cadence this time. His horse was unfazed at the second volley.

The echoes were distinct. He reloaded his pistol, scanned the scene one last time, mounted his horse, and rode back to the ranch house. He wanted to see if there was any reaction at ranch headquarters to the shots fired.

As he approached the bunkhouse and barn, there was a flurry of activity. The boys had stirred and were leading the horses out of the barn, saddling up, some stumbling from being still half asleep and half-hungover, clumsily fiddling with saddle straps and stirrups. Smitty emerged from behind a clump of trees and the guys turned around one at a time.

"Where were you? Did you hear those shots?"

"Yeah, I was out on the prairie—they were mine—chasing off some coyotes that cornered a calf."

"Oh, good. We were worried."

"Did I wake all you up?"

"Yeah, think so. I think we were all asleep."

"And you heard the gunshots while sleeping, passed out drunk?"

"Yeah." Two other guys nodded in agreement.

Jesse Albright came out of the ranch house, "Smitty? You hear them shots?"

"Yes, sir. I fired them."

"Is everything alright?"

"Yes, scaring off a few coyotes."

Jesse looked at Smitty with a stare of doubt in the story. It was a look that could kill and Smitty saw the look without any doubt in his own mind why he was given that look. Jesse knew what Smitty was trying to prove—that 35 gunshots to the head of 35 head of cattle could be heard at the ranch house—even at that distance. He knew Smitty was the clever type and never stopped until he got a sensible answer to something.

"Did they wake you up?"

"I was already awake, in the outhouse. Heard the echo."

Smitty dismounted and lead his horse to the barn.

"Anyone seen Jorge and Wilson?"

"When we left the saloon last night, they were still there playing cards."

"All right, glad you guys are up. We got lots of work to do. I don't know how much sleep y'all got, but y'all are up now and it's time to get to work. Get your coffee and breakfast in and meet met me by the windmill in ten minutes. We've got repairs to make."

Albright went back inside. The ranch hands unsaddled the horses they had saddled in haste and went about breakfast before they were put to work for the day.

Smitty gave his orders to the men and showed them what to fix. They needed to ascend the windmill structure, fix a couple of blades, the windvane, and shore up some of the planks that had weathered. Wilson showed up a few minutes late looking like death warmed over. Smitty told him to get his morning routine done twice as fast as normal and join the other guys at the windmill. There was still no sign of Jorge. After he showed them what to do he asked one of the guys to ride out to the prairie midday and count the cattle to get an accurate head count.

Smitty then rode into town.

He went to the sheriff's office. Both Deputy Donnelly and Sheriff Cooper were in.

"Morning gentlemen."

"Morning Smitty."

"Donnelly? You show Cooper that badge?"

"We were just discussing it."

"What do you make of it? You know I know that's one of your boys."

Sheriff Cooper was quiet for a moment. "I do."

"And?"

"I can't explain it."

Smitty gave him a glare, "All of your deputies have their badges? Do you have extras in a desk drawer? Have they all been accounted for"

"I deputized two of my ranch hands, just in case we ever need extra men for something."

"So then?"

"I haven't asked them yet."

Smitty glanced over to Donnelly in disbelief. Donnelly was expressionless. He glanced back at the sheriff. "I think I know when it happened."

"When?"

"This past Tuesday."

"Why do think that?"

"Because it had to happen one day when there was no one at the ranch. We were all in town that day getting provisions. We would have heard the gunshots. The only ones at the ranch were Albright and Jorge Sanchez."

"How do you know you can hear a pistol shot from that far away."

"It's not as far as you think and the hills out there echo. I know because I rode out there this morning at first light, fired several shots, and rode back to the ranch. When I had left there were three drunk cowboys, passed out, snoring up a storm in the bunkhouse. When I got back, they were all scrambling to get their horses saddled because they heard gunshots. They not only heard them; they heard the shots in their drunken sleep."

"That's interesting," replied Donnelly. "So why didn't Jorge and Mr. Albright react to the gunshots that day if they were at the ranch? They didn't say they heard them, did they?"

"I haven't talked to Jorge. In fact, I haven't seen him since before y'all were out there yesterday. I guess he's here in town somewhere. Boss man says he didn't hear anything."

Sheriff Cooper chimed in, "Are you saying what I think you are saying? Albright killed his own cattle?"

There was a pause before Smitty answered. "I'm not saying anything. I'm only giving you facts. Y'all can piece them together."

"Why would he do such a thing?"

Smitty had no answer. He just kept staring at the two lawmen, hoping their brains would come up with an answer. Cooper sat down behind his desk, crossed his arms, and stared up at the ceiling as if in deep thought. There was an extended silence in the room.

Donnelly made eye contact with Smitty while the sheriff's eyes were diverted at the ceiling. Donnelly glanced back at the sheriff, then back to Smitty, and cocked his head a couple times to the right in rapid succession as if to motion Smitty out of the office, or to follow him out when he left. Cooper moved his head back level and looked at Smitty.

"Smitty, I can't explain any of this, and it all sounds weird to me. Let the deputies put all these facts together and we'll look into it. Anything else you can add?"

Smitty made eye contact with Donnelly briefly before answering then looked back at the sheriff, "Nah, I think that's it, sheriff. You know where you can find me. Thanks." He turned and walked outside.

Donnelly piped up, "Sir, if you don't mind, I need to go check on something quickly. I'll be back shortly."

"Sure."

Donnelly followed Smitty out of the office.

They turned the corner on the street and Donnelly grabbed Smitty's arm, "Walk with me." They went down the adjacent street about a block. Donnelly looked behind them and then ducked behind a corner.

"What's going on?"

"Jorge Sanchez?"

"Yeah."

"He was at Gertrude's house last night."

"Go on."

"He was beating up one of the girls. Pulled out a knife and was yelling and threatening her. He yelled 'I'm going to gut you like a dead cow.' Some of the other men in the house busted in and stopped him. He was drunk and fought back, stabbed one of the guys, slashed at another one, and then ran out of the house. The girl's face was beat up pretty bad, but he didn't stab her or anything."

"Know where he is now?"

"Don't know, he got away. I suspect he rode out of town quickly."

"No one chased him?"

"I started to…" He stopped his sentence abruptly and had a guilty look on his face.

"You… You were there… At Gertrude's?"

"Don't say anything."

"I won't."

"He ran off into the night and I wasn't… fully dressed. I ran out of the house and I couldn't see him anymore. There were three or four saddled horses outside Gertrude's when I got there, I didn't know one was his."

"Was Wilson there, too? He didn't get back until this morning."

"I don't know. Do I know him?"

"Maybe you don't. Hard to describe, looks like everyone else, I guess. Always has a beard until he comes to town to get a shave. Does it once a week. Blue eyes and brown hair. Roan horse."

"Fits a lot of descriptions up here."

"*I'm going to gut you like a dead cow*? That's a strange thing to say."

"Think about it. You know how it is when you're drunk. Your mind loosens up and you say things that are fresh on it. Things maybe you shouldn't say. Secrets."

"You think Jorge said that because he was the one that killed all those cattle?"

"I think so—he was drunk—probably had a guilty conscience and not about his wits. His mind went there and his loose mouth quickly followed."

"And, if that's so, Boss Albright would have to be involved too?"

"Probably."

"Why would he do that to his own cattle?"

"How well do you Mr. Albright?"

"I've worked for him for about eight years now. I've been his ranch boss for five. The job was mine when Hutchins died."

"Did you grow up around here?"

"Arkansas. Born in the Territory before it was a state. Came up through Kansas and made my way up here trapping for a while. Been in the territory here almost twenty years, but I never knew Albright until I started working for him."

"Well, here's what I know." He looked around the corner again and up and down the street to make sure no one was close by. "Cooper and Albright go way back. I don't know if they were friends when they were kids or not, but they were both orphans down in Shannon Creek. They were housed in the same home until they were kicked out, or were old enough to leave.

"Albright's money and ranch are ill-gotten. I don't know the whole story. People around here think he won it in a card game—

154

Cooper said that isn't so—but he won't tell me the whole story. Cooper said the two of them rode with some outlaw gang for about a year when they were young, not yet twenty years old, and Cooper got out of it when they killed a family for their money and horses. He saw them gun down the father, mother, three children, and another woman. Cooper said he was sick about it and fled when they were going through the wagon. Albright stayed with the gang.

"Cooper went down range for a year or two and returned when he heard the gang was all shot up in a gunfight. He became a deputy up here. Then he found out Albright owned the ranch. Somehow, he got the ranch or got the money to buy the ranch, but either way, he probably killed for it. All the older people from that time are almost gone now, so no one really knows the real story, or won't tell the story out of fear. I grew up in Shannon also—we were neighbors to Miss Mabel's house, where the orphans grew up—but those guys are a lot older than me. Oddly, I was orphaned too. Both of my parents died when I was young. Anyway, right before I became a deputy, there was a big shootout in town—lots of people murdered—lots of innocent bystanders. I was still in Shannon Creek, but my older sister was in town that day with a friend of hers. They were huddled together in the general store while the gunfight was going on.

"That gunfight changed this town. It wasn't a rough town, but some folks were vindictive. There had been several gunfights before, but none like that one. Albright was in the middle of it, and so was Cooper. Cooper came out of it with his ranch. I don't know how, but I can tell you this—many of the older men and business owners of town were killed that day—the leadership of the town changed hands. If someone wasn't killed, they were probably forced to be loyal to Albright. It was bloody. A lot of families lost their fathers, and a lot of wives lost their husbands. Some of the families moved away.

Albright took over most of the businesses in town, as the years went on, he sold them to others, probably with stipulations. I started working for Cooper about a month or two later. Albright built his ranch house and moved out there. Ever since, Albright has been the king of this town. You know this. He runs the mayor's office, he runs the sheriff's office, he even has some influence over the territory governor."

"Yeah. The governor was out at the ranch last year. Stayed a few days. The boss man then left with him for about a week or so."

"Over the years, something has soured between Cooper and Albright. I don't know what it is, but Cooper talks ill of him often."

"Tom, that ain't hard to do, honestly. Albright is a scoundrel; I can attest to that."

"Well, you know the power he has over this town. Cooper wants to be mayor, but Colton Richards is Albright's guy. I also think Cooper wants to be part of the territorial government eventually. He thinks we're going to be a state soon and he wants to position himself to be in office when that day comes. I don't think so, I think we're a long way off from statehood. Anyway, my thought is this, Albright has some control over Cooper, knows a secret, or something no one else does. Cooper ain't the squeaky-clean sheriff he appears to be.

I think Albright gave him that ranchland way back when and holds some kind of power over him. Now, listen to this—Cooper left town last month—I think to visit the territory governor. He didn't tell us where he was going. I think Albright knows whatever Cooper is up to, has blackmailed him by slaughtering his own cattle, and will cast the blame on Cooper to destroy his political aspirations."

"This is all about politics?"

"I think so. Cooper talks about it a lot. I know the power Albright has. I think Albright and Cooper both have secrets that they each know about each other and Albright is throwing his weight around."

"But Albright could have just killed about four or five head to prove a point and still blackmailed Cooper, he didn't have to kill three dozen."

"I think he went overboard to make it really look as bad as possible—to make it look really evil—it's all over town this morning. Everyone's talking about it. Next week, most people would forget a story if four or five cattle are slaughtered at a ranch. But thirty-five? People will remember that forever. Albright is trying to smear and destroy any political aspirations Cooper has. He has that kind of money and power."

"And I gave the evidence away. The badge."

"If you hadn't seen it, he would have pointed it out. He needed it to be found and needed us as witnesses. He knew it was there or he planted it—one or the other—he wanted to make sure us deputies saw that it was found at the scene."

Smitty rubbed his chin in thought, "Actually, he said something to me as we rode past it. *He* pointed it out. It was glinting in the sunlight."

"There you go. He knew it was there."

Smitty was quiet as he processed all this information. Then he spoke up, "It still seems far-fetched he would kill that many of his own cattle just to prove a point."

"And something else, Cooper fired two of his ranch hands last week."

"He did?"

"Yeah."

"Why didn't he say anything to me when I asked him?"

"I'm telling you, Cooper ain't the man everyone thinks he is. Besides, he doesn't have to answer to you, he's the sheriff. He knows Albright is going to try to pin this on him and is trying to figure out how to get out from under it. The problem is Albright is crooked too. It's going to be tough to figure out what's truth here."

"I just thought about something."

"What?"

"I rode down here this morning by myself after I woke up everyone to try to prove you can hear the gun shots back at the ranch. Albright didn't seem too happy I did that. Since I've been gone, he may have talked with the rest of the crew. I might be in trouble when I get back there."

"You want me to ride back with you, just to make sure they won't try something? I can say I came back out to look at the cattle again."

"No. If they're up to something, and want to do something to me, they'll do it to you too. Tom, there's bodies buried out there on the prairie. Trust me. Albright would have no problem having two more out there: you and me. He'll say he never saw you and that I never came back. Just know this, if I wind up dead, you'll know who did it. If you don't see me back in town next week, you will know I'm dead."

They shook hands and Donnelly walked back to the sheriff's office.

Smitty walked off down the street to the general store. He bought a second pistol, ammunition, and a new holster. He paid the store clerk and walked outside, putting on his new holster as he walked. Without missing a step, he loaded the new gun and checked the chambers of his old gun, making sure it was fully loaded. He got some food at the café and took a shot of whiskey at Carpenter's saloon.

Armed with a shot of courage and a second pistol, he climbed into the saddle to ride back towards the ranch. He was ready for whatever was about to come his way, but also fearful he was soon to be dead.

A lot of thoughts went through his mind as he was riding. He could just ride off now, abandon the ranch, and find work in another territory. The dead cattle were not so important that he might lose his own life if he were to keep probing into the matter. He was sure Albright was going to kill him when he got back to the ranch. The dirty looks earlier were telling.

No, he needed to show back up. He was not about to leave. He thought it might be suicide to return at this point, but he was not completely convinced—he just needed to know—but his mind raced back and forth rapidly. If he were murdered, at least Donnelly, and perhaps a few others would get the hint, and investigate it further. Something about this whole scenario was not right.

Smitty stopped riding about a mile before the ranch gate. He could see the roofs of both the ranch house and the bunkhouse in the distance. Smoke from the campfire was still rising up above the horizon.

Smitty stared for ten long minutes, still contemplating if it was better for him just to disappear, or face an ambush. If he disappeared, no one would know he was not killed and his body hidden by Albright. If he was killed, would anyone, including Donnelly, even know? Albright could just say he never showed back up to the ranch.

It was not in Smitty's nature to run from problems, but this problem was not his. It was bigger than him, and the more he thought about it, the more he considered he was probably going to get executed if he rode back into that ranch right now. If he disappeared and did not say anything, Donnelly and maybe even Cooper might get suspicious enough to challenge Albright on his ranch foreman's sudden disappearance.

Smitty could wait it out somewhere, write Donnelly in the future, and tell him he was alive. His own disappearance would raise concern. If he were dead and his disappearance spurred an investigation, he would still be dead, but if he disappeared and his disappearance spurred an investigation, he would still be alive.

He spurred his steed, turned his reins to the right, and galloped off to the foothills of the mountains. He would stop in Sour Creek for some supplies and keep riding.

This was in the sheriff's hands now.

Sheriff Cooper received a visit that afternoon from Carl Strathmore, another local rancher. The irate man walked into the sheriff's office waving his revolver erratically and cursing Cooper's name. The deputies drew their pistols in defense, but Sheriff Cooper calmly remained seated behind his desk, and only put his hands up defensively.

The deputies talked Strathmore away from hysterics and back to sanity. They had always known him as a rational and mild-mannered gentleman. This was a moment of rage for him. It should not be something that would define his fate, should he murder the sheriff in cold blood. None of the deputies wanted to shoot the man, but would if they had to.

Strathmore eventually dropped his revolver on the desk. Everyone breathed a sigh of relief. One deputy reached over cautiously and took possession of his pistol. The distraught man slunk down into the chair on the opposite side of the sheriff's desk, visibly embarrassed by his actions.

"Carl? What's going on?"

"I'm… I'm sorry sheriff. I'm so sorry. I… I don't know what came over me."

"What's all this about?"

Strathmore caught his breath and took a deep sigh, "I discovered twenty head of my cattle dead this morning, shot in the head and disemboweled."

The rest of the occupants of the room were stunned silent.

"And I found this…" Strathmore threw a deputy's badge onto Cooper's desk. It clinked and rattled and came to a rest in front of Cooper.

The sheriff stared at it in disbelief.

"Wasn't me. Wasn't my guys."

"I knew you would say that."

"Trust me, Carl."

"We shot one of the guys that was doing it. They would have killed more of my cattle if we hadn't happened upon them."

"Who?"

"I don't know his name. I shot first and he didn't live long enough to answer questions."

"I fired a couple of ranch hands last week. Might have been one of them. Mind if I ride out and take a look?"

"Not at all, because I'd like some answers."

"Did you hear about Albright's cattle?"

"Jesse Albright? No."

The sheriff told Strathmore the story. It was apparent to him that Albright was trying to sully his name.

The sheriff turned to the deputies, "Let's head out there. Give him his pistol back." Cooper turned to Strathmore, "Just to let you know I trust you. I hope you trust me."

"For the moment."

Two of Strathmore's ranch hands were waiting outside, still in the saddle. Along with Sheriff Cooper, and his deputies, everyone rode out to the Strathmore ranch.

They followed the rancher to the pasture were the cattle killing had taken place. The lawmen looked around and saw the same gruesome pattern they had seen at the Albright ranch.

"Let me see the man you shot."

"I've got his body back up at my bunkhouse."

They all headed to the bunkhouse where they had covered up the body. The ranch foreman pulled the blanket off the corpse.

"Yep. That's Simons. I fired him last week along with Kendricks. I bet they were together."

"We only managed to hit this one."

"The question is are they working for Albright."

"Same situation?"

Deputy Donnelly spoke up, "About the same, yes. Except one of Albright's men might be in on it."

"Which one?"

"Jorge Sanchez."

"Don't know him."

Cooper piped up, "I don't either. Ol' Smitty said he hasn't been around the Albright ranch since it all happened."

"What's he look like?" asked Strathmore.

"Don't know," replied Cooper.

"I do," added Donnelly.

"You know him?"

"I know what he looks like."

"Tom, stick around town then and see if you see him around."

"Sir, I don't think he's hanging around town anymore."

"How do you know?"

"He got into a fracas the other night. I... I heard someone say he rode out of town in the middle of the night."

Strathmore looked at Cooper, "Think we should all ride out to Albright's and get to the bottom of this? Whatever it takes?"

"Carl, let's just cool down and figure out the best way to do this, all right?"

"I think you better round up a bunch of men and let's go get them. Sounds like he's trying to ruin your reputation."

Cooper did not respond. He turned and stared off towards the mountains. Everyone was silent for a few minutes as Cooper thought.

He turned back around to face the group. "Right now, I just think we better ride back into town. Let me do some thinking before we do something rash all full of vim and vinegar. If we do something, we'll plan it… Methodically… Let me think about it. I do my best thinking when I'm riding. Maybe sleep on it." He looked back at Strathmore, "Carl, come by the office tomorrow morning. We'll have a plan. Bring all your boys and anyone else you can rustle up."

"I'll be there."

Cooper looked at his deputies, "Boys, Let's head back."

Strathmore, his ranch hands, and about five or six other friends of Strathmore's were mounted in their saddles, impatiently waiting for the sheriff and the deputies when Cooper arrived at the sheriff's office at daybreak. Donnelly came up to the building a minute later. The other deputies arrived a few minutes after that.

"What's the plan, sheriff?"

"I guess we ride out and talk to Albright."

"*Talk?*"

"Yes."

"I don't think there will be much need to talk with that bastard. If what you say is going on, then we need to go out there and arrest him. Maybe even kill him on the spot."

"We need to get to the bottom of things before we start killing anyone."

"Sometimes killing men gets to the bottom of things a lot quicker than talking."

"Carl, pardon me, but I thought a night's worth of sleep would you calm you down a bit and make you think rationally. It obviously didn't. Looking at the redness in your eyes, you either didn't sleep a wink last night or drank through most of it."

"Sheriff Cooper, honestly, I did not get much sleep last night. But that's beside the point. I'm ready for action." Cooper shook his head, "Give me one minute."

The sheriff walked inside his office. Everyone else just sat in their saddles quietly staring at each other. Cooper re-emerged a moment later with two long arms in each hand. He slid them into their sheaths on his saddle and mounted his steed. He looked at the group of men around him and made eye contact with each one before looking squarely back at Carl Strathmore.

"Follow my lead, Carl, and don't do anything stupid until we've talked to Albright. I will ask him some questions and we'll see where it takes us. Understand?"

Carl nodded reluctantly. He turned to looked at his men, "You heard the sheriff." To Cooper, he detected a hint of sarcasm in Carl's voice, but nonetheless, the message was received.

Cooper turned his reins and spurred his horse to a gallop. The rest of the men followed.

The clouds above the mountains were tinged with the vibrant colors of morning. The rhythmic pounding of the horse hooves shattered the calm as they approached the Albright ranch. Birds were stirred and flew up from their roosts as the posse rumbled over the foothills.

They pulled up at the ranch gate, and one of the men jumped off his horse to open it so everyone could ride through.

The thunderous galloping receded to a rumbling trot as the horses neared the ranch headquarters. Albright's men, huddled around the morning campfire and drinking coffee, took notice and turned to face the troupe heading their way. They all put their hands on their pistols, readying themselves for a potential ambush.

Cooper, leading the pack, held up his left hand and pulled back on the reins with his right. Everyone else pulled up, and a cloud of dust drifted across the clearing in front of the bunkhouse. Thirty yards away, Albright emerged from the ranch house—his hands were empty—but Cooper noticed he was double-holstered.

A grin developed on Albright's face as he walked towards the posse that had invaded his compound. Sarcastically, he greeted them, "Good morning, Cooper. To what do I owe this pleasure so early in the morning? Oh heck, is that Carl Strathmore I see?"

Strathmore shifted in his saddle and answered, "You damn right, you scoundrel!"

Cooper turned and glared back at Strathmore, "Let me do this."

Cooper turned back to face Albright, "Jesse, good morning. We've come to talk and ask a few questions."

"And you felt the need to bring a dozen or more men to *talk* to me? An old man living peacefully out on his ranch?"

While that exchange happened, Tom Donnelly scanned the proximity and counted Albright's men. No Smitty, but he did recognize Jorge was back in group.

Cooper answered, "We don't mean any harm, Jesse, unless we're provoked of course."

Albright laughed. "You have trespassed on my property. The act of provocation is yours."

"Official business. I am the sheriff; I have that privilege."

"Really? Have you figured out which one of your deputies went rogue on you and slaughtered my cattle?"

"Maybe. Same thing happened to Carl's cattle. Carl's men shot one of my former ranch hands dead in the act. That's why we came out here."

Albright interjected, "Carl? You had some cattle slaughtered?"

"Yes, Jesse. But I think you already knew that."

"And you shot a former ranch hand of the sheriff's that had a deputy's badge on him?"

"Yes. But…"

Albright interrupted, "And yet you trust him and rode out here this morning with him to talk to *me*?"

"Well… Yes…"

"Do not all fingers point to Sheriff Cooper and his former men?"

Everyone was quiet for a moment reflecting on what Albright just said.

Tom Donnelly broke the silence, "Where's your ranch boss, Smitty?"

"Smitty? Haven't seen him. He rode into town yesterday and we haven't seen him since."

Tom leaned forward in his saddle, "Is that so?"

Albright answered emphatically, "Yes."

Tom looked at Cooper, Cooper looked at Tom, and glanced back at Albright. Tom continued, "Are you sure?"

Albright smirked, "Yes I'm sure. The bastard just left. We haven't seen him. Just as well, I guess."

"Well, Smitty came and talked to us."

"Really? Just to ya'll?"

"Yes, Tom and I."

"And what did he have to say?"

"That he thinks you and Jorge were the only ones here the day it happened because he proved you could hear gunshots up here at the ranch house from where the cattle were killed."

"Yeah, he told all of us the same thing."

"What do you have to say about that?"

Albright shrugged his shoulders, "Nothing. Maybe none of us were here when it happened. I don't know. But we found one of your deputy badges at the scene. Carl there just said he killed one of your ranch hands in the act of killing his cattle. Looks to me like you've got a problem Cooper. It's either you ordering them to do it or they went and did it on their own. Either way, the problem is yours."

"They no longer work for me."

"So, you say. A convenient way to cover it up. One man is dead so he can't corroborate the story. Where's the other man?"

"I don't know."

"Carl? You believe the sheriff?"

Carl paused—looking confused—and replied, "I'm not sure, Jesse."

"Sheriff, why would I slaughter my own cattle? Why would Carl? We are two prominent landowners in this community who have had their livestock butchered for no apparent reason and evidence of two men, whether previously in your employ, or still in your employ, as having been at one scene, and a badge at the other. One is dead and can't tell us anything, and the other one is God knows where. Perhaps you know? I think we should be the ones asking the questions and possibly arresting you!"

Cooper was quiet. The look on his face was that of a cornered animal in fear. He did not want to turn around and make eye contact with Carl. He hoped, but was unsure if Carl was still on his side. He did not want any doubt to creep into Carl Strathmore's mind, and if his fearful eyes would give any credence to that doubt, he did not want Carl to make eye contact with him.

"Jorge?" Tom piped up.

Jorge made eye contact with the deputy.

"Smitty said he had not seen you since the day it happened. Where have you been this whole time?"

Jorge stayed quiet as Albright answered for him. "He went down to Denver to see about some cattle for sale. I sent him."

"And you're back already?"

"My horse is very fast."

Tom looked back at Cooper. Cooper just stared straight ahead. He sensed the sheriff was not going to be able to prove anything here and that this trip was worthless. He turned back to look at his fellow deputies. They had confusion written all over their young faces.

Tom backed his horse up a bit and shifted around so he could see the faces of all those that rode up with them and the Albright ranch hands, still standing next to the campfire.

The scene was deathly quiet.

"Sheriff? I think you need to ride out of here. If anyone has any talking to do with each other, it's Carl and me. We are both victims here. Now, If you don't have anything further, I suggest you leave my property before something drastic happens."

Silence.

The eyes of almost every man there started to dart around. Tom noticed it. Doubt was creeping into everyone's thoughts. The tension was thick, and moments like these were ones that would tend to lead to violence. Tom began to think that Carl was changing his mind about Sheriff Cooper. If something erupted, Cooper and the deputies were suddenly going to be the bad guys, and grossly outnumbered.

"Sheriff? Do I need to get the judge?"

Cooper remained quiet.

"Sheriff?"

He still did not answer.

Tom was beginning to wonder what was going on in Cooper's mind. He was usually stoic when faced with adversity, but this was stonelike stoicism he had never seen before.

"Carl? Are you with me or against me on this? You didn't butcher your own cattle. I didn't butcher my own cattle. And there's evidence that points toward the sheriff. Do you not think the sheriff has some questions to answer?"

Carl's face was visibly confused. He popped the reins on his horse slightly and advanced a few feet to square up to Cooper's face. Carl looked Cooper straight in the eyes and tried to read him. Cooper remained quiet but made eye contact and then looked away. Carl turned his horse around and faced Albright.

"Jesse, I don't know what to think. I'm on no one's side at this moment but my own."

Albright smirked, "Then I guess this conversation is over. I would kindly like to ask the sheriff and his deputies to please leave my land. Carl, if you want to stay and discuss this further, you are welcomed to. I've a got a fresh pot of coffee going and my boys over there can share some of theirs with your men."

Albright turned to walk towards his house—Carl stayed in his saddle and turned to look at Cooper—there was no reaction from the sheriff. Carl then turned to look at his men. They rode out to the Albright ranch looking for a fight and they still had that bloodthirsty look in their eyes. Carl looked back at the sheriff and leaned forward, "This is not going as planned."

Cooper finally said something. "How did you want it go?"

Carl did not want to admit he was just simply looking for a fight and to exact revenge, whether properly exacted or not. Someone needed to pay for his mutilated cattle or some sort of sacrifice was in store for at least some mental compensation in Carl's mind.

"Not like this. I'm more confused now than ever."

Cooper reluctantly said, "Let's get out of here."

"I'm not so sure you should leave!"

Carl Strathmore's raised voice echoed between the bunkhouse and the ranch house. Everyone took notice of the strong statement. Jesse Albright stopped walking and slowly turned around to face the verbal confrontation.

Tom backed his horse up a few steps attempting to distance himself from the sheriff. The other two young deputies followed Tom's lead and did the same. Cooper was on an island with Strathmore staring him down.

"What are you accusing me of?"

"I think Jesse is right. All evidence points to you."

The clicks of a few pistol hammers were heard in almost unison as that sentence ended. Cooper looked at Strathmore's eyes, reddened with rage and insomnia. He saw Albright had turned around to take notice of Strathmore's accusation.

"And how do I know you two haven't conspired against me?"

Carl laughed. Albright snickered.

"Well? Maybe you two set all this up?"

Albright cut in, "I haven't seen Carl here in three or four years."

Carl nodded in agreement. "True."

Albright added, "You know I never go into town anymore."

"Then how did you not hear the gunshots that killed your cattle? Smitty said he proved the other morning that gunshots could be heard up here at the bunkhouse."

Carl turned to look at Albright for an answer to that. "I may have been out on the back side of the valley—I do ride around my own land—I guess I just didn't hear them. What can I say?"

Cooper did not like the answer he got and looked back at Tom. Tom quivered because whatever went down here—if Cooper was blamed for this by either Strathmore or Albright, and they retaliated against him, the deputies were guilty by association—even though they had nothing to do with any of this. He did not want to acknowledge Cooper and was now scared to add to any argument Cooper had in his defense. But then Tom's mind shoved the fear away for a brief moment and logic entered. "We could easily find that out."

Suddenly all eyes were on Tom Donnelly.

Albright squared up in Tom's direction and approached him courageously on foot while looking up at the young man tall in his saddle. It was a power move on Albright's part. "How deputy? How can you prove it?"

Tom got a lump in his throat and swallowed. "We have enough men here. All from the different parties involved. We can ride out to the furthest extents of your ranch in pairs or threes, someone can go to the spot where the cattle were killed, fire several shots, and see if everyone can hear them. Just like what Smitty did."

The confident look on Albright's face degraded. He thought quickly of a retort before the brilliance of Tom's methodical thinking sunk into anyone's else mind. All he could come up with was an excuse.

"Son, we don't have that kind of time. My men were just about to start their long workday when you all arrived and interrupted their duties. It's a nice thought, but we have been delayed too long this morning as it is. Now, we've kindly obliged your unexpected visit out here. I think you all need to leave so my boys can get some much-needed work done."

Carl interjected, "Jesse, I actually agree with the deputy. It makes sense. It would help prove your point."

"And what's my point, Carl?"

"That you could not hear the gunshots from everywhere on the ranch and that it could occur without your knowledge."

"Carl, it's just nonsense. And we don't have time for it."

Tom interrupted, now fully back on the side of the sheriff's department, "Or I could ride out to the farthest fence, all of you could just sit here and wait, and I'll fire my pistol. We're all here. Maybe I could borrow Jorge's very fast horse." He glared at the unsuspecting ranch hand as he unleashed the sentence with sarcastic wit.

There was a moment of silence until broken by Carl. "I think that is fair."

Albright looked back at Tom with disdain. "It will prove nothing."

"On the contrary, it would prove everything," added Carl.

"Maybe I was gone that day. The rest of the men were all gone that day in town."

Emboldened by Carl's defense of him, Tom interrupted Albright, "You said just a moment ago you haven't been to town in quite some time."

"I go places sometimes. Just not into town."

Cooper broke his silence, finally, "Then where were you last Tuesday?"

Albright answered quickly and defensively, "I don't know."

Tom added another layer to the sudden accusation, "For someone who claims to be a hermit on his ranch, you'd think you'd remember an odd day when you left. Especially just last week."

The tensions grew thicker—as if that were possible—Albright looked across at his men. They seemed at the ready to shoot and defend if needed. He smiled, backed away, and headed to his house.

"Where are you going?" asked Tom.

"I don't have to answer to you, kid."

Cooper jumped in, "No, but you do have to answer to me."

Albright kept walking.

"You found out I fired Kendricks and Simons, you hired them to set up some scheme to make me look bad because you knew I was going to run for mayor, and maybe eventually seek out the seat for territory governor. You wanted to end my political career before it ever got started. I've been your pawn for too long, Jesse. You killed your own cattle and planted that deputy badge there to make it look like my own doing. And then, just to make it look even worse, you did the same to Carl's cattle. You don't want me out of your reach, because you can't control me if I'm out from under you. You fear me in any position other than the sheriff's office where you think you can control me. You know I know everything Jesse—I know all the secrets—you know I can bury you!" Cooper's voice raised to a level of anguish that Tom had never seen.

"You don't know what you're talking about."

Carl interrupted, "Wait? What secrets?"

"That gunfight in town several years back? Jesse orchestrated that entire thing to get rid of everyone in power and basically steal the businesses for his own. He made money by selling them for far more than they were worth."

"We! *WE* put that together to take over this town." The admission came from the devil's mouth himself. "You ain't that innocent in all that!"

"I was only following your orders! You ended up with all the power!"

Carl jumped back in, "My brother was mayor at the time." He looked at Albright, "Did you kill him? I thought it was a random gunfight that started in the saloon that he got caught up in?"

Cooper answered, "Yeah, part of the plan—make it look like an accident by some saloon ruffians—Jesse wanted your brother dead."

Albright cleaned it up, "Yeah, but you shot him! In cold blood you killed Andrew Strathmore."

Carl looked at Cooper, "Is that true?"

Cooper sunk in his saddle and fessed up to Carl, "Yes. I killed a lot of people that day. And so did Jesse."

Without a conscious thought, Carl Strathmore instantly drew his pistol and held it at arm's length. He found himself pointing a gun at Sheriff Cooper's face for the second time in two days. Everyone froze—most still shocked at the verbal exchange and admissions by Albright and Cooper—but now further shock with Strathmore's gun drawn and pointed at the sheriff.

Stoic as always, Cooper faced Carl and spoke defiantly, "Jesse Albright ordered me to do it, and he killed your cattle to make it look like it was me. That pistol should be pointed at him."

Not a cunning gunfighter or marksman—and definitely not cool under pressure—Carl Strathmore's eyes danced back and forth between the two men. His trigger hand quaked, but maintained a shaky aim on his intended target: the sheriff. There was a sudden realization that everyone was everyone else's enemy at this moment.

He cleared his throat. Anxiety built within him. "Ordered? What do you mean by ordered?"

Cooper took his eyes off Strathmore. Not that staring down the barrel of a gun could stop a gun being fired, but he looked back at Albright. Strathmore's anguished gaze shifted to Albright. Then his gun moved to aim at Albright—then back to Cooper—confusion and rage were exploding inside Strathmore's mind. Albright remained silent. Carl Strathmore shook with rage, "What do you mean ordered!?"

Albright knew he had said too much already.

Cooper turned back toward the gun pointed at his face, "Jesse Albright took control of town that day by hiring a bunch of outlaws and paid his ranch hands to start a saloon fight, purposefully cause the chaos to mask the fact he ordered myself, and several others, to murder your brother and…"

He never finished his sentence. A shot rang out from behind him, he slid from his saddle and plopped on the ground, his left foot caught up in the stirrup. His horse bucked at the gunfire and Cooper's dead body flopped under his horse, his boot still hung up in the stirrup. The horse settled just as a second shot rang out. Tom Donnelly put a bullet in Jesse Albright's head. Albright fired the first shot that killed Cooper. It would be his last shot. Albright's body fell in the grass. Blood pooled around his head.

Chaos ensued.

At the time of Albright's shot, his men were more or less slightly behind Strathmore's men. Not having a vantage point to accurately see who shot their boss, the Albright ranch hands began unleashing a barrage of gunfire into the crowd of men that were unwelcomed in the first place. They did not care what their bullets hit; all their adversaries were in front of them. Several of Strathmore's men fell instantly—horses whinnied—blood spurt all around the area. There was the heavy thud of men's bodies hitting the ground. The screams of pain and groans of agony of the dying filled the air between the deafening cracks of gunshots.

All of that discord erupted in a whirlwind of gunfire, smoke, and dust. Tom turned his reins quickly as the first volley of bullets swept through the Strathmore men. He pressed his spurs into his horse and galloped off through the clearing to take refuge behind some old fallen trees fifty yards away. Donnelly jumped off his horse and pulled the horse down to keep it shielded from the gunfire. He was at a safe distance. This was not his fight and he was not about to die for this. He killed Jesse Albright because Albright killed his boss. He felt in the heat of the moment it was the right thing to do as a lawman.

The two young deputies—taking their cue from the more veteran cohort tried to run for cover also—one made it, the other did not. Vickers slid in right next to Tom behind the fallen tree trunk— his horse down behind it as well—young Williams was not as lucky. A bullet found his back. Whether the shot was fatal or not was irrelevant. As he fell, he landed face first breaking his neck. Tom looked over at the contorted body and saw Williams's head at an unnatural angle to his torso. His horse galloped away through the trees.

Carl Strathmore turned around in time to see his executioner. Jorge fired a fatal shot that hit Strathmore in his chest. He fell backward off his saddle and his body crumpled awkwardly in the dirt. One of Strathmore's men fired at Jorge Sanchez. A fatal blow. The gunfight seemed to last for an eternity, but really only took a few chaotic moments as the Strathmore clan and the Albright clan exchanged shots. There were two men left alive outside the bunkhouse when the gun smoke and dust cleared, both of which were cowhands for Carl Strathmore.

Tom heard the gunfire cease and poked his head up over the fallen tree trunk he'd been hiding behind. Vickers peeked also. Tom cautiously worked his way over to Williams to check on him—definitely dead—and then he approached the last two men standing. They wheeled around at the sound of Tom's footfalls, but Tom put his hands up. They pulled their pistols down, but kept them ready to draw again.

Tom kept his hands up, "You know I have nothing to do with the sheriff's past and nothing to do with the butchering of all those cattle, right?"

They both nodded. One said, "We figured."

"Thank you." Tom put his hands down.

Vickers walked up behind him. "Now what?"

"Lots to process and clean up."

Vickers surveyed the bevy of dead men and looked back at Tom. "I guess you're the sheriff now?"

The carnage was cleaned up. The families of the slain men were notified and the bodies were prepared for burial. The judge went out to the Albright house, more curious about the scene than for any legal reasons.

Some of the cowhands had no immediate families or relatives close by. Their graves were marked in the local cemetery and joint funerals for those men were held. Carl Strathmore's funeral was attended by what seemed almost everyone in town. Jesse Albright's was attended by no one other than the presiding pastor. After all the funerals happened, and with the testimony of the surviving Strathmore ranch hands, the mayor authorized Thomas Donnelly to be the new sheriff of town. He took his oath in front of a small crowd at the town square and quipped afterwards, "I'm only qualified because I already know where everything is." The townsfolk laughed. It was a welcomed moment of levity after the severity of the funerals.

A last will and testament was read in the judge's chambers concerning the Albright ranch. It all went to Lawrence Kendricks, Sheriff Cooper's former ranch hand.

The newly christened Sheriff Donnelly was visited by Judge O'Neill. "I just thought you should know. Albright filed it a few days before the incident. His lawyer brought it to my office, Simons and Kendricks were to split the ranch and Sanchez was to get half the remaining herd. Since the other men were killed, it all went to Kendricks. I assumed it was still an active investigation."

Tom looked at the piece of paper in front of him and handed it back to the judge. "Not so much anymore. I think that about confirms everything, wouldn't you say?"

"Unofficially? I'd say so. Is there any other proof he did it? Could you arrest him?"

"Maybe. I have something else in mind. Is he out there now?"

"I'm not sure."

"I'll pay him a visit soon. I need to look around the property for a fresh grave."

Six weeks later a telegram came across his desk:

Deputy Connelly,

Never went back to Albright's that day. I'm in Kansas. New ranch job. No need to look for my grave. Not yet! I thought you'd like to know.

Smitty

The End

4

The Streets of El Paso

Frank Fuller slinked around the side of the wooden building. He had his pistol drawn, cocked, and loaded. He inched his way down the wall to the next corner. Gingerly, he peered around the corner and saw the outlaws hunched over a body in the street.

The dust and smoke from the gunfight were dissipating. Several dead bodies lay about the street and sidewalks. Frank lost track of who shot whom, who was dead, and who was still alive. It was not apparent if they were gathered around the body because it was one of their own or one of the good guys.

One man raised his hand at about a thirty-degree angle, pistol in hand, and fired. The body jolted from the impact and the blast echoed down the street—if the body was not dead prior to that gunshot—it was now. It was one of the deputies. Frank still was not sure which one, though. He pulled his head back behind the building so as not to be seen. He counted five outlaws in the semicircle around the dead deputy—there were eight originally. Frank remembered shooting two—killing one in his tracks—the other he was not sure about; he had crawled back out of view. None of those five looked wounded.

He looked up and saw his fellow deputy Michael Towson creeping along the roof of the building adjacent to him. His shadow was behind him. The building was a store and had a raised area on its front for its marquee. Towson had his rifle drawn. He crept up to the edge of the marquee. Frank figured he was mostly shielded by the raised front from being seen by anyone on the street. If they saw him and fired—the wood front might provide protection from the bullets—depending on how well it was built.

Towson took position and lowered the muzzle to aim. He blasted off a shot, cocked the lever-action rifle to engage the next bullet, and fired again. Both shots hit targets. The first was a kill shot and the outlaw he hit dropped hard with a shot to his chest. The second—because the covey of outlaws scattered when the first shot was fired—hit another outlaw's arm. Frank could see he was bleeding. The outlaw ducked behind a horse trough and fired back with his good arm.

It appeared the outlaws had to take a moment to figure out from where the shots came before they scattered for cover. Towson's third shot was a miss. He cocked and aimed again. The wounded outlaw fired up at Towson's position, but was unsuccessful in hitting Towson. It did not even hit any wood. Frank crept around to get a better position on him. He found a straight shot at the wounded outlaw's back. Frank fired. The outlaw was no longer just injured, he was dead. His body fell backwards his mouth gurgling and gasping for air for a few seconds before succumbing.

A shot rang out towards Frank's position. It was over his head and hit the building behind him. Frank turned to face where he thought that shot came from, but could not see the shooter. Another shot came his way and splintered the wood pillar that held up the awning above him. He dove down to protect himself better, but he still did not know where the shots were coming from.

Towson had reloaded and was firing down to the street level. He had the optimal vantage point. Another outlaw went down due to Towson's gun. He had tried to run from one spot to another to get better cover and Towson's shot sliced through his torso. He fell immediately and never moved again.

Another shot was fired at Frank. He ducked down to the point where he could not see the street at all. *Where were these shots coming from?*

He moved behind another horse trough that was in front of the building and he dropped down stealthily under the wooden-planked sidewalk that ran lengthwise with the street. Under the sidewalk was a crawlspace. It did not give a good vantage point for seeing what was going on, but it protected him from being seen and provided protection from gunfire.

Several shots were fired upwards towards Towson's position. Two outlaws were across the street huddled together and they stood up at the same time to fire. One the shots was successful. Frank saw Towson hit the dusty street below with an ominous thud. Several planks of splintered wood fell with him. The outlaws approached the fallen deputy's body and one pulled out his pistol and shot Towson in the head, just to make sure.

Frank was now alone on this street. Towson was dead—Marlowe was the one who the outlaws circled around in the street before this round of the gunfight started—Ferguson was killed about ten minutes ago. All his fellow deputies were now dead. He was not sure where Lefty Gorman was. Frank was hopeful Lefty was still alive and arriving soon to help Frank.

While their attention was diverted for a moment—as they eliminated another foe—the outlaws did not forget entirely about Frank. Whoever had Frank pinned down shouted across the street. Frank could hear approximately from where his voice came, but still did have a visual. Frank's vision was greatly obscured by his position under the sidewalk planks, but he was shielded about as good as one could be considering the situation. The group on the street heeded the words of their cohort and began crouching down and scanning under the planks. One of them noticed Frank's boot and pant leg. Frank looked around through a gap and felt he made eye contact with his foe. Several shots penetrated the wood planks and nearly hit Frank. Frank was not sure if it was one of the outlaws on the street or the original hidden shooter. His body quivered and he jostled for a moment in the tight space to gain his composure.

Now where was this guy?

He tried to turn over onto his back, but did not have the clearance in the tight crawlspace. He started crawling forward rapidly. He got to the end of the sidewalk overhang and had a clear view of Towson's killers. Frank wanted to exact revenge. Whoever and wherever this guy that was shooting at him would probably figure out where Frank was, but he was going to get these other two first, if it was the last thing he ever did. He got his arm in the right position considering the confines of the crawlspace, aimed, and hit the one closest to him with a kill shot. He immediately aimed at the other as he lurched and pivoted to get away from the gunfire. Frank fired and hit that guy in the gut. He fell backwards in pain.

The outlaw, flat on his back, raised his head up over his body to look in Frank's direction. Now that the outlaw was on the ground, he had the correct vantage point to see Frank under the sidewalk planks. He raised his pistol slowly and aimed. Frank wondered where the first outlaw that was shooting at him was and this guy was going to give away his position if the other guy had lost track but Frank aimed and fired again. His shot pierced the side of the abdomen of the wounded outlaw. Blood spurted upward from the impact. The outlaw instantly dropped his hand and head when the bullet hit him.

Another shot rang out towards Frank, but was not that near to him this time. Frank was still blinded to the shooter's whereabouts. He was not sure if he should crawl out from his position or not. This much he did know, this guy was the last one left.

He pulled himself forward another foot or so and peaked out to get a better look across the street. He still could not see the last outlaw. He carefully inched his way on his belly outward. He knew with each movement he was going to expose himself more—he had to be careful—he was risking everything. He peaked upward again—nothing—he got about halfway out, rolled on his back, and slowly sat up. A shot whizzed past his head.

"I know where you are now!" he yelled across the empty street.

Drenched in sweat and caked in dust, Frank pushed his body with his hands and eased his legs out from underneath the planks. He rolled back over onto his belly and crawled behind a horse trough. Another shot came his direction and penetrated the trough. Some water trickled out onto the dusty street. Frank had an idea now where the shooter was. He was across the street and Frank thought he had the trough perfectly in between them. He still could not see the shooter in the shadows, but he narrowed down his location.

Frank, hunched over, eased his way back in the direction he had crawled from, using the trough as a shield. He thought he was completely covered, but he left one boot exposed. A shot rang out across the street and struck Frank's ankle. He buckled over in pain. The shooter could see Frank's feet under the trough. The shot was on target. Frank tried to keep his body upright. He knew if he fell and hit the ground—even though behind the trough—the shooter could make the same shot again and hit his body if he were lying on the ground.

His ankle screamed in pain. He finally fell forward, his torso doubled over. His knees and elbows were propping him up, but were exposed for a potential shot from the gunman.

Another shot pierced the silence of the death-filled street, but it had a different sound to it. It was not from the gunman. Frank heard a body hit the planks across the street. The body tumbled two feet down off the sidewalk and onto the dirt street. Still in excruciating pain, Frank pulled himself up over the rim of the trough and looked across the street. The outlaw was slumped over, presumedly dead. He looked down the sidewalk and saw Lefty walking up with his rifle. Lefty had taken the guy out with a precise shot.

Frank pulled himself up the rest of the way and stood up on his good leg.

"You alright?" came from across the street.

"Got hit in the ankle."

Lefty, not taking his eyes off the outlaw, went up to him to make sure he was dead. He was. Lefty's shot hit the neck. A warm pool of blood was staining the dust. Lefty had hit his jugular. He nudged the body with his boot just to make sure. No movement. He came across the street to help Frank.

The streets of El Paso saw a lot of death that day. Lefty knew more was to come. But now he had three dead deputies and an injured one. He was the only one left at full capacity.

Lefty got Frank to the doctor. The bullet had grazed Frank's ankle. His boot had two holes in it: an entrance and an exit. The gash in his skin was deep, but clean. The doctor stitched him up and Frank was going to be heal eventually. The wound was going to hurt for some time and the doctor told Frank to stay off his feet, but both Frank and Lefty knew that was not going to be possible. They knew more outlaws from this group were coming to town tomorrow— Frank and Lefty were all that was left in the marshal's office and Frank could barely walk. The sheriff would need to help.

Sheriff Logan did not like to help the marshals out. He was funny about jurisdiction and such. He felt when one law enforcement group or the other got into a fracas, that group needed to finish their own job. Logan did not interfere or assist the marshals and he did not like when the marshals interfered with his business. Lefty always figured Logan was running some contraband over the river or doing something nefarious. It was nothing he could ever prove. He heard all the rumors and always thought Logan was shady.

Most of Logan's deputies appeared to be shady also. The only thing that made them lawmen were their badges. Their actions were questionable most of the time and their ethics were largely non-existent. They took their lead from their sheriff. Logan could not be trusted as far as Lefty Gorman was concerned.

El Paso was still an unincorporated town, but an advantageous gateway to Mexico. Gold, guns, and whiskey flowed across the river unchecked. As the western half of the Old Texas Republic was ceded to form the eastern part of New Mexico, El Paso remained in Texas, as the state boundary was drawn on the 32nd parallel just north of town, and the international line drawn at the river. But those mythical lines drawn on maps rarely meant anything to men with bad intent. With the agriculture and trade of the region on both sides of the river, El Paso was not particularly associated with the rest of Texas, mostly due to the remoteness of the area. Six hundred miles of scrub brush and cacti separated El Paso from San Antonio, the heart of Texas at that time.

But the Gadsen Purchase of a decade earlier brought more commerce into the area, as it becomes a southern route to California. This caused an economic boon in El Paso. Legal and illicit activities both offered myriad of business opportunities, and while the city had no formal city government at the time, the new inhabitants demanded the law be enforced in the wild town. With the new territories to the west becoming United States possessions, the US Marshals office dispatched its assistance as best it could provide.

The nation had been in the throes of civil war and El Paso was largely a forgotten outpost to those back east. A Union outfit from California began occupation of the area, driving out Confederates in 1862, and using Fort Bliss as its headquarters. As the war took a turn in the Union's favor, the Californian outfit left at the end of 1864, and returned home. Even though the Union troop presence was not far away, they were tasked with keeping the Apache at a distance from the town, rather than keeping the peace within the town. The small town was left to its own devices and rudderless with any official leadership.

Logan was basically a self-appointed sheriff and the highest person of authority with no one else to report to. As the Union troops left, the US Marshals stepped in. Lefty Gorman was offered the position as Marshal at a young age. It was an opportunity to move up in the ranks. It was also a job no one else wanted—thankless— in an area full of ruthless ne'er-do-wells. *Frontier* did not even begin to describe the area, and the new marshal position was really a position set up to fail. *Law* and *order* were ill-defined and existed mostly in the abstract.

Lefty Gorman had the chance to start something new there. He could mold it in his own image. It was easy enough to break the laws out there without the help of a corrupt local sheriff. With a corrupt local sheriff, lawless gang activity flourished. Lefty's first goal was to keep the peace. He second was to establish law and order. The first goal was hard enough on its own to accomplish. The second goal was a dream.

Lefty and Logan had a soured relationship from the get-go. Lefty was a greenhorn marshal deputy, cocksure, but ethical. Logan was older and a remnant of Colonel Doniphan's outfit from the border wars. He played a part in the Battle of El Brazito and the occupation of Chihuahua City. Logan was never a soldier, just a citizen who tagged along from Missouri and helped in the conflict. He stayed in the El Paso area and proclaimed himself as a part of law enforcement, capitalizing on his involvement in the border battles. Somehow he was eventually proclaimed as the sheriff and in due time was well-known on both sides of the river.

Lefty thought he was known on both sides mostly for illicit reasons. He knew the line Logan walked was a thin one between legal and otherwise, but it was something that Lefty had no concrete proof of; only rumors. He stuck his head into Logan's business as much as he could, but was never successful in proving anything. Lefty was new to the area and had a difficult time establishing any rapport. Sheriff Logan had deep connections with some of the businessmen in town and that was all a crooked sheriff needed. With no organized city government, Logan was king.

Nonetheless, Lefty needed some help after this latest gunfight in the streets of Logan's town. He went to the sheriff's office to talk with Logan.

"Well, look who's here, Marshal Gorman."

"Sheriff, how are you?"

"I'd be a lot better if my town hadn't gotten riddled with bullets earlier. What the hell were y'all doing out there?"

"Getting slaughtered, no thanks to you. We could have used some help today."

"Sorry, we were looking into some cattle rustling down by the river when all that broke out. When we got back, I guess it was all over."

"Well, it's over until tomorrow. Word is more of them are coming into town. I'm going to need all the help I can get. I'm just down to myself and Frank, and Frank is gimpy. Got shot in the foot, he'll be okay, but won't much help tomorrow other than to shoot from one spot or another."

"I'm sorry to hear that, Marshal. We don't want to see any more El Pasoans shot. How can we help?"

"I figured we need to formulate a plan to ambush them. We know where they are going."

"How do you know that?"

"Earlier we captured *Diablo* Garcon, I have him behind bars in my jail cell, but no one else knows that. His two henchmen are dead. We were going back to clean up their bodies when this group of outlaws came to his hiding spot. Carrasco's Tavern, by the way. He has a secret backroom to that bar. Did you know that?"

"How would I know, I don't go to taverns."

"Well, Garcon had been wanted by the Marshal Service for quite some time and we tracked him down. We got tipped off he had been hiding there. I'm holding Carrasco, too. I don't know if the rest of the group that's coming into town tomorrow will know that their guys are all dead, but if they don't, we might have a chance to capture them in the bar."

Logan was silent and thought for a moment. "Who are these bad guys?"

"Collins Gang."

"From Las Cruces?"

"Yes."

Logan was quiet again for a long minute. "What are they doing with Garcon?"

"Robbing banks in Mexico apparently. What I got out of him was that they were going to hit the big bank downtown in Del Norte. Garcon wanted Collins and his men to be backup because they were going to try to get back across the river with the money. The plan was to ride straight through to Las Cruces, divvy up the money, and then split up."

"And Collins is supposed to meet him at Carrasco's tomorrow?"

"Yes, apparently at noon."

"And, as far as we know, George Collins has no idea his men were killed or that Juan Garcon is in your custody?"

Lefty nodded, but with a shadow of doubt in his eyes, "Unless someone reports to him that saw the shootout earlier."

"Why was part of Collins' gang here already?"

"I think they just got here a day early. Near as I can tell they had been down at Presidio and rode into town to rendezvous with the rest of them. They just got here a day early and went to the tavern. Carrasco said they had just got there after we raided the place and apprehended Garcon. My deputies went back because Garcon's two men were dead and that's when they ran into them and the shootout began."

Logan pondered the situation further and then came up with the beginnings of a plan. "I guess we can all be in the bar as patrons. Have one or two guys outside to be backup, across the street, and then have someone in the back. You maybe? Or Frank, since he's lame. We can also have someone on our side behind the bar. We'll all be heavily armed with rifles and pistols. We can take them all out or, if we're lucky, they'll surrender. How many are we talking about?"

"I'm hoping no more than five."

"I think my boys and I, with you and Frank, can handle up to ten, if needed. We'll have the element of surprise in our favor. I know some guys I can trust that can populate the bar with us and help out. If I remember correctly, I don't think Collins has more than ten or twelve in his gang. You took out eight today?"

Lefty nodded.

"He's got a big group, probably the biggest this side of the Pecos, but I don't think he's got more than twelve plus himself. Y'all took out the bulk of them today."

"I just don't know what connections Carrasco may have and if they're sending someone out to warn them."

"Collins will approach with caution regardless. He'll stage a guy or two outside the bar to keep watch and would probably go to meet Garcon alone or with only one other guy. They probably would not even hang out in the bar. If this is a friendly meeting to discuss details of robbing the bank, then Collins will have no need to worry about any funny business when he arrives… provided he's not warned ahead of time, like you say."

"So, this might be easier than I think?"

"I wouldn't say that. Carrasco is the one I'd be worried about. If the bar is not open tonight, someone will know something is up. It depends on how many others know what is happening. Collins has connections here. We probably should just have a couple of guys hanging out in the bar but others nearby to rush in should something go wrong. I think we just let Collins walk in and walk to the backroom like he's probably not expecting anything.

If he hesitates, then we'll know he already knows. There's an anteroom nestled between the end of the bar and that backroom. If Collins is to meet Garcon back there, he'll just walk on back. One of you can be in the anteroom and the other in the backroom and get him. We'll take care of the outside. There's no back door or exit out of that room except back into the bar. The only back door is back down the hallway."

Lefty interjected, "We should probably get together first thing in the morning and plan this out. An hour after first light? Meet you here?"

"Sounds like we should."

Lefty reached out a hand to Logan, "I'm glad you can help us out. Thank you."

"No problem. And Lefty…"

"Yes."

"Let us handle the dirty work. Decide whether you want yourself or Frank in the backroom, but my boys will do all the dirty work. If one of you has to take out Collins, do it. But, let us do this

195

one. I've been gunning for Collins for years. It will be nice to take him down once and for all."

"Will do. It's your operation. I'll see you here first thing in the morning."

Lefty Gorman went to see his wounded deputy one last time before the end of the night.

"I had an interesting conversation with Sheriff Logan."

"Yeah."

"I told him that Collins is coming into town to meet with Garcon tomorrow and that there is a back room to Carrasco's bar, where we got him."

"Yeah."

"Well, at first, he said he never knew there was a room in the back. Then he mentioned a minute or two later that he knew the layout of the area, mentioning that side room. He suggested you and I should hang out back there, wait for Collins, and his deputies will take care of anything in the bar or out on the street."

"Huh. Sounds like he's a little too much familiar with the place."

"Yes."

"You think he's in on it? Or that he knew all along Garcon was hanging out there?"

"I don't know what to think. While the doc was stitching you up, I was talking to Father Cunningham, who had come down the street to see what had happened, and I told him the story. He said he saw Logan and one of his deputies at Miller's hardware store. Father said he could hear the shootout on the street. What is that? Two blocks, maybe? And he went inside the store and you could still hear all the gunfire. He turned around and saw the sheriff and wondered why they didn't rush to scene to see what was going on. He said they just left the store in no hurry at all and casually walked down the street in the other direction."

"That's disconcerting."

"What's worse was that Logan told me just now that they were all out taking care of some cattle rustling business on the edge of town, or somewhere down by the river. He said they had no idea of what happened to us until afterwards."

"The lying bastard!"

"Yep."

"He basically left us to die!"

"I'd say so."

"So, what do we do?"

"We're going to meet up at the sheriff's office in the morning to discuss the plans. I told him it was his operation and we'll play a part. He wants you and I to be in the back room to take custody of Collins if he just walks in and heads back there."

"Sounds like a trap for us. There's no exit to that room."

Lefty agreed, "Exactly."

"So, what do we do?"

Lefty was already planning. "I think we'll counter with Logan, call his bluff. I think we'll see if he, or one of his deputies, wants to be back there, and see if he dismisses the idea. There is logic that since you can't walk to have you back there to hold Collins at gunpoint, but at the same time, if the sheriff is as crooked as I am sensing he is, he wants Collins to go back there and kill us both.

Then they can all get away, blame our deaths on the *outlaws*, and the Collins gang and Garcon can rob the Del Norte bank. Logan will just let them escape, probably getting a cut of the bank money."

"You've always suspected Logan of being crooked."

"Yes."

"It does sound like he wants us at a disadvantage."

Lefty was quiet. After a moment he said, "I'm most concerned of what to do with you since you can't walk very well. Like I said, it's logical to have you in the back room where you don't have to move much, but that's if we knew Logan was on our side. If we suggest his men should be back there, what can you do? Where would I stage you?"

"At the bar?"

"Perhaps. Sleep on it. We'll see what Logan is thinking in the morning and we'll see how the plans work themselves out. If you and I end up back there, and even if we shoot Collins dead, I think we're going to run into a bar full of corrupt deputies that will kill us. If they eliminate the rest of Collins' gang, then the sheriff deputies may become Garcon's bank robbers. They'd split the money with fewer people. Logan's guys are tight-knit. I'm sure they already know what their plans are."

"Let's sleep on it and discuss before we go over there in the morning. Maybe one of us will come up with a plan by then."

"Sounds good, Frank. I'll come by here in the morning and we'll talk and then head over to Logan's together."

"See you in the morning."

The sun had not yet shone itself over the Franklin Mountains, but the early glow of dawn made a silhouette of the range. Lefty Gorman was already on his horse and approaching Frank Fuller's house. He had been awake most of the night contemplating today. He could see that Frank was already up and a kerosene lamp was glowing in the kitchen window.

He knocked on Frank's door and heard Frank call towards him to enter. Frank was still getting used to walking with the crutch the doc gave him.

"G'morning."

"G'morning."

"I've got an idea, Frank. I'm going to insist, that since you're gimpy, to be staged on top of the building across the street and offer sniper protection. Logan knows you're a good shot. If he disagrees, I'll stress that you can't move that fast, which it doesn't look like you can, and that I can't afford to lose another deputy if something goes down bad in that backroom. If he still doesn't agree, I may just pull us out of the operation all together. That may call his bluff."

"That's a good idea. But I've got a better one!"

"All right."

"You go to Logan's this morning and tell him, since I can't walk very well, that you decided to give the Del Norte bank the courtesy of warning them of the information we found out, and to secure their money or get more armed guards. I can't walk well, but I can still ride my horse."

"Frank, that's brilliant!"

"It's calling his bluff before he can make a bet. Now, I can still be up on that roof top like you want. We won't tell them. I can hide myself and be there to protect you. But they'll think I'm across the river. We can send someone down to the bank with a letter from you to inform them we have word of a potential bank robbery."

"Who can we trust at such short notice?"

"I was thinking Kel Riley. He lives just down the road here."

"Perfect. And he hates Logan."

"Well, we can tell him what's going on with that, if you want. But it'll be true that we are warning the Mexican bank of what we know."

"Let's do that."

"How do we get you on top of that building?"

"There's a staircase on the back. I think I can get to the roof from there. I remember there's a ladder next to the chimney. I saw it a week or so ago."

"If the ladder isn't there anymore?"

"I've got one, I'll just take it with me."

"Good. So, you and I are going to be out of contact. If you're up there I'll motion to you if I'll be in the backroom of the bar or not. I'll look up at you when we arrive. If I take my hat off to wipe my brow, it means I'm in the back. If not, I'm at the bar. I'm sure you'll see all of us ride up there and stage ourselves. I have a feeling Logan has this all planned out himself. I'm just going to counter with suggestions. Since I will tell him I sent you to Del Norte, he has to come up with another scenario."

"Sounds good."

"We should visit Riley before he gets his day started. Tell you what. You go to him. Tell him the details. And if he can do it, tell him to meet me at our office and I'll have the note for the bank for him."

"On my way."

Kelly Riley arrived on horseback at the Marshal's office, alongside Fuller. When he walked in the door, he gave a hard look over at Garcon and Carrasco in their respective jail cells.

"Hello Marshal, how are you?" They shook hands.

"I'm doing well, all things considered. Did Frank brief you on what's going on?"

"Yes, sir."

"And you can help us?"

"In any way I can," answered Riley.

"Here's a note for the bank manager. He lives a block west of the bank."

"Frank told me about your thoughts on Logan. Yes, he's corrupt, alright. I could never prove it while I was in the department, but we all knew. Before he even became sheriff, we all knew how crooked he was. You need to watch your back. He's probably involved. Do you know if they were planning to rob it today?"

"That I'm not sure. I think the robbery would be tomorrow." Gorman turned around and looked toward the jail cells. "*Diablo*!?" he yelled in a mocking voice. "Were y'all robbing that bank today or tomorrow?"

Juan Garcon did not acknowledge the question and kept his head down and ate his breakfast. Lefty turned back to Riley, "He ain't talking anymore."

Riley walked up to the prisoner. "Look at me." Riley paused. "Hey! Look at me!"

Slightly startled, Garcon looked up at Riley. "You remember me?"

"Si."

"You know what you did to my wife?"

"Si."

"You are damn lucky you are behind those bars. If I were you, I'd stay there. Don't try to escape, because I will hunt you down and kill you, you bastard."

Garcon lowered his head and kept eating. Riley spit into his jail cell and made contact with Garcon's face. He casually wiped it off his cheek and rubbed his pants. Riley glanced over at Carrasco. "You either. You'd best stay back there, also."

Ernesto Carrasco did not acknowledge Riley's threat and Riley walked back to the front of the office.

Gorman asked, "Bad blood?"

"A story for another time. Let me get across the river."

Gorman added one last thing, "With today being Easter Sunday, they might just try to hit it this afternoon. Just tell him we are not sure what day they are coming."

"I will."

The three men dispersed.

Frank found his way to the top of the building and secured his location and remained hidden. Kel Riley rode across the river to warn the bank. Lefty made his way to the sheriff's office.

"Where's Frank?" asked Sheriff Logan.

"I sent him to Del Norte."

"What?"

"I figured it was courtesy to warn the bank down there of the information we had. He can barely walk and wouldn't be much help in a gunfight anyway, should there be one. They can take whatever precautions they need to further secure their money."

Logan was silent. He realized Gorman was playing him.

"Are you going to take position in the back room?"

"I was thinking we just don't be back there at all. If Collins goes back there, and he can only exit through the bar, then he's cornered. None of us can get caught in any crossfire."

Logan was silent again.

One of his deputies spoke up, "He's got a point."

Logan shot a look across the room at his deputy that could kill. "Not wise. I don't want Collins out of sight for one second, even if he does just go straight back there. If we had someone on both sides of him, it's easier to apprehend him. He'll surrender when he realizes he's surrounded."

Gorman did not respond immediately.

Another deputy spoke up, "One of us should be back there."

Gorman immediately piggy-backed that comment, "Yes! I think any one or two of your deputies is capable of taking position there. I'll hang out at the bar or take a position outside. We still don't know how many men he's bringing with him."

Logan was visibly frustrated with Gorman's verbal poker playing.

The room was quiet for several minutes. Everyone was searching their thoughts. Gorman could see some of the deputies looking back and forth across the room at each other. He caught the eyes of the outspoken deputy looking at Logan, trying to indicate with a slightly dismayed look on his face that he was sorry he spoke out of turn.

Gorman decided to break the silence. He stood up and said, "So, is this our plan?"

"I'm not sure we have one, yet."

"We stage one your deputies in the back. We have someone posing as the bartender. We have a couple of us outside, possibly across the street, and the rest inside. We see how many men show up with Collins and take him down once he realizes it's a trap."

There was silence again.

Logan, still sitting, glared up at Gorman. "And where do you wish to be, marshal?"

"Across the street. There is an empty building two doors down and I can see from there how many ride up with Collins. If they all go inside the bar, I'll follow them in. You can have all the personnel inside you want, or have one or two men outside, also. They can be on either side."

Logan stood up, dismayed his plans were getting augmented, and looked around the room at his men, "All right. Jackson? Salazar? Y'all flank the bar on either side. Stay out of sight until after Collins arrives. If all the men that are with him come into the bar, follow them in. I trust the marshal will be right behind you two."

Gorman nodded.

"Diego? You'll be behind the bar, and Carl, you'll be in the back. No one make eye contact for more than a second and just let them walk in. If we have to open fire to take them, we will. The priority is to arrest them."

"On what charges, sir?"

"Huh?" Logan turned around to face Jackson.

"All he's doing is walking into a bar, what do we charge him with?"

Logan was stunned one of his men was asking him this absurd question. Gorman tried to contain himself and a little smile formed on his otherwise placid poker face.

"We have suspicious activity that we've long suspected Collins as having done. He's out of our jurisdiction in Las Cruces, but he'll be here now. Remember that, son." His voice rose authoritatively at the young deputy as he finished his statement.

Jackson nodded, "Yes, sir. Sorry."

Logan added one more quick quip to stymie the legal doubt of arresting a man simply entering a place of business, "However, Las Cruces is within the marshal's jurisdiction." He glanced over to Gorman. "Perhaps the marshal can think of something between now and then to warrant an arrest? Marshal?"

"I'll think of something."

Logan looked at the roster of his deputies one by one in the eye, the tension was thick in the room. "Good, we all know what to do. Let's go do it."

Logan looked back toward the marshal one last time, "Marshal Gorman, when are you going to be position?"

"I'll ride up with y'all."

Logan did not like that answer. "Well, you can go on ahead if you like. Get your bearings across the street. We'll be right behind you."

Gorman paused—he knew what was going to happen when he left the room—Logan was going to brief his men to not do anything with Collins. Gorman tried to think quickly of something to say so as not to give Logan that opportunity but was not sure just how well briefed all his men were.

"Marshal?"

Gorman could not stall any longer. "Right. I'll see myself out. See y'all there."

Gorman walked slowly out the door and lazily to his horse. He glanced back through the windows and saw Logan watching him, but Logan quickly refocused his attention to address his men. Gorman got on his horse and rode off behind the nearest building to observe when they left.

He saw the whole crew leave the sheriff's office about five minutes later: Logan, Salazar, Jackson, Diego, Carl, his oldest deputy Richards, a kid named Mitchell, which he had just met this morning, and another deputy who he had never met, nor was introduced to. They all mounted their horses and rode towards Carrasco's tavern, except for Mitchell. He rode off in the opposite direction. Gorman figured he was riding out to meet Collins to tell him the changes to the original plan. Gorman mounted his horse and trotted towards Carrasco's, taking a short cut to get back ahead of them.

He came down the street and looked up to Frank's location. The street was quiet on that block. He whistled to get Frank's attention. Gorman saw a hat poke up on top of the building. He stopped and looked back to see if Logan's men were behind him—there was no sign of them—he motioned to the building he was going to be in. Gorman turned back around to see if they were close yet—they were not in view yet—he motioned back up to Frank. He pointed at himself, made a gesture across his throat, and then pointed

206

back to where they will be coming from. Frank got the message. They planned to kill Lefty. They did not know Frank was up there and assumed his boss would be all alone. Frank lowered himself out of view.

Gorman rode behind the building, tied his horse up, and went to take his position in the empty building across from the tavern. A minute later the sheriff's men rode up and dispersed. They all tied their horses up in various places up and down the block, so as not to be in the line of fire. Gorman kept his eye on all of them to see if they all went in the directions they were supposed to go. It was still too early for Collins to arrive.

Jackson went to the left and was directly across from where Gorman was. Salazar went to the other side of the tavern and sat down on a bench on the sidewalk. He placed a rifle behind him on the wood planks. Everyone else went inside. Still no sign of Mitchell, but Gorman was not expecting him.

Lefty Gorman was still not sure what he was going to do when Collins arrived. He was convinced that Sheriff Logan was involved and they were going to try to execute him and blame his death on a shootout with the outlaw gang. After the bank robbery happened—without a marshal's presence—they easily could come back across the border with the gold and the money, and then escape to the mountains up north. Gorman was relying on the young Frank Fuller above him to help take out a few of the bad guys if they came his way. Surprise was their only advantage. Fuller had been with the with US Marshal office about two years. He opted to join them instead of going to war. He met Lefty in San Antonio while working in the local sheriff's department there. Frank then joined Gorman in the marshal's office. When the Marshal Service offered Gorman the El Paso assignment, Frank followed Lefty to El Paso.

The areas out west were not much involved in the Civil War raging across the eastern half of the United States. There were strong opinions and even stronger loyalties, but those out west mostly stayed clear of the action. Some of the criminal element, with vim and vigor to be satisfied, gravitated towards the war to enlist in the fighting, and others, perhaps the more entrepreneurial spirits, headed west. They were consolidating themselves into gangs and strongholds across the western states and territories. Much of the country was preoccupied with the war and little attention was given elsewhere. Marshals were the only federal presence and sometimes the only legal authority in many places, but word of the surrender of the Confederates had just hit El Paso and Gorman hoped things would change out west for the better.

Gorman wondered if this was his last day on earth, what would happen in the short-term to this border town if Sheriff Logan was the only law enforcement left standing. Yes, the US Marshal service would replace Gorman, but Logan would be now be rich and even more powerful, if he chose to remain in town. He also worried about Frank. They would eventually get to him on top of the building and kill him. He would only be able to hold his position for so long. He wrote a letter last night and dispatched it to the neighboring forts in Texas: Fort Davis and Fort Quitman. He also sent one to the marshal in San Antonio.

He knew they would get them long after him and Frank were dead, but at least they could come to El Paso to investigate and perhaps prove that Logan was involved in all of this. Although deep down in Lefty's gut, he figured they probably would not. They had enough problems of their own to attend. If he could not prove any of his suspicions about Logan, they probably would not either. He just wanted to let others know what he had suspected for some time. He did not want to the sheriff's office to go unchecked for years to come and continue to be corrupt beyond Logan's tenure there.

After that meeting this morning, he was at peace that the letters he dispatched were right to assume that Logan was crooked and his deputies were in on it, too. A successor would undoubtedly come from this group, whenever Logan decided to give it up. It would not bode well for the future of the town.

Gorman was not even sure about the future of the country. It had been fractured for so long, its strength was in doubt. Since the Confederacy was coming to an end, he hoped Lincoln could bring the country back together. So much had already recently changed, but one thing that would be tough to change was the corruption locally. Perhaps his letters would convince others to investigate his suspicions should he not live to see another day.

Gorman kept watch across the street. He had no game plan other than to play it by ear. He could see into the tavern but only a few feet deep into the building. The back part of the bar was in the shadows. He saw two deputies sitting on the end of the bar, but could see no one else. He kept waiting.

Eternity crept along. It was the longest morning of Lefty Gorman's life, and possibly his last. He kept checking his pocket watch—his mind drifted to thoughts of his wife—she gave him that watch for their first anniversary. It was a mail order from the east coast. He did not say anything to her this morning, she was still sleeping, and kissed her on the cheek when he left. He always had a letter written to her in his desk drawer if he was ever killed. He updated it last night anticipating him not making it home today. He thought about her for a few more minutes and then refocused his attention across the street.

Ten or fifteen more minutes went by and Mitchell came trotting up on his horse to the tavern just ahead of what he perceived to be Collins and the remainder of his crew. Five in total were behind Mitchell. As they dismounted Gorman glanced around at Salazar and looked for Jackson. Salazar was reaching behind him to pick up his rifle. Still convinced Logan and his men were going to kill him, Gorman assumed Salazar was doing that for the benefit of playing up the fact that the plan was to capture Collins. He could not see Jackson.

One outlaw was more nicely dressed than the rest and had a cigar in his mouth. Gorman assumed it was Collins. He wore a wide flat brim black hat whereas the other four wore lighter colored hats of various brim styles. Collins looked around the street in all directions. It was eerily quiet. A few wagons had trundled down the street, but turned at the corners. The entire group that rode up entered the bar.

Gorman looked at Salazar. He stayed put on his bench but held his rifle now. Salazar watched the group enter the bar. Gorman still had no clue where Jackson was. He glanced at his watch; it was a quarter to noon. He looked up and something caught his eye on top of the building across the street—the one next to the tavern—it was deputy Jackson. *What was he doing up there?*

Gorman decided to make a move of his own. He thought the best way to survive was to join Frank. Salazar's attention was still on the tavern's front door. Gorman retreated into the shadows of the empty building, turned, went out of the backdoor as discreetly as he could, and ran around the back to the building Frank was on top of. He scurried up the stairs on the backside of the building, ascending the ladder with the prowess of a cat.

Frank turned around when he heard the footsteps behind him. "Why'd you come up here?"

"We're about to find out if Logan is in on this or not. Look across the street on top." He pointed towards Jackson. "They're changing up their plan. They think I'm down there in that building. Let's see what they do."

All was quiet for several minutes. Frank and Gorman waited quietly.

Salazar got up and walked toward the front door. That was one of the cues that Gorman was to follow. However, nothing happened inside. No shots had been fired—no loud voices—nothing.

Salazar did not enter. The front door opened and Mitchell, Carl, and two of Collins' men came out and joined Salazar on the sidewalk. They looked around and then started making their way across the street to where Gorman was supposed to be.

Gorman whispered to Frank, "I knew it."

They kept watching.

"Take out Jackson up top."

Frank aimed at Jackson, who was still oblivious to Frank's presence across the street. He leveled his rifle and fired. Direct hit. Jackson fell. The shot shattered the silence of the street and the exposed men in the middle of it scattered. Gorman aimed and shot two of them, they laid dead in the street. Frank hit another, he was wounded, and tried crawling for cover, gasping for his last breaths. His body collapsed on the edge of the sidewalk. Salazar made it across the street and took refuge under the awning. He figured out where the shots were coming from.

Some of the rest of the party emerged in the doorway and in the windows, but did not step outside. Frank reloaded and took pot shots at the windows. Some blood splattered but he was not sure if the targets were just wounded or dead. The remainder retreated into the building. Gorman surveyed the dead on the street, the one gasping for air had succumbed; the dead were Collin's two men and Carl, the deputy. Mitchell and Salazar escaped. He knew Salazar ran towards their side of the street but he did not see where Mitchell ran.

The door to the tavern opened, but no one came out, instead it was Logan's voice, "What are you doing, marshal?"

Gorman did not want to answer and give away their position, although he was sure they knew both men were on top of the building across the street.

"Marshal!?"

Gorman remained quiet.

"Marshal?"

Frank tapped Gorman on the shoulder. One of the Collins gang had scaled the back of the building where Salazar had been in front of. He must have gone out the back door of the tavern. Gorman acknowledged and motioned for Frank to take him out. Frank fired but had a rare miss. The gangster was more exposed than he wanted to be and ducked, but he did not have sufficient cover. Frank fired again and hit him this time. His body slumped down behind part of the roof. Someone from within the tavern fired up through the open door at them. They were errant shots. Frank and Gorman had good cover where they were, but their position was now revealed.

"Marshal? I know where you are. You are outnumbered."

Gorman tapped Frank's shoulder again and whispered "I'll be right back." He rushed over to the chimney and pulled up the ladder onto the roof. If they were trying to get to them, they had nothing to climb up beyond the stairs which ended at the second floor landing.

As Gorman came back to Frank's position, he noticed one of Collins' men running across the street about two blocks down from them. He pointed. Frank saw him.

"Marshal, we know where you are. Just come out!"

He finally answered Logan, "Why are you doing this?"

"Doing what?"

"Betraying the citizens of El Paso!"

"I don't know what you mean." Logan's voice was half laughing at the accusation.

"You partnered with Collins and Garcon to rob the bank in Del Norte. I foiled your plans."

Logan remained quiet, searching his thoughts, but finally answered Gorman with a vague statement, "I don't know what you are talking about."

"I know you've taken allegiance with them. Probably were going to split up the money."

Another man went darting across the street to their right. They were going to try and surround them.

"You don't know that... and even if you did, you're going to be dead soon and no one will be able to prove a thing."

"Why would you kill me if you are working on the right side of the law?"

"Because history will not be recorded that way. I will be the victor! The story will say *you* were working with them and they got away."

Gorman rushed over to the back of the building. Both men who had scurried across the street on either side of them were approaching from their respective directions. They were not going to be able to get to the roof but Gorman did not want to take the chance they could scale it in some other way. He took a shot at the closer of the two and took him down. Shot to the chest. The man recoiled from the impact and fell backward awkwardly. The other cowered for cover at the sound of the shot. Gorman rushed over to that corner of the roof and could just see the man's arm, the rest of him shrouded by the building. He shot at his arm. Hit. The man doubled over in pain and exposed the rest of his body. Gorman shot again at his torso and he dropped dead. He headed back to the front of the building.

Frank took a shot at Salazar who was running between the building, exposed for a split second, but could not hit him. He was directly beneath them.

"Logan… Your numbers are dwindling. Just keep coming at us."

Some citizens in a wagon came down the street, saw the dead bodies, veered off, and took a left turn. They knew better than to get involved in a shootout.

"Logan!?"

"What!?"

"I always knew you were crooked, you son of a bitch."

"Is that all you got to say?"

"What else can I say?"

"It's your last day on earth, make your words count if you're going say anything at all."

"I'll see you in hell, Logan."

Frank looked across the street at the rooftops. He saw the Mitchell kid up on another building. He turned to aim. The sunlight glinted off the rifle barrel and Mitchell ducked. "Watch him," Frank whispered to Gorman.

Several rifle blasts suddenly rang out in almost perfect unison from the windows of the tavern. The remaining occupants bombarded Gorman and Frank's position. Splinters flew all around them from the barrage of gunfire. They both ducked and were unscathed.

There was a pause in the gunfire, Frank popped up and fired into the window—nothing—they were probably reloading. He popped up again to shoot, but a second barrage of gunfire emanated from the tavern windows. Frank ducked back down just in time. He heard a groan and glanced over at Gorman. Gorman had been hit in the right arm and was lying on the rooftop staring at the cloudless midday sky. "Lefty!" Frank glanced back down on the street. The men were still inside the bar. He ripped off a strip of clothing and wrapped Lefty's wound. "Keep your hand on it."

He popped back up in position. Two brave souls were moving across the street: Richards and Diego. He aimed and fired two quick shots at both of them. Richards was hit in the leg and Diego reacted by firing up toward Frank's position while running to their side of the street. Frank took another shot at Diego and he fell flat on his face. He aimed at Richards, who was limping back towards the tavern, clutching his leg, and screaming in pain. The unnamed deputy came out of the tavern a step or two to cover Richards and Frank fired at him, hit him in the chest, and he crumpled on the wooden planks of the sidewalk. Richards was still dragging himself across the street slow enough for Frank to reload his rifle. Frank took aim and hit him dead center in the back. He fell forward with a thud; motionless.

Mitchell gathered up his courage and rose to fire at Frank from his rooftop vantage point. Frank ducked, let the shots go by, then popped back up, and returned the volley. The younger man did not stand a chance—he flailed from a bullet hitting his chest—fell over the side of the building, and crashed with a thud ten yards from where Richards lay dead in the street.

All that was left was Collins, Logan, and Salazar.

Frank looked back down at Gorman, "Lefty? You all right?"

"In pain, but making it. I think the bleeding has stopped. How are we doing?"

"Better than we were."

"That's good."

Frank focused back on the street. He wished he knew where Salazar was. He wanted to lean over and look, but doing so would probably expose him to a shot. He saw movement inside the tavern. He thought only Collins and Logan remained in there. They were not near the windows or door. He stood up quickly and looked over the edge of the building. He saw no one. He ducked back down as quickly as he stood up. His ankle had been throbbing this whole time. He looked back at Lefty. Lefty was staring at the sky clutching his arm—the bleeding continued—he needed to get him off this roof as soon as possible and to the doctor.

A shot rang out from behind him. He whirled and did not see anyone on the rooftop. He careened around and scanned all the roofs around him. *Where did that come from?* He heard a few thuds behind him. He looked back towards the bar—nothing—he slowly rose to his feet and walked to the back of the roof. He peered down from behind the chimney. He saw Salazar laying on the first landing, bleeding from a chest wound. Kel Riley was ascending the stairs. He stopped at Salazar's body with his gun still drawn. He reached down and felt no life left in him. He looked up and waved at Frank. Frank motioned him to come up. He slid the ladder down and retook his position at the front of the roof, overlooking the street. He could only see someone's boots through the window of the tavern; he figured them to be Collins' boots. They moved toward the front of the room, his legs slowly appearing, and then another set of legs. Collins bent over, glanced up at the rooftop, and pointed. He then saw Logan's face join him in the view of the window, both looking up at him. He drew his rifle. They both saw the barrel emerge over the rooftop and quickly shuffled back out of view.

Riley came up behind him. "Lefty... You alright?"

"I've been better."

He turned to Frank, "Is he alright?"

"Shot in the arm. He needs the doc."

"How are you doing?"

"I think we're just down to two, thanks to you. I wondered where Salazar was, but I don't think he could've gotten up here. Did you pull the ladder back up?"

"Yeah."

Frank looked back down at the tavern. It was quiet. "I'm not sure what they're doing. They could probably go out the back and get reinforcements, but I'm not sure."

Some more people could be seen coming down the street, but then walking away after seeing the dead bodies littering the street.

"They don't know I'm here, so I think could go back down, sneak around back, and see."

"That might work. Did you deliver the message to Del Norte?"

"Yes. They were very happy for the head's up."

"Well, unless these fools have more outlaws stashed away somewhere, this ain't happening today or tomorrow. I've taken out everyone here except Logan and Collins."

"Let me go down. Pick the ladder back up."

Kel went to the backside of the rooftop, lowered the ladder, and climbed down to the landing. Frank scanned the area once more before hobbling to the back of the rooftop, and hoisted the ladder back up.

Kel ran down the alley to the end of the block and edged himself toward the street. He peered around and then darted across. He quickly made his way down the next alley to the back of the tavern. The back door was ajar.

Walking slowly along the back of the building, he had his pistol drawn. He edged himself up to the doorframe and listened. He could hear the two men talking but could not make out what they were saying. They were probably in the bar room and not in the hallway, so he figured he could chance a quick look. He quickly looked and pulled his head back around. They were facing the street. He took another quick look. He took a deep breath and whirled around in through the backdoor with his pistol out in front of him. He took two long strides that got him halfway down the hallway and fired into the back of Collins. He crumpled on the spot. Logan spun around with his gun already drawn, but not quick enough as Kel fired at him—hitting his arm—causing Logan to drop his pistol. He fired again at Logan's left shoulder—the sheriff reeled backward— fell against a barstool, and slid slowly down to the floor.

Kel kicked Logan's pistol across the floor. Logan, clutching his shoulder, and grimacing in pain, rolled over and made eye contact with Kel Riley.

"Ri… Riley? What the hell?"

"Hello sheriff." His voice had a condescending tone to it.

"What... what are you doing... doing here?"

"Taking care of business. Business from long ago."

Logan and Riley stared each other in the eyes. "I just want you to suffer for a little bit longer until I put you into the ground." Logan made one last-ditched lunge upward with all his remaining strength, his body encased in pain as he slithered upward, but it was his last movement. Kel Riley fired the deadly shot at point blank range.

The echo from the shot faded away and only a deathly silence remained in the room. A solace came over Kelly Riley as he had finally exacted his revenge on his nemesis.

Suddenly, a gurgle came from Collins' body and Riley reeled around to look at him. He was near death, but trying to grab the pistol out of his holster. Riley watched him struggle, and then Riley fired his last round.

Riley went out the front door and waved up to Frank. Frank motioned to Riley to come help get Lefty down off the roof. He quickly crossed the street to help Frank.

Frank lowered the ladder down and the two carefully got Lefty down to the ground.

"Don't worry about me, Kel. Just get boss to the doc!"

Riley put Lefty on his own horse, mounted his own, and gathered Gorman's reins in his hands. Both horses trotted off to the doctor. Lefty sat upright in the saddle, but moaned in pain.

Frank limped into the street on his crutch with his rifle still in hand. He surveyed the death all around. If Hell had a waiting room, it would be busy on this day. He walked into the bar and saw the two dead men there. He wished it had not come to this, but circumstances were what they were. Some people started to gather at the end of the block, sensing the gunfight was over. Frank stumbled in their direction. He looked down the street and saw a restaurant one block down. A kid about ten or twelve years old came up to him and asked if he was all right.

"Thanks, yes, I'm fine. Can you do me a favor, kid?"

"Yes, mister."

"Can you run down to the church and get the padre for me? Padre Cunnigham?"

"Yes."

"Run down there and tell him that US Marshal deputy Fuller needs to see him pronto. I'll be right in that restaurant over there."

"Yes, sir." The kid ran off down the street.

Frank hobbled over to the restaurant, sat down, and ordered some water and food. He took a deep sigh and relaxed his body in the chair. He was exhausted. For a few short moments he held his head down trying to let the pain of his body leave him. It was a harrowing and excruciating turn of events they all just went through. This was not the first of these gunfights he had been involved in on the streets of El Paso. He wondered how many more he would be a part of and how many more he could survive. How many more could Lefty survive? His fellow deputies were not so lucky yesterday. They were all younger than him and would have to bury them in the next day or two. He could have been one of them. He pondered a career change or at least a change of scenery. He could move north to some unchartered territory or ask to be transferred east—Texas was becoming too wild for him—since the war was now over, maybe there were opportunities back east. He was still young by normal standards, but not for this still untamed land. He felt lucky to be alive, but saw these last two days as a warning. If this lawlessness kept up out here, he would not live to become an old man.

The evil in this world that men did weighed heavy in Frank's mind. He tried to be a just man, a caring man, a Christian man, a man of the law; but the world seemed to overwhelm him at every turn. It seemed his job was becoming increasingly more difficult—his moral code increasingly more rare—it haunted him on many sleepless nights.

Last night was one of them—he lied awake most of the night thinking it would be his last—he contemplated the choices he had made and whether they were the right ones. It did not change the fact that he knew he had to face what hell was coming their way in the morning. It was a hell he could not avoid—he had to face it today—he could not run away from it. He was bound by his duty to stand up to the thugs that were coming. He prayed the night before he would survive today—would have the chance to reevaluate his career choice—now he could do exactly that.

There were other avenues he could pursue. The war had just ended and there would be a lot of rebuilding to do—both on the east coast and down south—he could be a businessman like his father in some small town, or even move to one of the big cities. Perhaps he could settle down with a war widow and help raise a family, or move northward, and start again up there. All these thoughts raced through his mind as he tried to calm his nerves from the death and turmoil that had only just ended a few minutes before.

His food arrived—he was famished and the nourishment helped ease some of his pain—it also calmed his mind and his anxiety waned. His plate was empty within a matter of minutes. He leaned back and took a long drink of water. He stared across the room at the other patrons. They were going about their business—

having their midday meal—taking a break from their own daily tasks and chores. They were just trying to get through their day. Most probably did not know that the local marshal's office had three fewer deputies in it than yesterday—their local sheriff's department, due to their own corruption, was presently non-existent. These people ate in peace and had their own worries to take care of.

As Frank watched his fellow citizens eat, he realized more than ever he should remain a lawman. His oath was to protect the peaceful people of the community. No matter how much evil came to town, he was what stood between that evil and these people living peaceful lives and chasing their dreams. If he did not do it, who would? Someone like Logan?

He took another deep sigh. He hoped the priest would arrive soon. The deceased outside needed to be taken care of and Frank had to explain why the entire local police force was now dead. All things considered; the local priest was the only one outside of the marshal's office he could trust. He hoped Lefty was going to survive his wound—he was not ready to be the only marshal in town—he had to get back up on both his feet himself before that could happen.

Frank hoped the evil of the world would pause just a moment until this town could figure out what to do without proper law enforcement, but he knew that is not how it worked. He could hope for such things, but not expect it. Today evil was satiated, but tomorrow was another day.

He saw a newspaper on the next table and picked it up. He had not read one since Friday. He turned it over to the front page and read the headline: *PRESIDENT LINCOLN DIES FROM GUNSHOT!*

The End

5

God's Country

Ennis snapped the reins on the horse team, their hooves dutifully clip-clopped forward, and advanced the covered wagon westward. The rising sun was at his back, and the expansive plain stretched out in front of him. The grueling journey had taken its toll on the family, but the severe circumstances that the Carpenter family faced back home had led to them attempt the challenge of this demanding venture.

Ennis' father had failed to keep the family's whiskey business going. Two cousins suffered severe burns in a barn fire that consumed the entire inventory of whiskey, except for one full barrel that was inside the old Carpenter home. One cousin passed away the next day from his burns. The other survived, but was scarred for life. A long and harsh winter in the mountains of Eastern Kentucky all but wiped out all their food stores. The youngest of

Ennis' siblings, a baby boy born the day before the fire, developed a fever three days after Christmas, and did not survive into the new year. His youngest sister, having just turned three, died of a similar fever one month later. His parents—devastated by the hardships—decided to leave the Kentucky mountains behind and start fresh out west.

Ennis was fifteen. He was too young to have seen so much strife and suffering in such a short life: the two recent deaths of his youngest siblings during the winter; the deaths of all four of his grandparents within the last two years; and his two uncles on his father's side, which were both killed in a "whiskey war" that erupted in the area between rival families a year before that. More than a dozen local men had been murdered senselessly through nothing more than personal greed. His own father took a bullet in his right lower leg and had a permanent limp. Ennis was still a boy who had seen all this with own eyes, but he was also becoming a young man.

That limp his father had from the gunshot wound did not matter anymore. His father contracted cholera, or something like it, before they got to the Missouri River crossing at St. Joseph. He died within sight of its flowing waters. Ennis buried him where he died. He was left with only his mother, a sister two years younger than him, and a brother who was five years old. His mother had been in a weakened health state for the past few years, always having coughing fits. With every cold snap or harsh northern wind, she seemed to hover near death. His surviving brother had the same fever his deceased sister and infant brother had, but had managed to survive. The young boy was severely ill in each of the five winters he had lived through in his short life. Only Ennis and his surviving sister seemed fit as fiddles. They were rarely sick when the rest of the family came down with illnesses.

His mother's sister accompanied them out of Kentucky, but decided to stay in St. Louis. She had no desire to go into the wilds of the western territories of the United States. She had said the day her niece died that even Kentucky was too uncivilized for her. She pleaded with her sister to not go any farther when they arrived in the gateway city, but Ennis' father was insistent, and his mother did not argue with him.

Ennis was the man of the family now. He had to take care of his sickly mother, his sister, and a five-year old. He had a wad of cash from his father from the sale of the family land and other possessions before they left. That final surviving barrel of grandpa's whiskey proved to be worth more than the house and land put together. Sadly, grandpa's recipe disappeared forever after that. The only men who knew it were now all dead. His father never passed it along to him.

His aunt had her own money and even tried to give her sister some, but the Carpenter family refused her request. Everett Carpenter had plenty of money to make the trek out west, but his health outran his money in Missouri. The money was Ennis' now. The fifteen-year-old could have turned the family back around after his father's passing and rejoined his aunt in St. Louis, but he also wanted to venture west. His father's dream of seeing the Rocky Mountains was also his dream. He had heard the same stories of the trappers that had come home to Kentucky. The stories of the majestic mountains sounded a clarion call within the restless souls of both Everett and his son Ennis. The sagas told by these scruff adventurers were as if they were mythology. Legends of lore braved by demigods.

The tales enthralled the father and his oldest son, and to add to the lure, was the news of gold recently discovered in a place Ennis had never heard of before: California. He was suspicious that the claims were true, but if they were, it was better than where they were presently. The journey would be long and treacherous, but the potential reward was great. Ennis was excited to start his life out there, but he was not sure what he was going to do. His father had some ideas, but they were all dependent on what opportunities presented themselves wherever they landed. The western frontier had boundless prospects for one with an entrepreneurial spirit. Ennis was a hard worker and had that yearning deep inside his heart. All he knew was that he was ready to take on the frontier.

Some of the family's provisions needed to be replenished. His mother bought a couple of items needed for cooking while they were in town, but Everett had been explicit to his family when the journey began about wasting the family money on bought food. Between him and Ennis, they hunted or fished whatever protein source they could find. His father said, as they traveled, to stay near the rivers. You could always catch fish and the wildlife needed to drink. It was always easiest to hunt an animal while they were getting water. Ennis had kept the family well-fed in the past couple of years, all by himself, while his father tended the family business.

He was a crack shot that was taught well by his father and the other men who were around him as a youngster. None of those men were around anymore. He was adept at fishing and well-seasoned at hunting rabbit, squirrel, birds, and deer that were plentiful where they once lived. On the trail out west, Ennis quickly discovered that rabbits and birds were readily available, but deer could be scarce at times. They had left Kentucky with plenty of dried, smoked meats, and pemmican for the journey, but nothing beat the taste of fresh meat—when he could hunt it.

The Carpenter wagon crossed the river at St. Joseph the morning after Everett Carpenter was buried. They travelled about another dozen miles and stopped for the night to eat.

Ennis went out late in the afternoon after making camp and returned an hour later with five rabbits. Ennis and his sister skinned and gutted them. In her grief, his mother cooked one for the family to eat that night. She needed the distraction. They seasoned and smoked the others. The bounty would last them for several days while on the trail. When the preserved meat would run out, Ennis would have to hunt for some more, but today's kill would mean the family could progress down the trail for several days with very few stops.

The family bedded down for the night and continued their trek at dawn. They followed a trail that was becoming well known and met many others making their way to the frontier. Ennis travelled alongside them or followed close behind for several weeks. Sometimes the other frontier seekers were ahead by a mile or so in the distance, some days Ennis was ahead of them, and other days they were alone as far as the eye could see. At one point he had veered off the path that followed the river to take a slightly more northern route than they had been on. His father and him had talked about it as they moved through Missouri. If they turned northwest once they cross at St. Joseph, eventually they would hit the trail, and then head due west.

There was no map Ennis could follow, but he knew he needed to keep the morning sun at his back, and head in the direction of the afternoon sun, veering slightly northwest until he hit a river or a wagon trail. He knew all the rivers across the plains came from the mountains, flowing west to east. Ennis only had to keep trekking upriver of any he came across, eventually hitting the western mountain ranges. His father said that's where the opportunities would lie. There were small frontier towns all amongst the mountains and plenty of frontiersmen needing supplies and such. That was his father's goal, to start a business in one of those towns that attracted weary travelers—they just needed to find the right place.

A week went by. The moon was full and the trail was well-illuminated at night. He suggested to his mother that they could travel by night and follow the wagon tracks of those ahead of them. Not that Ennis was necessarily in a hurry to get to wherever it is they were going, he just wanted to keep moving. Where they were was not where they wanted to be. Ennis was as antsy as every teenager has ever been and ready for the next big thing to happen, but he also had the maturity of an adult, mostly because he had to be one now. His youthful exuberance drove his old soul. He just wanted to keep moving. His mother and his young brother went to sleep in the back of the wagon as it ambled along. His sister sat up front with him, they talked of their dreams, and the riches they hoped to find out west. His sister eventually fell asleep to the rhythm of the horses clopping their way along the trail.

Ennis watched the moon move gradually, but purposefully, across the clear night sky. He became drowsy himself but managed to stay awake. He estimated it was two hours past midnight based on the moon's position in the sky when they came across an encampment of about a dozen wagons. A few campfires were still just barely lit. He decided that safety in numbers was best and he needed a few hours of sleep so he pulled up to join the group.

228

He had been thinking about it as he travelled through the night that they could have run across some bandits or Indians looking to harm them. He had heard all the stories and was concerned, but there was no stopping him once he had set out into the night. The teenager was relieved of the dangerous thoughts that had occupied his lonely mind late in the night, as they arrived unscathed with this other group.

A lookout was posted amongst the other wagons. He approached Ennis, and he told the man with the rifle it was just him, his sister, brother, and mother. His sister awakened to the voices.

"You are lucky you are still alive. There are outlaws in this area. I suggest you stop for the night and not go it alone. You can continue on with us in the morning if you like."

"Thank you, sir. I'll take you up on that offer. I need to get some sleep."

"No problem. Where you headed?"

"Wherever. We're just heading west from Kentucky."

"We're part of the Mormon group."

"We're Baptist... mostly, if that's alright with you? Momma was raised Catholic, but Papa was Baptist, so that's what she is now."

"As long as you don't give us any trouble, we don't care. There's strength in numbers."

"Ain't much trouble a fifteen-year-old, a widow, and her two other children could give you, I suppose. We're just going until we don't anymore."

"Welcome to the group. Stay with us as long as you like. We know where we're going, but got a ways till we're there ourselves."

"You going as far as the Rockies?"

"Yes, past them, to the great desert on the other side."

"You're going to a desert?"

"It's where the rest of our people are. We are settling out there. Leaving the rest of the world behind us, those that persecute us. Our kind has not been wanted in many areas, so we've started our own society out west."

"I've heard the stories. It's sorry that people chase you away."

"It is. But we hope to get as far away from them as possible. It's our Exodus."

"Just like the Bible? The promised land?"

"You could say that."

"I'm Ennis... Ennis Carpenter."

"I'm Clinton... Clinton Jarvis."

The two shook hands.

"Good to meet you, sir."

"Likewise."

"I'm going to bed down for the night. We'll see you in the morning."

Ennis checked on his mother and brother, they were still sound asleep. His sister crawled into the bed of the wagon and curled up in a blanket next to them. Ennis grabbed a blanket of his own, and by moonlight, found a flat enough piece of dirt to lie down on.

The Carpenter family travelled with The Mormon group for almost two weeks. Some other travelers joined them along the way. Various wagons split off and went in other directions. Ennis met a girl one year younger than him, Susanna, who stole his heart. Her family joined the wagon train several days before the Carpenters first started with them.

For four straight evenings both families all ate dinner together and got to know each other. Ennis and Susanna would go for long walks and talked each evening until it was time to rejoin their respective families for the night.

On the morning of the fifth day, Ennis awoke to gunshots and shouting voices. An outlaw group was attacking the wagon train. The day had just broke. He quickly grabbed his father's double-barrel flintlock pistol, loaded both sides, and grabbed the Springfield flintlock rifle. He hid behind the wagon and peered out onto the scene to assess the situation. Several men were already shot dead. Two women lay by a campfire bleeding from gunshots and crying out in agony. One outlaw held another woman by her waist and was dragging her kicking and screaming out of the circle of wagons. Random gunshots were being fired in all directions. His mother was in the bed of the wagon her body draped over his little brother. His sister had the family Brown Bess shotgun poised to fight off any intruder at close range. She also had her father's pepper-box revolver at her side.

Two of the outlaws had new Colt Walker revolvers and were proving to be technologically the more advanced weapon in this gunfight. Ennis had seen some in Lexington last summer when his father and him went to town to sell some hogs. He wanted to own one ever since. Lucky for the wagon folk, Jarvis and Stevens, the other lead waggoneer, both had Colt Walkers of their own. Ennis watched Jarvis shoot three of the outlaws dead. Ennis figured there were four, maybe five left. Stevens shot one off his horse. The outlaw had just put a bullet in the forehead of two Mormon men.

Ennis looked back towards his left at the outlaw carrying the woman, stumbling towards his horse, dodging the woman's punches on his body. He was separated from the group and Ennis thought this was the perfect time to get him. He crouched down and moved briskly from the back of one wagon to the next and then to the next. The woman landed two blows to the outlaw's head as he attempted to pick her up and get her onto his horse. He slapped her across her face once his arms were free. She hit him again and he slapped her harder. Ennis got twenty feet behind him and raised his flintlock. The outlaw moved sideways slightly to grab the rope off his saddle horn and Ennis fired, shooting the outlaw in his back. He gyrated and turned slightly to see what hit him. Ennis quickly advanced on the wounded outlaw, and before he could reach for his gun, Ennis fired the second barrel and put the lead ball square between his eyes.

A trickle of blood spurted from the gaping hole above his nose. He attempted one last grasp of his horse or saddle, whatever he could get a hold of, but slid downwards quickly dying. His horse was startled by the gunshot but only moved a few feet sideways. The woman slid off the saddle and collapsed on the ground. Ennis ran to her aid and got her to her feet. "Come over here, to my wagon." He helped her get back to the Carpenter wagon and she climbed up into the back with his mother.

Ennis reloaded the flintlock and moved around to the front of the wagon. The horses were tied off on some trees forty yards away grazing. He looked up at his sister. She was still holding her position. From her higher vantage point up on the stage of the wagon she could see three of the outlaws to her right. She motioned to her brother, he stealthily moved around the front of the wagon, and shrouded himself behind the adjacent wagon. There were three men in front of him. He looked back at his sister. She saw him. He held up two fingers, pointed at his chest, then pointed at her, and held up one finger. She got the message.

He ran out from behind his cover. The outlaws had their backs to him. From five feet away he abruptly and successfully put a lead ball in the backs of two of them—one fell dead—the other one wounded. The third one reeled around to see Ennis running behind the cover of another wagon. He advanced on Ennis' position only to meet his fate as his sister fired the pepper-box three times, hitting the outlaw's head twice.

The wounded outlaw from Ennis' shot stumbled to his feet, and seeing her shoot his compatriot, clumsily fired at the Carpenter wagon. Probably in pain and discombobulated, his shot was high and went over the crown of the wagon cover. He fired again and it was off to her right side. As he got closer to her, she fired at him and struck him in the chest. He reeled backwards a few steps, blood spilling down his shirt, and then slumped to the ground.

Ennis took the shot and saltpeter bag out of his pocket and reloaded his pistol. The mayhem was still ongoing beyond their wagon. He motioned to his sister to stay put and he disappeared toward the inner campfire where the action started.

As he moved silently between wagons and saw the wagon belonging to Susanna's family. He peered inside. Susanna's mother was crying. She looked up to see Ennis and cried even harder. She was hugging her daughter and she moved upwards from her embrace enough for him to see his love interest drenched in blood. Susanna's head slumped and her neck went limp as her mother disengaged her embrace. Her mother's dress was stained with Susanna's blood. Ennis stared in disbelief. They made eye contact again and he jumped up onto the back of the wagon. He hugged Susanna and realized she was dead. He drew back in sorrow and tears ran down his young face. His face turned from sadness to anger and then to rage. He jumped off the back of the wagon and ran towards the middle of the wagon circle with reckless abandon.

There were three outlaws left, they were holding several of the Mormon men and women at gunpoint, and were taking money and belongings from them. Without thinking, he raised his pistol and fired his two shots at the outlaws. The first he hit behind the ear dropping him to the ground and the second hit the right arm causing the second outlaw to drop his gun. The third turned and fired at the now defenseless boy. Ennis quickly ducked behind the nearest wagon the moment he fired his second shot, knowing he was now defenseless. One of the Mormon men picked up the pistol dropped by the wounded outlaw and shot at the third outlaw, hitting him twice in the back, killing him. The wounded outlaw reached towards the armed Mormon but the Mormon was too quick for him and shot him in the face. That was the last of the bandits. The blast of the final gunshot seemed to hang in the smoky air for an eternity, but dissipated into the continuing cacophony of bawling and weeping from those left living—mourning the lives of their newly deceased loved ones.

Ennis emerged and went to check on those that were just previously hostages. The men shook Ennis' hand and thanked him for coming to their rescue. They turned to embrace their wives and kissed their tear-stained faces.

Ennis ran back to Susanna's family. He wept on his knees. He had only known her for four days, but he felt he knew everything about her. He wanted to marry her when they got to the end of the trail. He asked if he could help bury her, her father obliged, and the two of them dug her grave.

The rest of that day went that way for the entire trail-riding group. Everyone had someone to bury. Some children lost a father. Some children lost both parents. Some parents lost a child; some lost all their children. Ennis learned that the initial attack was quick. The outlaws came up unseen and unheard, and attacked those making breakfast. Most of the deaths occurred instantly before the men could react and grab their guns. Many did not have any guns on them where they stood, or where they would soon die. Their guns were several yards away in their own wagons. It was those still not yet at breakfast that heard the gunfire, grabbed their guns, and tried to defend of the rest of the group.

It was rare he slept late. He was usually up before the sun came over the horizon, but that night he had been up late with Susanna. They had exchanged their first kiss the night before, and he lied in his sleeping bag much of the night wide awake thinking about her beautiful face, her warm embrace, her smile, her laugh, the soft touch of her hand, and that kiss. It kept him up deep into the night until he finally fell asleep. His mind kept replaying that first kiss and the sensational feeling that tingles one's entire body. It was his first kiss ever and sadly, her last.

At the end of the day Ennis and Jarvis sat and talked. "I heard the Indians were the ones to watch for out here on the prairies."

Jarvis responded, "They can be. Some are. But some of the natives are friendly. It depends on which ones you run across out here. This is my sixth crossing. I've gotten to know some of them. If we were about two or three days farther along, we may have gotten some help by the tribe out there. They probably would have headed those bandits off before they got to us, or warned us they were coming. The chief has become a friend of mine. I call him *The Guardian* because he watches over the wagon train when we cross his territory."

"You've done this six times?"

"Yes. I lead the families out west. It can be dangerous, but it pays well."

"What about the Indians that aren't friendly?"

"We've run across them. Been ambushed a few times. There's not much warning when they attack."

"Why do they do it? Attack like that?"

"They're threatened by people moving in. Their land is being taken and they fight back to keep it. Anyone would do the same. Some call them savage, some call them brutal, but I've seen the way our people fight when our land and lives are threatened. It's not much different—like today—all men fight when threatened. Whoever or wherever they are. I've studied the history of Europeans and other peoples around the world—all humans fight when threatened—it's not just the natives here."

"I've seen it, too."

"Yeah? At your age?"

"My uncles. Killed in a feud. Families on one side of the mountain fighting families on the other side—all over territory and stills of whiskey. My father took a bullet in his leg. Limped the rest of his life."

"He passed away?"

"A few weeks ago. Outside St. Joseph."

"Sorry to hear that."

"Thank you."

"Yeah, there isn't much difference with mankind wherever you go. The tribe or group may change, but the heart and mind of most men are the same. A man's desire to defend his earthly possessions is a common thread. It overwhelms most men's sensibilities. If it's worth fighting for, it's worth fighting to the death for."

"And the bandits like those today?"

"Just pure evil. The natives of this land are considered savages by some. I don't agree with that prevailing sentiment—as uncivilized as they are considered to be—they have more conscience than those trail bandits this morning. The Indians live by a moral code. They are a spiritual people who answer to the power of nature. We are a religious people who answer to a higher power. It may not be the same as ours, but it is morality. Those outlaws earlier today live by no moral code at all. We live to be at peace. They are ruthless and do not care one wit of human life. They live only for themselves and that is all. They live to rape and steal—earthly possessions are all they live for—kill or be killed is their only credo."

Ennis and Jarvis waxed philosophically for some time into the evening. Ennis returned to his wagon and wondered about the job Jarvis did, leading families across the prairie to their promised land. It seemed adventurous. He considered it for about a day and then his thoughts drifted back to being a business owner in a frontier town—growing a business as a town grew—that was what he wanted. He was enthralled by this voyage across the country, but he wanted to put down roots in a town. He wanted a home, a wife, children, and to settle down, and live out his days in peace in the mountains. Maybe he could find a gold mine out there too.

The wagon train chugged westward. After a few more days they crested a ridge. As they descended into the next valley, Ennis saw a gathering of hundreds of wagons. Ennis remembered seeing violent thunderstorms in the distance the night before. Being out on the plain the travelers got some rain that night and lots of thunder. Other getting drenched, nothing else was troublesome about that stormy night.

However, the valley beneath them now displayed the aftermath of that violent night. The creek that ran down the gut of this valley before them was swollen with floodwaters. Much of the alluvium was submerged. The creek flowed into the Platte about a mile downstream. Torrents swirled at the confluence of the two. It was one large, tempestuous lake of silty water.

Wagon trains had bottled up along the nascent shoreline of the breached river, unable to cross. Everyone had to wait to cross what was described to Ennis later as normally a mild stream and easily traversed. Evidence of receding floodwaters were apparent, but it had quite a way to go before a wagon could cross.

Some travelers were contemplating just settling there. About a dozen were standing on the top of a hillside looking down at the floodwaters. Ennis could see they were having a conversation even though he could not hear them, but the gesturing and pointing in all directions gave it away as to their intentions.

The arrival at this place, at this time, was serendipitous as far as seeing just how bad the flooding could be after a storm. Plans for a town free from a natural annihilation were easy to make. You would need to build it safely up on the hillside were the men stood. Some other men were dragging lumber up to the peak of the hill. Ennis watched them and saw they were laying boards down to mark plots.

The hill was flat on top, encompassing about a hundred acres, with a gentle slope downward to the current torrent of the river. There was nothing higher around it as far as one could see to the horizon. Ennis wondered what the stream looked like under normal conditions. Perhaps these men had crossed a few times before, like Jarvis, and knew that this might be a good spot to set up a town for frontier-bound travelers to rest for a day, or a night, and gather much-needed supplies before continuing. This was the American entrepreneurial spirit incarnate. This is what Ennis Carpenter wanted to find—but not here—he wanted to find a mountain town.

He observed the flurry of construction activity that began as the days went by. There was a small forested area two miles upstream that quickly turned into an ad hoc lumber enterprise.

Another sojourner used his team of oxen to pull the lumber to the promising settlement. It took several days for the floodwaters to recede to pre-inundation levels and then several days for the mudbank to dry out. Then it took a few more for the hundreds of backlogged, westward wagons to cross. The impatient waggoneers were the ones that got stuck. It discouraged others from attempting the crossing for at least another day. The traffic continued to pile up behind the group the Carpenters were in as the days slowly went by. Ennis grew restless and spent several days helping with the carpentry, but then became anxious and unfocused as their wagon group inched closer to the receding shoreline. He hunted up on the plateau for a couple of days while his sister and mother minded their campfire and prepped food for when their journey continued.

Ennis sensed some were going to stay and not continue. Some families moved about the hilltop, staked claim to their own little corner, and started working independently of the others.

The Carpenters finally reached the water's edge and crossed. The water was still murky as the traffic had been constant, stirring up the muck of the streambed. Ennis could see upstream that the tributary water was pristine.

The bottleneck of wagons gradually diminished as the prairie miles went by and the individual groups fell back into their ranks as they got farther away from the swollen stream. A week later it was just the Jarvis wagon group as far as Ennis could see from his wagon stage.

The group followed the North Platte towards the mountains. The Carpenter family broke off from the Mormon wagon train several days later. They had just arrived at a fort on the edge of the prairie. Ennis said goodbye to Susanna's family and to Jarvis. Jarvis tried to convince Ennis to stay with them, but it fell on deaf ears. He thanked Jarvis for all the advice and help along the way. He wanted to head farther north than where the rest were going.

The wagon trail had been fascinating. The trails were carved into the landscape and helpful because of the lack of landmarks through much of the monotony that were the prairies. The tracks along the ground made the journey easier to navigate. Now he was about to progress through a less-charted area.

Two other families that had recently arrived at the fort went with the Carpenters. A third family that had been at the fort for several days joined them. Ennis and his mother grabbed provisions there and talked with the soldiers about which way was best. With their advice, they moved on. Two soldiers on horseback rode with them for the rest of the day. They said Indian attacks were common west of the fort, but once they made it to a pass in the foothills, they were generally safe. The soldiers escorted Ennis as far the pass.

Summer was at its height, but the weather was pleasant in the foothills of the Rockies. It was vastly different than the summers in Kentucky, of which Ennis had been accustomed. This entire journey was a new experience for him. He was mesmerized by the vastness of the plains west of Missouri. On clear nights, he could see every star in the universe. At first, the days were hot, but as they drifted northwesterly, the days became more tolerable. He was stunned by the size of the bison when they came upon them. Sometimes they were like gentle giants that just wanted to graze, but once or twice he saw them charge a wagon.

As they neared the Rocky Mountains Ennis marveled at their grandeur. Their most unbelievable aspect was that of the snow-capped peaks. The season was not right for snow, but nonetheless, there they were. The smattering of people along the way were usually gracious and helpful. Everyone had their own dreams and aspirations of what their futures held. He was always interested in the conversations. They had a Methodist pastor travelling alongside them for a few days, on his way to a fledging western town to start a new church, and then they picked up a Catholic priest later on doing the same thing. His mother participated in a Catholic mass for the first time since before she was married. She asked the priest to baptize her children and receive the sacraments of confession and first communion. Her persistent cough raised concern by the priest. He even asked if she wanted him to give her the Last Rites. She refused his offer. "Not now. Not yet." The tone of her voice was melancholic, as if she knew something.

His sister met a boy along the way. They followed their wagon for several days until his family parted ways and went off somewhere unknown. She begged her brother to stay on their course, but he had some other plans. He saw a map at the fort and he had an idea where they should go. It did not have a name yet, but it looked intriguing on the map. It was up in the mountains on a river. He could only imagine it was a crystal-clear mountain stream with brisk clear air. He thought it would be like back home in Kentucky. He liked their mountain home in Kentucky. He wanted something similar but he knew the mountains up here would be different. He was finding that out. Their majesty was unparalleled.

Traversing this continent continued to impress him with each day and week spent heading towards the setting sun. Despite the tragedies, he remained excited about tomorrow. Each day meant a new adventure, and he was maturing into a man ready to face every hurdle.

Summer gave way to autumn instinctively. The air was crisp and the foliage was vibrant with change. Ennis embraced the change. He was changing along with the leaves on the trees. The mountains were another challenge. The group of wagons grew to seven along the way. A mountain lion attacked a child who had wandered off from the confines of the wagons one early morning. The child survived but would be scarred across his face for the rest of his life. One of the waggoneers shot at the lion—missed the animal—but scared it away from the child he had already mangled. Another night a pack of wolves proved to be a nuisance to the group—but they were easily frightened away before any human casualties were amassed—only a day's worth of smoked meat was dragged away by the wolfpack.

The wagons traversed the foothills of a range and dropped back down into a valley. A river flowed in the distance. Another range of mountains were beyond the river. A small settlement was up on a high plain above the river, next to a mountain spring-fed creek.

The travelers stopped in the small settlement for an extra day before pushing on. There was a small hotel that only had four rooms. The young families with infants checked into the rooms and the rest of the party stayed in their wagons as if they were still out on the prairie. An early season snowfall lightly dusted the town overnight. His mother's cough was getting worse. Ennis was concerned for her health, but could not do anything about it. One of the townsfolk told Ennis there was a doctor in the big town down along the river. The Carpenters and a few others traveled down that way. Everyone needed to stock up on supplies as the days were getting colder.

Ennis found the doctor's house. Her cough had become relentless. He looked for a place to stay and could not find any lodging. His mother stayed in the doctor's house, and Ennis and his two siblings slept in the wagon outside. The priest visited before the night was over. As night fell Ennis could see a lit lantern through the window of the room his mother was in. The doctor and priest were both standing next to her bed having a discussion. Ennis feared the worst as he watched them from a distance before he eventually fell asleep.

His sister woke up the next morning with only her younger brother next to her. Cold, foggy air encapsulated the mountain peaks. She peeked out at the dewy mountain morning and looked across at the doctor's house. She could see Ennis in the window. He looked like he was crying. She got up and walked to the house. He gave her the sad news; their mother had passed away.

At Christmas, they were a family of seven. They left Kentucky in the late spring as a family of five, and now they were a family of three orphans in less than a year. Later that day Ennis buried his mother in the town cemetery. The priest administered the funeral. He decided this was the place they would settle. He did not want to be far from his mother's grave. His sister agreed. Now he needed to find a profession. Starting a hotel was not something he ever thought about, but there was a need for lodging in the budding town. Plenty of travelers were coming through it. Those travelers would need to eat, too. There was a timber operation across the river and lumber was readily available. A hotel and a restaurant seemed a logical opportunity.

Ennis drew up the plans for his hotel. He worked at a livery stable right next to the city plot that he had purchased with his money. He started working on it himself and had some help from a local carpenter. Winter interrupted the work most days, but slowly and surely the hotel and saloon took shape as the spring months turned into summer. As the months went by, his sister worked at a dry goods store down the street.

The town was growing and Ennis knew his venture would pay off. When finished, his was the only hotel in town. His saloon and restaurant were the second ones in town. His sister helped in the evenings after working at the store. He hired a guy just a few years older than him to be his bartender: Thomas Donnelly. Donnelly had seen the hotel being built, was looking for a job, and was hired before the building was finished. Donnelly was an orphan from a neighboring community, Shannon Creek. With no prospects in Shannon Creek, he went to the neighboring big town to look for work. When Donnelly saw how young Ennis was, he was curious how such a young kid could afford to start a business.

They shared their stories and bonded over the fact they were both young men that had lost both parents. By the time the building was finished, Ennis was almost seventeen. The last two years had taken a toll on him physically and mentally, and he looked a few years older than he really was. He was proud to finally take up roots in the mountains. All he needed now was to find a local girl, start a family, serve the people of his town, and the passers-by.

The night the saloon opened, his sister helped Thomas behind the bar serve drinks. The crowd was large and the revelry went on late into the night. Thomas had to break up a few bar fights. Ennis' sister said to Thomas after he threw some rowdies out the door, "You could be the sheriff one day."

"You think so?"

"Yeah. Why not?"

He shrugged his shoulders at her comment, went back behind the bar, and continued serving drinks.

The next morning Ennis was in the soon-to-be restaurant area. He had already cleaned up the bar and was working on some final details of the restaurant. His sister walked in to find her brother working hard.

"Good Morning."

G'morning."

"Last night was good, yes?"

"Very good. I was surprised. If every night is like that, I'll be a happy man."

"Miss Mabel told me she might be giving up the store. She wants to move back home to be with her daughter in Texas."

"You've got a job here, sis, don't worry about that."

"That's not it. She says she wants to sell the store. She said she'll sell it to me."

Ennis stopped his busyness and turned to look her in the eyes, "That's great news!"

"Can I borrow the money from you? I mean, it's papa's money really, isn't it both ours?"

Ennis was quiet for a moment before he replied, "Yes. It's yours, too. Is that what you want? To own the store?"

"Yes. I think so." She paused. "And that house down the road back here behind the stable? It's for sale. I think I should buy it. I think this is home, Ennis. I had my doubts at first, but this is home now. You have your hotel and by this time next year, I can have a store."

He looked at his sister, "I think so, Gertrude. We've arrived at our promised land."

The End

6

A Demon on the Loose

Chester Flanaghan rode through the wintry twilight. Normally, his horse was at a trot when heading home from the sawmill, but tonight, his horse was as tired as he was from the long day. He had left before daybreak this morning to go to work. Flanaghan's house was three miles outside town. He knew his wife would have dinner ready when he got home. The blueish glow of the snowy ground in the fading sunlight cast an eerie landscape as far as Flanaghan could see. He circled around the base of one of the mountains outside town, and then eastward onto the high plain.

He rode across the plain like he did every day for about a mile and then veered northward to a passage between two foothills that dropped him down into the valley where he and his wife had their homestead. The mountains north of town circled eastward, creating the western rim of the valley they lived in. The aura from the setting sun silhouetted the sawtooth peaks of the snowcapped mountains. When he crested the ridge between the hilltops, he could see clear to the other side of the peaceful valley. The highest peaks on the northern edge were catching the last vestiges of sunlight for the day; the snow on the caps aglow in a comforting orange and pinkish hue. His house was in the center of the valley, a thousand yards past the mountain-fed stream that wended its way through the valley floor.

Every evening as he came home and arrived at this vantage point, he could see the smoke from the chimney of their house. When conditions were just right, he could smell his wife's cooking. It was his first sign that he was almost home. No one else lived in the valley. He feared someone else might encroach someday, but for now, it was just his family. He did not have the land rights to the entire valley, but he treated it as if it were all his.

Curiously enough, this evening, there was no smoke coming from the chimney, none that could be seen from this distance. Even if Margaret had finished cooking, on cold nights like this, the fire was kept going for warmth. He was concerned and sensed something was wrong. He popped the reins on his steed, and they trotted downhill with urgency.

As he raced down the hill along his normal path, the view of his house was shielded by an outcropping that he rode alongside for quite a while before dropping down to the valley floor. He rounded the outcropping, and as he got closer, he noticed six horses tied up to the hog pen. His anxiety heightened.

After he crossed the frigid stream on the valley floor, he slowed down his horse so as not to make too much noise. The other horses were unknown to him, and he wanted to have the element of surprise riding up to his house, should surprise be warranted.

A hundred yards before his house, Flanaghan dismounted, led his horse by the reins, and tied his lead to a tree not far from the front gate of his fence. He grabbed his longarm from its sheath on the saddle and checked that his pistol was fully loaded. The light of one lantern shone through a window. Although he could not see it earlier from a distance,

Flanaghan now noticed a very thin wisp of smoke coming from the chimney, reminiscent of dying embers of a campfire, telling Flanaghan that whatever Margaret had going had been extinguished. That was not a good sign.

He cautiously peered through the front window of the house from a distance. There was not much frost on the windowpane, telling him it was not warm inside. He saw a few dark figures moving across the beam of light from the lantern shining in the kitchen. As no one inside seemed to be looking outside, and their focus was faced inward towards the kitchen, he decided he would have better cover if he went around back to the north side of the house. There were two smaller windows, head-high, on either side of the chimney. He would not be seen creeping around from the back. When he got to the back of the house, he eased himself upward slowly from a crouched position to peak into the kitchen. The lantern had a weak beam that flickered through the windowpane but did not appear to be bright enough to illuminate his face.

Flanaghan could see five men in the kitchen and his wife—tied up and gagged—her face battered. He gasped, and tears ran down his face. He could not see his son. He counted six horses so there was another man unaccounted for. He repositioned himself to look through the other kitchen window. He still only counted five. From that vantage point, he could see one man pointing a gun at his wife's back. Their voices were muffled as they talked. He saw blood on the floor next to the table, but could not tell where the blood came from. Tears and blood were streaming down his wife's face—he had to do something. Surprise was on his side. Assuming one horse per outlaw, he was still missing one.

He went back to the first window, looked back in, and took a mental note of where everyone was. One outlaw moved close to the window, his back to it, almost directly in front of Flanaghan. He grabbed a log off his firewood pile, and wedged it up under the latch of the backdoor. This would prevent anyone from coming through that door at him.

Flanaghan trembled at what he was about to do next. He quickly thought through what his immediate actions were about to be. He was not a killer. He was a peaceful man. All he wanted was to live a peaceful life with his wife and son on his own plot of land. He never bothered anyone. He went to work in town during the day, and came home to his family at night. He never visited the saloons in town. He was never caught up in anything nefarious from all the scoundrels and bandits that roamed in and out of the area. He did not know who these men were, and he did not know what they wanted, but after weighing his options, he knew he did not want to find out.

Walking into his house to confront them was not going to end well for him or his family. He needed to take advantage of the fact they did not know he was outside, so that he could try to stop whatever was going on inside. He glanced back in at his wife. She was obviously badly hurt. Her clothing was torn, her left eye was almost completely closed, and her face was puffed up from the bruising she took from these evil men. Blood and tears continued to run down her beautiful cheeks. Her teeth were clenched on the bandana gag in her mouth. He feared they had already done their worst to her. He trembled more. This was not how he ever wanted to end any day of his life. He never wanted to ever have to face this situation, but evil came to his house on this night, and he had to do something.

A knife was produced by one man. He was pointing it very close to Margaret's face. He said something but his voice was muffled by the walls of the cabin. She wept after hearing whatever he had said. Flanaghan knew he needed to act and act swiftly. His fear was transforming into rage.

As he studied the man with the knife, he noticed he held it in his right hand, and the man's holster was on his right side, his shooting hand. He would not be able to react quickly if Flanaghan started shooting.

Flanaghan took a deep breath, followed by another. He looked up at the sky to ask God's forgiveness for what he was about to do. He had never been this nervous in his whole life. He checked his pistol again: fully loaded. He checked his rifle: loaded. He took one more deep breath to muster the courage.

As swiftly as he has ever moved, he fired into the window, and shot point blank into the back of the man that was standing in front it. The man dropped dead instantly. Without flinching, Flanaghan fired straight ahead at the man standing in the doorway of the kitchen. That shot hit him in the face, and he also dropped instantly. The man with the knife swiveled to see what was going on, instinctively ducked, and dropped to the floor behind the table, and out of view of Flanaghan. With his arm sticking partially inside the window, Flanaghan rotated a quarter turn to aim at the man behind his wife. With little confidence, he would not hit his wife; he hesitated to fire. The man pivoted from behind Margaret and fired at the broken window. Flanaghan ducked out of the window, using the log wall of the house as a shield. A shot whizzed past, through the opening.

Flanaghan rushed over to the other window and shot through it at the man standing in that corner next to the stove. He dropped dead. The man who was previously behind his wife pivoted his attention toward the second window. Flanaghan's wife, not being held any longer, but with her hands still bound behind her back, ducked to the ground. Flanaghan fired through the window before the outlaw was able to completely turn to face him. Flanaghan put a bullet in him, and he fell. He saw his wife on the floor. He also knew there was one man unaccounted for, and the man with the knife was still on the floor somewhere, out of his view. He raced around the eastside of the house to confront whomever was left, potentially standing at the front door. He stopped at the corner of the house and quickly peaked at the front door.

It creaked open, and one peaked his head out to look around. Flanaghan fired at him, but missed. The man's reaction was to fire in his direction, just as he ducked back inside. He heard his wife scream, which meant he knew the gag was removed, or she freed herself somehow. A shot rang out through the front window. A desperation shot, or a shot to hold Flanaghan at bay. Leaning against the east wall he reloaded his pistol, and holstered it. Lost in the confusion of the moment of chaos, he nervously double-checked his rifle, though he had not used it yet. He could hear one of them trying to force the back door. Luckily the log held in place. He had them cornered inside, but his wife was also inside with them. And he assumed his son, whom he had not yet been able to get a visual.

Flanaghan's heart was jumping out of his chest. He was still trembling; he holstered his pistol, and was now holding his rifle. He amazed himself a minute ago that he was able to keep a steady aim through the kitchen windows. He took a deep breath, tried to calm his nerves, but his anxiety was racing as fast as his heart. His water well was in front of the house. A trough was twenty yards off from the porch. The windmill towered above, silhouetted against the nascent moonlight. He formulated his next move, went over it in his head twice, and quickly moved around the corner of the house. He turned his body, and fired two shots from his rifle rapidly through the front window of the house. He was not expecting to hit anyone, it was more to cover his movement until he was safely behind the water trough. He discarded the rifle next to the trough, as he was out of ammunition for it. One shot rang past him as he ducked behind the trough, but the shot was way off by whomever shot it, basically shooting into the dark.

Flanaghan unholstered his pistol. From the safety of the trough, he addressed the outlaws inside, "Who's in my house? What have you done with my wife and son?"

There was no answer. He asked the question again. Still no response.

He readjusted his crouching position—eased around the left side of the trough to see if he could see into the windows from there—nothing. The lantern from the kitchen produced a faint glow, and a silhouette or two was seen, but it was too dark inside for detail. The movement inside the house was minimal.

He crouch-walked himself back over to the other side of the trough, keeping his head and body behind it for cover. He compared both vantage points, and realized neither was to his advantage. Still nothing verbal came out of the house.

He yelled back towards the house once again, "Who are you?"

Silence.

"What have you done to my family?"

A shot rang out. The blast from the gun momentarily lit up the darkened landscape. Flanaghan knew where one man was based on where the shot came from. He could not see because of the shadows of the house, but he had his position. He raised his pistol over the edge of the trough and fired in the direction of the gun blast. The outlaw must have ducked after shooting his first shot. Then a second shot was fired towards Flanaghan. Same location. Flanaghan raised up higher this time, and fired two quick shots into the window at the where the shots came from. Still nothing. No scream of pain, no thud of a body. He was unsure whether he hit his target.

The evening was eerily quiet for a few moments. Another shot rang out from the house in Flanaghan's direction. It pinged off the water trough. Shortly after that shot he heard his wife screaming, and a struggle going on inside.

"Maggie!?" he cried out.

She started to scream again, but her voice was quickly stifled. He knew one them had her in their grasp again.

He stayed silent.

Suddenly the door banged open, and the unaccounted-for outlaw came rushing out the door; bullets blazing toward the water trough. Several sharp metallic pings squealed into the still night. Water dripped out. Flanaghan stayed in his covered position until the bullets stopped. As he sensed a lull in the rhythm of the firing, he stood upright and saw the outlaw face-to-face, fifteen feet from him. In the moonlight, he could just barely make out his face. The outlaw raised his gun higher at Flanaghan, but Flanaghan fired first—two rapid shots—putting the outlaw down on the ground.

Blood poured from the holes in his body, the dark liquid oozed out in the moonlight. Flanaghan ducked back down not knowing where the last man was. He assumed the last man standing was the man who had been holding the knife in the kitchen. The dead man in front of the trough was the one he had not seen yet when he looked through the windows. Flanaghan looked back toward his house to see if he could make out anything but everything inside was dark.

He reloaded his pistol, took another deep breath, and raced back to the east side of his house. No shots were fired from within. He raced back around the back side of the house, and peaked cautiously into the kitchen window. Nothing but dead men. He still did not know where his son was. He raced back around the eastside of the house again. He peaked cautiously around the corner at the front door. There was no movement of anyone. He tiptoed carefully down his porch. The last man had to be in the front room of the house. Broken glass littered the boards under his feet. He tried to step as lightly as a cat, so as not to alert this outlaw of his presence, but still crunched some of the glass under his boots. He got close to the door when he heard his wife whimpering in pain. It was faint but distinguishable. She was still alive.

He took another deep breath, scared out of his wits at what he was about to do, and kicked the door open. A gunshot blasted toward him from within, but missed. He fired at the spot he saw the blast come from. He heard a grunt from the outlaw, so he must have hit him. The lantern glow from the kitchen was no longer bright. A second shot blasted toward Flanaghan, he ducked back behind the wall, and pulled the door shut. He heard his wife's agony again; muffled. Perhaps the gag had been put back in her mouth.

"Who are you?" he cried out once again from his front porch.

The last man standing calmly answered, "Billy Pearson."

Flanaghan did not recognize the name. "And what do you want?"

Sarcastically, but stoically, the outlaw responded, "Nothing. Everything. What do you want?"

"Nothing? Everything? What does that mean?" He paused, "I just want my wife and son to be safe. Just let them go. Take whatever we have, take everything we have, I don't care. Just don't harm my family."

Still in a calm demeanor, Pearson replied matter-of-factly, "Your son is dead."

A tremendous wave of grief and disbelief rushed through his brain at the statement. "Wha... What?" He screamed.

"He's dead. He tried to be a hero when we showed up. He's dead."

Tears gushed down Flanaghan's face, and an anguished rage enveloped him.

"Why? Why are you here? What do you want with my family? Why did you come here in the first place?"

With a lilt in his voice, he answered, "It's just who I am."

Flanaghan did not know how to react to that statement. He had never met a killer who had no reason to kill. Hunched down behind the wall next to the door, he was contemplating his next move when suddenly the door flung open, and Pearson came shuffling out onto the porch holding Margaret—still gagged—with his pistol pointed at her head. Flanaghan—startled by the suddenness of the door opening—lost his balance momentarily, but scrambled upright against the wall, and regained his footing. He gripped his pistol tight, but was frozen at the sight of his wife—beaten and bloodied—in Pearson's clutches.

"Don't move, and everything will be alright. Don't try to be a hero like your son."

Flanaghan remained frozen. He noticed Pearson was bleeding from the arm that was wrapped around Margaret. That must have been the shot from Flanaghan. The blood continued to drip slowly, but the wound looked superficial.

Pearson inched his way down the steps of the porch to the snow-covered ground. The footsteps of his boots crunched the snow beneath him. Flanaghan's wife was barefoot. She had cut her heel on a shard of glass. He could see her fully for the first time. Her clothes were torn, one sleeve of her dress ripped down to her elbow. Her dress was torn in several other spots. She had a sweater half on her, half-ripped, draped over the other shoulder, barely clinging to her frame. Most of her clothing was blood-stained. Her breath was visible in the cold night air. She had an absolute look of fright in her eyes as she looked at her husband, tears streaming down her face. Her blonde hair was disheveled, and she had clotted blood matted on one side on her head. Flanaghan knew these outlaws had done their worse to her. He was mortified by the sight of her in this condition. He was trying to process this entire scene, while remaining motionless so as not to trigger any more violence from this Pearson guy, whoever he was.

Pearson and Flanaghan stared across at each other as Pearson eased backward with each step. Flanaghan did not know what to do next, and he was thinking this guy did not know what to do next, either. He decided to speak calmly, despite the rage and fear coursing through his mind. "Why did you come out here tonight and do all this? Do I know you?"

"No. You don't."

"Why did my family deserve this tonight? Why her? Why my son? Why us?" Flanaghan's voice began to tremble with anguish as he completed the last two questions.

Pearson shrugged his shoulders. Flanaghan furrowed his brow, and several more tears ran down his cheek. This was the face of evil. He had never quite seen it before, but there was no doubt in his mind that what was in front of him—with a gun held to his wife's head—was evil incarnate. He did not know how he was going to get out of this. He was running scenarios through his mind of how he was going to save his wife. How was he going to save both him and his wife? All this was going through his head while still trying to process the fact that his son was dead. It was daunting, terrifying, and maddening all at once. He had never been put in this situation before, and it was overwhelming his thought process. All was silent except for the footfalls of Pearson on the snowy ground as he slowly eased his way backward, still holding Margaret hostage.

"No reason? No reason at all? Money? At least tell me it's about money. Maybe I can understand that." Flanaghan's voice cracked at the end. More tears ran down his frozen face.

Pearson grinned and replied, "Nah. Money is good, but you can't take it with you. This is a thrill! Don't you think? Isn't this thrilling? I'm having fun... Are you?" He started laughing. His diabolical laugh seemed to echo through the valley before hitting Flanaghan's ears. Pearson was an insane man, turning a peaceful man insane. Flanaghan was being tortured mentally. He looked at his tortured wife. Rage welled up inside. He began to shake. He did not want to further provoke this madman, but he felt like he was about to burst. Before Flanaghan had time to act on his billowing rage, Pearson suddenly let go of Margaret. Stunned, she froze and then tried to run. But before she could take her second step, Pearson fired two rapid shots into her abdomen, and she dropped to the frozen ground.

Flanaghan let out a rageful cry, "NO!"

He pointed his pistol at Pearson, now some twenty yards away, and fired. His tortured demeanor caused him to shake and not be in control of the shots he frantically fired in Pearson's direction. Pearson ducked, but did not have to, as Flanaghan's shots were errant. The madman returned a volley of gunshots. Flanaghan ducked, still standing on the porch. He went down behind one of the posts holding up the eave over the porch. It was not anything ideal to duck for cover behind, but it was all he had. One of Pearson's shots splintered a chunk out of it two inches above Flanaghan's head. The other shots hit the wall of the house behind him.

Flanaghan stood upright and braced himself for a hopeful, steady shot. He took aim and fired, but it kicked up the ground and snow behind Pearson. Pearson, still diabolically smirking, did not even flinch. He aimed back at Flanaghan, who was standing in full view of him—pulled the trigger—but the chamber was empty. The hammer ominously clicked to Pearson's chagrin. He realized in the volley of gunfire he forgot how many rounds he had fired. Flanaghan leveled his pistol at Pearson. Anticipating death, Pearson just grinned at him. Flanaghan took several steps forward and pulled the trigger, but the same empty click was produced. Flanaghan did not keep track of his shots, either. Pearson turned and ran out of the gate, into the darkness of the night. Flanaghan holstered his empty pistol and gave chase.

Moonlight provided some discerning details to the snow-covered ground they ran upon. A few holes and rocks were visible, or at least the shadows produced by both. They weaved and leapt over the obstacles that were barely visible. Flanaghan gained ground on Pearson and lunged at him when he was close enough to be tackled. They rolled around in each other's grasp, and punches were thrown. Both men tried everything to disable the other: punches to the face, blows to the abdomen, and attempts to hit one another in the crotch.

The two men hit the ground together and wrestled for a few minutes until Flanaghan escaped from Pearson's grasp, rolled away, and stood up in a boxing stance. Pearson scrambled to his feet as well. The two traded punches back and forth again. Flanaghan landed one on Pearson's gunshot wound. Pearson let out a whelp, grimaced, and doubled over, but managed to stay on his feet and duck a few more of

Flanaghan's parries. He backed away eventually and grabbed his knife. His grimace of pain turned back into the devilish snicker he had had a few moments earlier. He swiped the knife back and forth several times at Flanaghan's torso. Flanaghan backtracked to avoid the knife. Pearson laughed under his breath. Flanaghan could see his teeth in the moonlight. The two settled into a standoff five feet apart and circled around each other. A couple of Pearson's punches landed on Flanaghan's brow and opened up a wound. Flanaghan's face dripped with sweat and blood in the frigid cold.

The faceoff in the middle of the snowy valley punctuated the violence that disturbed the otherwise peaceful, winter evening that this corner of the world expected every night. The stars above watched these last two men going at it. The stars silently witness all the evil that goes on in this world. Twinkling with hope, they stood their position in the cosmos and watched in disgust as this evil man continued his reign of terror on this innocent family man.

After the two men circled around each other three or four times, Pearson finally made the offensive move and lunged at Flanaghan, knife-blade first. Exhausted, Flanaghan managed one more graceful move to avoid the stabbing assault. He grabbed Pearson's forearm as he lunged past his torso, and wrangled the knife out of his hand. Disarmed, Flanaghan thrust Pearson forward and shoved him to the ground. The knife stealthily landed somewhere in the snow. Pearson looked around briefly to no avail until Flanaghan came at Pearson with his fists flying. Flanaghan landed a couple of punches on Pearson. Pearson returned the volley and landed a few punches on Flanaghan. Flanaghan managed to land one more to Pearson's face. Pearson backed away, still desperately searching for the lost knife. He backed up even more from Flanaghan, got his bearings, turned, and took off running back toward the house. Flanaghan pursued, but tripped about ten yards into his pursuit. Pearson gained a sizeable lead on his pursuer as Flanaghan gathered himself to continue.

The cold night air proved too much for Flanaghan's lungs. Halfway back to the house, he doubled over with his hands on his knees and stopped to catch his breath. Pearson ran the rest of the way. When he no longer heard footsteps behind him, he looked back to see the exhausted Flanaghan in the distance, trying to gather himself. Pearson continued running until he got to his horse. He mounted him and rode off into the night back towards town.

Flanaghan walked several more yards, and then his body collapsed to the ground with exhaustion from the violent ordeal that was stacked on top of a grueling twelve-hour day of work. The frigid air pierced his lungs. He lay there for a few minutes, trying to catch his breath and crying at the same time. He had no wife and no son anymore.

He eventually gathered himself and stumbled in pain back towards the house. He knelt next to Margaret and pulled her body to his. He wept for what seemed an eternity to him.

He collected himself, picked up her body, and carried her inside. As he walked inside his house for the first time that evening, he noticed a trail of blood on the floor. He followed it into the kitchen and realized what the pool of blood on the floor was that he had seen through the window earlier. The blood was from his son's body, riddled with gunshots, lying next to the table. The table had blocked his view from the outside.

Flanaghan knelt next to his son, hugged his body, and wept some more. "*Billy Pearson, Billy Pearson, Billy Pearson...*" he kept saying to himself, to remember the murderer's name. "I'll kill him if it's the last thing I do."

His mind was in complete disbelief that this had happened, one day that changed his life forever. A day that started like any other, but ended in a way unfathomable to anyone. It was a cold night made even colder by tragedy. He sat there incapacitated with grief. His breath in the frigid air was the only breath in his house. A house full of death. And the cold, moonlit night harbored a demon on the loose.

The End

7

Seven Deadly Sins

She gracefully walked up the wooden stairs from the saloon with a cowboy behind her. Her dress flowed and rippled as her hips wiggled up each step. The cowboy was fixated on her figure as she swayed in front of him. He was mesmerized and had a hundred thoughts coursing through his head about what he was about to experience. She had an exquisite beauty any open-range cowboy would desire after a long month out on the prairie, and her body matched the beauty of her face.

They turned down the corridor and headed to her room. She opened the door, led him to her bed, and he sat down; his eyes wide with anticipation. She turned around to undo her top, and the cowboy's eyes somehow became even wider. The grin on his face told his whole story; he could not keep his eyes off her, and there was still even more he had yet to see of her body. "You want me to go on?" Her smile could melt the ice off the mountain peaks.

He nodded in anticipation.

She shimmied her skirt down past her waist, revealing her hourglass figure, curvy legs, and silky, soft skin. She stood naked in front of him. He just ogled her and took in the entire scope of her beauty. She was worth every penny of the day's wage he had paid her.

She leaned over, helped unbutton his shirt, and slipped it over his shoulders. He stood up, and she unbuckled his trousers. Before she even got them unfastened, she saw how excited he was. She looked up and smiled at him as she pulled his trousers down to his ankles. Completely aroused, she teased him with her sensual touch. He melted in her hands. He sat back down on the bed. His boots needed to be removed for him to get his pants off, and she assisted.

They rolled onto the mattress together and began to explore each other's bodies. He was in more of a hurry than she because of how long he had waited for this, but she reciprocated in every way possible with the same enthusiasm.

Their naked bodies became entwined, and they started doing what came naturally. After a few minutes, he asked her to get on top of him, she agreed, and they switched positions.

Around her neck was a silver cross necklace, adorned with turquoise. It bounced between her breasts and moved in synchronicity with each sensuous movement as she worked her magic on him. A month of frustration for him was relieved in a matter of minutes. She slid off him and plopped down on the bed beside him. They both caught their breath. He reached over to fondle her while they lay together side by side. She did not object and let him do what he wanted. He explored her entire body tenderly. The cowboy was her fifth customer of the day, third that evening.

The raucous entertainment from the saloon below filtered upstairs through the old wooden building. Laughter and music permeated the room. Every few minutes, you could hear the footsteps of another couple making their way down the hall. She was tired for the night, but it was Saturday, and the saloon was full of men. Men with money to burn, and she had what they desired.

The cowboy had dozed off, and she wanted to try and get a few more customers for the night, so she got up, and got dressed. She did not want to tempt him anymore when he woke up, even though he was very nice and gentle, but she wanted to make more money. She doubted this old boy could go another round anyway; he appeared exhausted. She shook his shoulders to wake him. He stirred, and groggily looked at her.

"Time to go, cowboy."

"Huh? Already? All right." He moved to sit up. He sheepishly asked, "Can we go again? Do we have time?"

"I don't think you have it in you, do you?"

He moved his legs open to show. "How about it?"

She smiled a devilish grin at him and crawled onto the bed in a sultry manner. "How about I just do this?" She licked his bare thigh and worked her mouth over to between his legs. "If I keep going, it'll cost you a little extra."

"Keep going. I got the money."

She did not ask for the extra money up front. She always had a certain level of trust with the cowboys. She knew they worked hard, and they needed a sensuous night of pleasure once in a while. Most of them did not have families of their own, so they were never concerned whether they kept their money or not, and cash was useless out on the prairie. When they were out on the range, they ate as a group at the chuck wagon and slept under the stars. They had nothing to spend their money on. But when they drove the herd into town, and the trail boss sold the cattle at market, the boys all got their money and were ready to get rid of it as quickly as they got it in their hands. There were usually only three things a cowboy would spend money on when they got to town: women, whiskey, and poker. They usually spent almost all it before the end of their first night with it.

It was the outlaws she could not trust. She would demand all the money up front from them, even for extras like what she giving to this cowboy. It was the outlaws she had to watch for.

He groaned with pleasure as she continued to please him. He leaned back against the pillows and enjoyed the sensation of her mouth and tongue. She finished him off and stood back up. He stood up, reached for his pants, and pulled out the money for the extra service he received. He was still naked, standing there holding his pants. Mabel kissed him softly on his cheek. He was gracious and still excited to be there.

She looked down and could see he was not ready to quit. She looked back up at his face. He was hesitant to get dressed. She smiled, "Don't tell me you want more?" He just stood there grinning. "You still in town tomorrow night?"

He nodded.

"Tell you what. Come back tomorrow night and I'll give you two for one. How's that?"

He nodded again and put one leg into his trousers. She pecked him on the cheek again for being so nice. He balanced himself, put his other leg in his pants, pulled up, and kept getting dressed. She did not always get nice fellows like him. He was a breath of fresh air. Common with the cowboys like him, almost always nice and gracious, and always leaving happy, but most nights there was just not enough of them. She enjoyed those nights when the cattle drives came to town, business was plentiful, and she rarely had to worry about a ne'er-do-well. Other nights it was more common to get the outlaw or rough-and-tumble type; drunk, rowdy, and they did not care if they roughed her up a bit in the process. Unfortunately, being bruised and beaten was the end result some nights. Not that there was not a rough cowboy here or there, once in a while, but the cowboys were usually grateful to spend some quality time with a lady. They liked to lie in bed for a few moments next to her before leaving. The outlaws only wanted a whore, and usually left quickly after they were done.

Normally, she could pick both types out of the crowd. The outlaws usually had more money; they were always cleaner, better dressed, and did not smell like a herd of cattle or the back end of a horse, but ran the risk of a violent disposition. As a lady of the evening, she had to weigh the pros and cons of the clientele in the saloon every night. Some nights, the big spenders were the economic choice for her, despite the consequences. Other nights, she would rather spend it with five different cowboys at a discounted price, and a nice goodbye kiss at the end of every hour. She had to make money like everyone else.

After the nice cowboy left her room, she tidied up and went back downstairs. She had made a hefty sum for the evening and was enjoying the night. A whole troupe of open range cowboys were in the saloon enjoying the evening, and she figured she had done business with almost half of them since they arrived yesterday afternoon. Word got around, and it was good business for her. She was floating in the air as she moved through the salon. The other half of the saloon clientele were mostly miners—off shift until Monday, with a week's wages in hand—some regulars, and a few strangers comprised the rest of the crowd.

She was in high demand by most of the regulars, but she could not attend to all the men in the saloon at once. The regulars will still be in the saloon tomorrow night; the strangers usually are just passing through. Luckily, any one given outlaw was rarely a regular. They usually came and went. There is no shortage of them, however. Even though one leaves town, there is always another one arriving right behind him, and they always want a woman for the night.

She was moving between the poker tables when someone grabbed her from behind. She playfully turned around and saw another one of her usual men. He was a local who lived about a half-day's ride out of town: Roddy McIlwain. He owned a large ranch and visited town once or twice a month for provisions. He would spend the night at the hotel—sometimes in her room, paying her for the whole night, or sometimes in his own room by himself—and ride home the next day. She turned and smiled at the familiar gentleman. "Hi, sweetheart. Ready for a good time?"

"Always. You still entertaining prairie herders tonight, or are you ready for a real man like me?"

"Always ready for you."

"Let me finish this hand, and I'll be up there."

He looked at his cards. The cowboy next to him raised the current bet. He smiled and folded, "She's better than this hand, that's for sure." The men at the table all laughed. He picked up his money and strolled upstairs to the familiar room.

She knew what he liked; it was old hat for her. He was older, probably sixty, she was not sure. He was a lovely gentleman, remembered her birthday, brought her wildflowers for the vase in her room, and always treated her like a lady. When he opened the door, she was standing next to the bed, already undressed. He liked to always start that way. He was not going to be quite like the young buck she had finished with a few minutes ago, but she knew she was going to enjoy her time with him. She enjoyed his touch as much as he enjoyed hers. He was gentle and respectful with her. She knew he just needed some female companionship for an hour; he was lonely out at his ranch, and this was his escape.

Roddy even proposed to her once, and often reminded her about it, keeping it an open invitation to join him on his ranch. She was flattered, but she enjoyed her life in town too much. Even though she would be safe out there and would not have to deal with dangerous men night after night, she did not relish living out on a ranch, cooking, tending animals, and all the hard work outside in the elements. Her work was much easier in town, and always under a roof in a warm room. Still, she thought about it from time to time. He was forty years older than she was, and she was enamored by his demeanor and gentleness. They would make love, and usually converse the rest of the time. Tonight, he just needed something quick. He had his own room for the night.

Roddy approached her naked body, grabbed a hold of her shoulders, and kissed her passionately. She tingled at his kisses, long and sensuous. He worked his way down the curves of her body. She loved the sensation. He stopped at all the right places and did all the right things, especially the one spot that mattered most.

Eventually, they found their way to the bed. He always undressed slowly and folded his shirt and pants nicely. She always liked watching him doing it, a real gentleman. Not overly rambunctious and impatient, he took his time, the only man she ever really knew who folded his clothing for the short time it was off of him. The normal undressing activity of her patrons was flinging pants, shirts, and boots on the floor. Roddy was different. She understood why the other men did that. When you spend a month out on the range with no one but cattle and other smelly cowboys around you, you are desperate to get going with a beautiful woman.

Despite his age, he was strong and lean. Accustomed to ranch work his entire life, he was as strong as a bull, but with her, he was gentle. It was in these moments that her mind would consider the invitation to marry him. Roddy was a different man for her; he would make her feel special, but the next customer would walk in the door, and it would change her mind. The money was too good for her to walk away from this life.

He was still a customer through all of it, regardless of her fondness of him, and vice versa. Whatever he paid for, and whatever he wanted, she would do. When he would embrace her and caress her body with his strong, rough hands up and down her soft body, she felt guilty that she was being paid for it. It was a routine process, rarely any changes, but nonetheless, she enjoyed every moment of it. After he was done, they would lie for the rest of time in each other arms, talking briefly, catching up on what had happened since the last time he was there.

It was usually him who did all the talking. Her life was not one that she wanted to share with him as far as details were concerned. He did not want to know how many men, or how often, or what other things she may do with them. Some of the men had strange or unusual requests, but it all paid the same to her. She kept all that to herself. He never asked, either, not once. He just asked for his time with her, and never concerned himself with what she did with other men.

When their time was up—and she was usually loose on the clock with him—they got dressed, and she opened the door to the room. He gave her his usual long and passionate kiss at the end, and headed back down to finish playing cards. She stood in her doorway watching him walk away again, with his offer still being open to marry him. 'One day,' she whispered to herself, and sighed. 'One day I'll take you up on that offer.'

She straightened up her room, and made it ready for her next customer. She went back downstairs and surveyed the crowd of rowdy men, enjoying all their vices. She was tired, but it was still too early for her to turn in for the night. She knew a good night of business when she saw one.

It would be odd to necessarily say she learned everything about the business from her mother, Gertrude, but it was her mother who begrudgingly gave Mabel her start in the business. Gertrude ran a brothel on the edge of a town farther south. She set it up when her dry goods store burned down. The career her mother chose lead to a pregnancy. She had other girls work for her, and before Gertrude realized it, her new career was much more profitable than her old one. Her reputation grew, and she had connections with local law enforcement, so she was largely left alone. The rumor was that Sheriff Donnelly and Gertrude had an ongoing love affair, and he never hassled her business.

Gertrude wanted Mabel to have a better life, but a better life was hard to come by on the frontier. One had to make the most of what life dealt you. When Mabel was old enough, Gertrude thought it was good for her daughter to be out of the house during the busy times, so Mabel worked at her uncle's inn as a waitress in his diner. Despite her mother's attempt at discretion, Mabel knew exactly what was going on in the house. The other girls all lived there and told her what they did, but Mabel stayed away from it at first. She wanted to marry a boy who worked at the local livery stable, but he was killed in a gunfight. Another boy who struck her fancy died of cholera the following year. She was downstairs one evening when a bunch of cowboys were in town, and one took a liking to her. She accepted his offer, and the rest was history. Her mother found out too late and was livid, but realized the environment she had put her daughter in. The temptation was going to take over eventually, and it finally did.

Gertrude did not want her daughter to follow her same path, and tried to stop her from pursuing it, but Mabel did not want to stop. She went outside the house to conduct business a few times, and her mother was even more furious. They had a falling out, and Mabel left the territory. She took a stagecoach out of town, heading farther north. That was three years ago.

Mabel was back downstairs and walked through the saloon surveying the crowd of men. There were even some rich, fat cats in the saloon tonight. The rich men usually had a pocket watch tethered to their vest pockets, had pressed clothing, usually completely unsoiled, were clean-shaven, rarely wore their hats indoors, and often they were portly or overweight. They were not the type that spent all day working animals, riding horses, or doing sweaty, dirty work. These men who got off the train at the station, trains they owned, had businesses, or even owned entire towns. They rode in railcars, drinking whiskey, eating three hefty meals a day, smoking cigars, reading newspapers, and sat and counted money all day long.

She knew the type; though rare to see this far north, they came to town from time to time. As more people were moving into the territory, she saw more businessmen like these guys in the saloon, looking to further develop the town, invest in existing businesses, or establish new ones. Not too long ago, she had one pay her for an entire week, and got a glimpse into his ritzy lifestyle. She rode the rails with him into the next territory. Once they arrived, he had to go back to his wife and family, so he put her back on the train, and she returned to her frontier town. It was just some fun on the rails for him while he traveled home. She enjoyed the ride and the money; however, the rich man was not to her liking, but business was business. She still had the two dresses he bought her in Boise; they were her best ones.

There were three men sitting at a corner table, and two who fit the railcar description. One man was tall, thin, and handsome, but the other two were the opposite of him. She passed by and glanced back at the handsome one, hoping to catch his attention. He was impeccably dressed, well-kempt, and looked completely out of place in the smoky, raucous, small-town saloon. Maybe she could go on a weeklong railcar ride again? He smiled at her as she walked by, but turned his attention back to his business colleagues. She went to the bar and got a drink. Rarely did she ever have to pay for drinks; usually, the act of her sauntering up to the bar would elicit a bevy of would-be suitors to rush up to pay and start a conversation. She ordered a whiskey from Rico. No man approached her. Odd for a saloon full of men.

"On your tab, Miss Mabel?"

"I guess."

She passed back by the table of businessmen, wiggling her assets playfully, and then in her best flirtatious manner, turned around, leaned up against it so her low-cut blouse would be noticed, and purposefully interrupted their conversation, "Can I interest any of you men in some fun?" She turned to the handsome one and winked, "...especially you."

The other two men laughed at her direct approach to their friend, and the handsome man blushed, both startled and flattered by the invitation. They egged him on, "Go for it!"

"I think she's worth whatever she's offering."

"She looks like a great investment to me!"

They laughed and clanked glasses together, saluting their drunken wit.

She did not acknowledge the two fat guys; she just stared into the handsome man's eyes and waited for a response.

He nervously tried to avoid eye contact and smiled, "Ma'am, I'm married, sorry, but thank you."

She winked at him and answered, "I won't tell if you won't. Where's your wife?"

"Home."

"Where's home?"

"Denver."

"That's a long way away." She grinned even wider and playfully rubbed a finger up and down his cheek.

One of the other guys piped up, "Might have to pay me not to tell!" He laughed, thinking he was funny, but no one else at the table did.

She kept staring at the married man.

"I'm sorry. I'm faithful to my wife. Thank you."

"Why are you here?"

"In town? Or in this saloon?"

"Either. Both. Tell me your story."

"It's not that interesting."

"I bet it is." She winked. He blushed again. She invaded his space by pushing him back away from the table a foot or so, and plopped down on his lap. Not invited to do so, he avoided touching her with his hands. She leaned over and whispered in his ear, still trying to entice him with her feminine ways, "I tell you what. You can remain faithful to your wife, but still tell me your life story. I'm very interested. But I'd like to make a little money tonight. I have a room upstairs, and I'm a good listener. I'm even a better listener naked. You'd have to pay, but you don't have to get undressed. But I guarantee you'll like what you see."

He smiled, intrigued by her offer. He pulled his face back from hers, "I'm sorry, ma'am. You are very beautiful, but I can't. But I'm sure one of these two men might want you to listen to them. Naked or otherwise."

"Ooooohh," came out of the mouth of one of them, and a whistle came out of the other. One started stomping his foot at the thought of it.

"Well," she said, "word of mouth spreads. I guess I could start with one of them first. After I get finished, you'll be begging for me after that."

The other two men laughed and made whooping noises. She knew they were drunk.

"My price goes up after midnight; don't think about it too long."

She pivoted around in his lap, and faced the two men across the table. The pivot was a purposeful grind into his crotch, hoping to entice him. She traded glances with both men. "Who's first, boys?"

One spilled his glass and exuberantly proclaimed, "Me! Me!"

"I like the eagerness."

"Let's go, honey."

"But I haven't told you my price yet." She winked at him.

"It doesn't matter. You have any idea how much money I have?" He grinned with all his ego.

"You might not have enough. Am I not the prettiest girl in here?"

"Sweetheart, you are the prettiest girl I've seen in a month!"

"You aren't that good of a businessman, are you?" She smiled at him and playfully reached across the table and caressed his hand. "You just played your hand, that will now cost you more! My value just went up!"

"I don't care."

She giggled and slowly rose up from the handsome man's lap. "Well, then. Let's go."

She turned around and winked at the handsome man, "You can still have me at regular price, even if you just want to watch."

He shook his head and smiled, "Sorry. Go have a good time with Murray there."

"It will be his best time, ever. But it could be yours, too. Think about it."

Murray laughed at the brief exchange, "Watch? You mean like the peep shows in Paris? Except we're all in your room?"

"Careful for what you wish for." She cracked a devilish smile.

She grabbed Murray's hand and the two went upstairs, arm in arm. Murray's booming laugh could be heard across the rowdy saloon.

The other man turned to the handsome man, "She really wanted you. Why didn't you take her up on her offer?"

The handsome man picked up his drink and took a swig, but did not say anything. He reached inside his jacket, and pulled out a silver case from an inside pocket. He lit a hand-rolled cigarette, inhaled, and blew out a satisfying puff of smoke. He then looked at his colleague across the table. "Anderson, you see, I am happily married. She is a gorgeous woman, and I was tempted. But how good would my reputation be if I succumbed to her for some cheap thrills? I'm trying to do business with you two, and I need to establish a level of trust with both of you. If I can't keep my integrity, then what good is my word?"

Anderson, who was very drunk, and not very coherent, looked at him, a bit stupefied that the conversation turned so serious and philosophical. He was stunned and speechless for about thirty seconds. The married man took another long draw from his cigarette, and exhaled.

Seemingly not gripping the heaviness of what the married man was conveying, he just spouted out, "Somehow I don't think her thrills are cheap." He laughed again at his own supposed drunken wit.

The man across the table inhaled more smoke and smirked at Anderson's comment. "Fair enough, I guess." Bored with the sophomoric conversation, he turned in his chair to observe the rest of the activity in the saloon, still puffing on his cigarette.

Anderson stared across the table, worked his drunk mind into a more lucid moment, and responded more seriously, "You don't have to prove your morality to either of us. Trust me, we don't care."

"I know. But I do... I care."

"Eh. Go on up when Murray's done. He shouldn't be too long. You've been away from your wife for a couple of weeks, go have a good time with this girl."

The married man inhaled again. He looked across the table at Anderson's face and exhaled. He turned away, looked across the room at the other men enjoying their night, and took his last swig of whiskey. "I was just showing you that when I give someone my word, I mean it. My integrity is my worth."

Anderson took a drink and ignored the comment.

The married man snuffed out his cigarette, stood up, collected his overcoat from the back of his chair, and put his hat on.

Anderson looked up at him. "Going somewhere?"

"Nice knowing you two. Too bad we cannot do business."

Anderson sat there staring up at the man, stunned.

The man tipped his hat and went to the bar. Rico gave him his bill, and he paid up. "Oh, that beautiful girl that was over here a few minutes ago?"

"Mabel."

"Mabel. I noticed she had a drink. Does she have a bar tab?"

"Yes."

"Allow me to pay it."

The married man exited the saloon doors and disappeared into the night.

Murray came down the stairs about twenty minutes later, his hair all ruffled, half of his white shirt not tucked in, and his belt askew. It was obvious to anyone who cared, he had enjoyed his time with her, the ear-to-ear grin was a dead giveaway.

"Anderson! You're next! She's still naked. Get up there! She's wild!" He took a deep breath and looked around their table. "Where's George? She still wants him to go up, too."

"He left."

"Why?"

"Integrity."

"Integrity? About what?"

Anderson shook his head and downed the remainder of his whiskey. "He left, and he's not doing business with us."

"What!?"

Anderson got up. "Maybe he'll change his mind in the morning. I don't know. But he's gone for the night."

Murray was dumbfounded.

"What room is she in?"

"Room six."

"How much is she?"

"I don't care, and I didn't ask. She's worth every penny, though."

Anderson passed out on her, naked, and in her bed. After she had run through both of those rich guys, she knew she could rest for the night. The second guy did not say anything about the handsome man to her. She was hoping there was still a chance with him, but she needed to get this drunk guy out of her bed. She got dressed, went downstairs to ask Murray and the handsome guy to come up, and help her get their friend out of her bed.

When she got down there and found out the handsome guy had left for the evening, she was dejected, but still needed Murray to help her with Anderson. Murray obliged.

They got him dressed and got him out the door. Mabel had overcharged them for her time greatly. She knew they would not care, and she took advantage of their deep pockets. As Murray plopped Anderson outside into the hallway, he turned to face her and asked if he could have another go-around with her. She was exhausted. She had made almost a normal week's haul between these two. "I don't think so. It was lovely."

"Please? I've got money."

She was tired and was not even remotely interested in him in any way. There was nothing about him that turned her on.

"I said my price went up after midnight." She hoped that would discourage him.

He grabbed his pocket watch and looked at it: 12:35.

"Okay. How much more?"

She hung her head, "Double."

"I've got it on me." He grinned.

"What about your friend?"

"He's passed out cold. He doesn't even know he's on the floor of the hallway right now. He'll be alright."

"OK. But you're not spending the night. Only one more time. Got it?"

"Do you have an overnight charge?"

She hung her head again, disgusted at herself that she let that out; her tiredness got the best of her. "I do. The hourly charge. Well... the double hourly charge until the sun comes up. If you want to go again in the morning when you wake up, it'll cost you even more."

Murray had more money than anyone in the territory. He did not care. "It's a deal."

"The hour? Or the whole night?"

"The night."

She shuddered at the thought of sleeping next to him for the rest of the night, but the money was ridiculous, and he was willing to pay. "What about your drunk friend? We can't leave him in the hall all night."

Mabel thought maybe that will drive this guy out.

"Can he just sleep on the floor in here?"

She grimaced, but thought about the money. She was intrigued that the he did not mind being naked in bed with her, with another man in the room, even if the other man was passed out.

"Sure. But you have pay me for him being in the room all night, also. I get paid by how many men are in my room." It was an ad hoc rule that came to her tired mind. "And if he wakes up, and wants to have a go with me, that's an extra charge for him."

"He's got the money."

"And you can't watch."

"Watch? Huh. What if I pay to watch?" Murray asked with a grin on his face.

She sighed. "Everything. *Anything!* That you do extra will cost you extra. It's a charge per man, per event. If you want to watch me and your friend go at it, I don't care, but it'll cost you plenty. Apparently, you got the money."

"You have no idea how much I have."

"How much?"

"I could go get every man downstairs to come up here, and pay for all of them, and still have enough left over to buy every building in this town, and the next town over."

"In the bank, or so you have that kind of cash on you? Right now?"

He dug into his pocket and pulled out his wallet. She did not notice the wallet the earlier, because she was getting undressed. She knew he was rich, but even she could not believe someone could have that much money on them. He opened his wallet to show her. She had never seen that much cash all at once. She came up with an idea to hopefully get him to spend the night elsewhere; but also, to capitalize on this foolish and rich man, get as much of his money as she could, and not have to touch him again tonight.

"You like to watch?" She asked suggestively.

"I've only done it once, at a peep show in Paris last year."

"Did you enjoy it?"

"It was definitely a thrill, and something new to me."

"Want to do it again?"

"Yeah, especially if you're naked." He smiled at her.

"I'll charge you double. One for a cowboy from downstairs, one for you. You can get naked. Do whatever you want to yourself while watching; over there, on the chair—not in bed with me or the other man—but the charge is for two. I'm pleasing both of y'all, and it's after midnight, so it's double that double charge. I get to pick the cowboy."

"Can I stay the rest of the night after that?"

She hesitated, but realized how much money she could make. "You can spend the rest of the night with me then, at the after midnight double-hourly rate. And don't forget about your drunk friend; you're paying for his time, also."

"Deal."

"Let's get your drunk friend in here; we can't leave him in the hallway."

Murray grabbed Anderson's shoulders, Mabel grabbed his pant legs, they dragged him inside the room, and plopped him down in the corner.

"I'll be right back. I'm going to look for a cowboy."

It took her a few attempts to find someone that would not mind some creepy rich man watch them. It was an odd and unusual request, and she knew something most would not be amenable to, but it was also a free roll in the hay with her to whomever took her up on the offer. A few of her regulars that were in the saloon did not like the proposition, but she eventually found someone interested; a man she had never seen before. He was dressed more nicely than the average cowboy, but had a grizzled look about his face. Perhaps he was an outlaw, but she did not care at this point. No one else was interested in the unusual offer. This man had a dark look in his eyes, a look she did not like, but this was about making more money than she had ever made in one night. It was more than she would have made in any one given weekend, and besides, she thought he was almost as handsome as the businessman that refused her advances earlier, he just needed a shave. She was still stunned that the handsome guy earlier refused her. Maybe this was her idea of getting even. Murray disgusted her but was willing to pay, and this gruff-looking man would make up for it.

"He's paying?"

"Yes."

"For me and you... together? He's just going to *watch*... us?"

"Yes. He will probably be naked and... you know... with himself."

When they walked inside her room, Murray was already naked. He was sitting in a chair across the room from the bed. The two men acknowledged each other. The stranger looked at his pudgy, naked body, and smirked. It was clear to the stranger this rich man did not belong out on the frontier, he looked like he was accustomed to being indoors, and probably would perish if left outdoors in the mountains, or out on the plains. He thought this guy probably couldn't rub two sticks together to make a campfire, and was only this far from civilization because the railroad made it out this far.

"So, let me get this straight." He looked at Murray. "You are going to pay for me to be with her while you watch me and her together in bed? And you are just going to sit over there and, well, I think know what you're going to do, and you are not expecting anything between the three of us, right?"

"Right."

"You're just going to watch us?"

"Right."

"You're not going to try to touch me while I'm naked, and you're staying over there on that side of the room?"

"Right."

"And you are paying for everything?"

"Right."

"Peculiar, aren't you?"

"I've already had her tonight. And I'm staying the night with this sweetheart after you leave. Have you ever been with her?"

"No. I've never met her before. First time in town."

"Just you wait. You are in for the time of your life."

"You must be loaded—and a little crazy."

Murray made a fatal mistake. He reached over, grabbed his wallet, and showed the stranger his stash. He was not shy about his nudity, or his money as he handed Mabel the money he promised for the double-double hour. The stranger's eyes widened at the wad of cash in the fat man's possession. Murray set his wallet down behind him, next to his clothes.

"Damn." He suddenly noticed the motionless body slumped over in the corner of the room. "What about that guy?"

"Passed out. Doubt he'll wake up anytime soon."

The stranger took off his coat and hung it up on the hook on the back of the door. "It's your money." He turned to Mabel, "Ready?"

She suppressed a yawn and nodded. The two got undressed. Murray's excitement was evident as Mabel disrobed. Even though she was disgusted by his naked body, she could not help but look over at him again. She noticed what he was doing with himself. This was new territory for her. The stranger was just behind her, undressing. Mabel turned around to look at him and liked what she saw. She grabbed hold of him as they were both still standing. She touched him seductively to get things going. He grabbed her shoulders and gave her a long kiss, something she wasn't expecting. She kept her eyes open and glanced over at the fat man. He was enjoying the moment. Even though she was not attracted to the money man, she was intrigued by what was happening.

Mabel wondered if the little fat man was aroused by just her, the strange, naked man in front of her, or both of them. She thought it all weird, but kept thinking about the money. Maybe she'll take some time off after this. She could travel by rail or go visit her mother. She had not left this town in quite some time. She could do a lot with the money she was earning tonight. She got into the moment with the stranger and quit thinking about the money. She reached around and pulled him closer to her. She slid down against his body and kissed him in several places on the way down. The stranger was enjoying her actions. She pleasured the stranger and made him climax. Her naked benefactor in the chair moaned as he finished himself off. She stood up, and the stranger jerked her body towards the bed with a rough shove. She was not too happy about the rough play, but did not say anything.

She looked over at Murray. "Are you done? I see what you did?"

"Just getting started."

The stranger looked over at Murray like he was taking a stage direction from him. After all, this was on the little fat man's nickel.

"It'll cost you some more to keep going." Mabel reminded him.

Murray did not even flinch. He just reached for his wallet and tossed more money towards the bed, landing on the floor. The stranger turned back to Mabel, got on top of her, and spread her legs. Murray watched eagerly. The two in the bed writhed and moaned together in passion.

After what seemed like an eternity of him being on top of her, he suddenly pivoted to one side and rolled her on top of him in one movement. Her naked breasts heaved against her necklace. The stranger reached up and squeezed her breasts hard—she winced in pain. While on top of the stranger, she glanced over at Murray again, who was still enjoying the moment. She just kept up the passion with the stranger.

Finally, the stranger climaxed, and he groaned loudly. The little man did the same. She was dripping with sweat. The stranger had a suggestive nudge on her torso to dismount. She did, and lay down next to him.

There was no way she was going to be able to do anything more tonight. That was it for her. If the little fat man still wanted to sleep in her room for the night, the money was going to talk, but no more tonight for her.

The stranger caught his breath and sat up in bed. He leaned over her body and sucked on her nipples. He paused before transferring his lips from the left one to the right one to admire the silver cross with the turquoise gemstones lying between them. "Beautiful necklace."

Murray got up from his chair and grabbed a towel from Mabel's dresser. The stranger got off the bed and stood up. Mabel, catching her breath, looked over at the stranger and smiled up at him. He did not return the smile. He just reached down and picked up his clothes. He looked at the businessman. "Is that what you wanted? Had your fun?"

Murray turned around to face him. "Yes. Thank you," he said sheepishly, wondering if that was some pointed remark. He decided not to think about it much. He was satisfied with the events of the night. "You want to watch me and her go at it?"

'*Oh God!*' she thought to herself. This little fat man thinks he is going to go at it one more time tonight? She told herself there is no way that is happening.

"Sorry, I'm not that weird." The stranger started putting his clothes on. Murray looked over at the bed with a smile. Mabel's naked body was sprawled on the sheets.

"Suit yourself. You are welcome to." He walked over and climbed in next to Mabel.

The stranger looked over at Murray's wallet. It was clear on the other side of the room. Murray started caressing her, and kissing her neck and shoulders. She was not amused, but went along with it, closing her eyes.

Suddenly, the stranger pulled his revolver out of his holster and put the gun to the back of Murray's head. Murray did not have time to react to the cold touch of gunmetal to his scalp. The shot splattered blood and brains all over Mabel. She had no time to react to the carnage as the stranger quickly pointed the pistol at her face, and did the same. Both naked bodies lay on her bed sheets with blood splattered everywhere. He turned to the motionless body in the corner and fired a third shot. Anderson never knew he was dead. He was still passed out drunk as he suffered the same fate as the other two.

The stranger figured no one downstairs probably heard the gun shots due to the piano playing, and all the bawdy noise from the poker players. If anyone was upstairs, they are probably naked, getting naked, or getting dressed, and in no condition to run out into the hallway to see what was going on.

The stranger grabbed the man's wallet. He reached over to the nightstand, grabbed what money Murray had already paid Mabel, and picked up all the money on the floor. He looked at Mabel one last time and ripped the silver crucifix, dripping with blood, off her neck. *This might bring some money.* He put it in his pocket.

He opened the door slightly and peered out. A few cowboys and frightened girls were standing in the hallway, but had their backs to him. He quickly exited the room and shut the door behind him. He walked down the hall swiftly, and someone asked, "Did you hear those gunshots?"

He nodded and said, "Were they up here or downstairs?"

"I think up here."

The small group started to go downstairs in haste. The stranger blended in, and moved with them. It looked as if the people downstairs either never heard the shots, or were just unconcerned. If it did not happen at their own poker table, they did not care. The stranger got to the bottom of the stairs, moved through the saloon with a purpose, but not too hastily as to draw attention to himself.

He exited the saloon and went out into the cold night.

The End

www.ingramcontent.com/pod-product-compliance
Lightning Source LLC
Chambersburg PA
CBHW051335020726
47501CB00007B/2100